SWANN'S LAKE OF DESPAIR

A HENRY SWANN DETECTIVE NOVEL

SWANN'S LAKE OF DESPAIR

CHARLES SALZBERG

FIVE STAR

A part of Gale, Cengage Learning

GALE
CENGAGE Learning·

Farmington Hills, Mich • San Francisco • New York • Waterville, Maine
Meriden, Conn • Mason, Ohio • Chicago

LIBRARY OF CONGRESS CATALOGING-IN-PUBLICATION DATA

Salzberg, Charles.
    Swann's lake of despair / Charles Salzberg. First edition.
    pages cm–(A Henry Swann detective novel)
    ISBN 978-1-4328-2936-0 (hardcover) — ISBN 1-4328-2936-X
(hardcover) — ISBN 978-1-4328-2937-7 (ebook) — ISBN 1-4328-
2937-8 (ebook)
    1. Private investigators—New York (State)—New York—Fic-
tion. 2. Mystery fiction. I. Title.
PS3619.A443S96 2014
813'.6—dc23   2014020033

First Edition. First Printing: October 2014
Find us on Facebook– https://www.facebook.com/FiveStarCengage
Visit our website– http://www.gale.cengage.com/fivestar/
Contact Five Star™ Publishing at FiveStar@cengage.com

Printed in the United States of America
1 2 3 4 5 6 7 18 17 16 15 14

"Life is a jest and all things show it,
I thought so once and now I know it."
                    —from John Gay's tombstone

"Go with the current."
                    —Ovid, *The Art of Love*

"That's a trail that nothing but a nose can follow."
                    —James Fenimore Cooper,
                    The Last of the Mohicans

1
A STARR BURNS BRIGHT

New York City/Long Beach

"Goldblatt, you gonna tell me what the hell you wanted to see me about?" I said, as I watched him shovel another forkful of pasta into his mouth, or at least in the general vicinity thereof. Believe me, it was not a pretty sight.

"Yeah. Sure. After we finish the meal."

"I don't know if I can wait that long. Watching you eat is making me sick."

"You got a problem with the way I eat?" he said, as a few droplets of red sauce shot through the air and landed on a glass I'd moved in front of my plate for protection from just such an assault.

"Exhibit number one," I said, pointing to the glass.

"Huh?"

"Never mind," I said, looking at my watch. I tapped it a couple times. "Look, I've got things to do. Tick-tock. Tick-tock."

"Yeah. Right."

He sucked the last tubes of penne into his face, dragged a half-eaten piece of Italian bread across his plate, stuffed it into his mouth in one piece, wiped his entire face with the napkin that had been tucked into his collar, and leaned back. "Ahhhhh. Good meal, huh?"

"Excellent," I said, not even bothering to hide my sarcasm. I doubted he'd get it anyway. My plate of spaghetti or linguine or fettuccine, I couldn't tell the difference, sat practically untouched in front of me. But I guess he didn't notice that. Quantity was always better than quality, when it came to Goldblatt. "Now maybe we can discuss the business you said you had for me."

"I haven't had dessert yet."

"Screw dessert. If I don't hear the reason you got me here, I'm leaving."

"Okay, okay. I need you to do a solid for me."

"I don't do solids. I learned a long time ago that solids always turn out to be work and, like beer spilled on a table, it tends to get sticky and spreads out. For work, I get paid. And I doubt that's going to happen with you. How much have you brought in since you got disbarred?"

"That's between me and the IRS."

I laughed. "When was the last time you filed your taxes?"

"That's personal."

"I rest my case."

"Hey, I'm no deadbeat. You wanna get paid, I'll see to it you get paid." He pulled a wad of bills out of his pocket and waved it in my face.

"What'd you do, mug an old lady for her life's savings?"

"Very funny. You may not believe this, Swann, but I provide valuable services to people and for those services I get paid."

"What kind of services?"

"They vary. I may not be able to practice law anymore, but I know how the law works. I'm a consultant. A facilitator. I get things done."

"I'm sure you do. How do I fit in?"

"I want you to pick up a package for me."

"Do I look like the FedEx man? I'm a skip tracer. I find people. I don't make deliveries."

"FedEx don't deliver packages where I need them to."

"Where's that?"

"Long Beach."

"As in California?"

"As in Long Island."

"I'm pretty sure FedEx services Long Beach."

"Not when and where I want them to. You familiar with the town?"

"Yeah. My father grew up there. He'd take us back there to see what family he had left. It used to be a dump, now it's a poor man's Hamptons, overrun with weekenders, real estate speculators, Guidos, and religious Jews."

He slapped the table. "I knew you were the man for me."

"Not so fast, Goldblatt. Truth is, it turns my stomach to go out there. I'm not a man who likes change. And as for nostalgia, that ain't my thing."

"Do I detect the hint of a beating heart, Swann?"

"Not unless you've got a stethoscope hidden under the napkin covering that growing by the minute belly of yours. I need to know what I'm getting into and for how much."

"What's the difference? You take the train out there, you pick up the package, you take the train back, and you give it to me. Simple as that."

"Do you think I'm stupid?"

"Why would I think that?"

"Because didn't you think I'd ask you why you can't do it? A man like you, Goldblatt, four years of college, three years of law school, assuming, of course, you actually got through law school, knows how to figure out a train schedule."

"There are reasons."

"Give 'em to me," I said, knowing that whatever he said would be a lie or at the very least a souped-up version of the truth. Goldblatt was an operator. And he knew that I knew he was an operator. But the truth is, I get a kick out of seeing him operate. It's a cheap, harmless form of entertainment.

"I got a bad knee. You saw me limp in here."

"You're full of shit. Maybe you take a few pounds off and those knees of yours wouldn't have to do so much work."

"Okay, I've got a little problem with some people who live out there, so if I show my face I might find myself in a little bit of trouble."

"That's almost believable, so you know what, I'm not even going to ask what kind of trouble, because I don't give a shit. What's in the package?"

"That's confidential."

"Find someone else to be your errand boy," I said, as I pushed myself away from the table and stood up.

"Wait. What about dessert?"

I had to smile. There was no way to deal with Goldblatt other than to treat him as a joke. But he was a friend. The kind of friend you can't trust but you know it so you still make like he's a friend. The kind of friend who amuses you in an inexplicably perverse way. The kind of friend you can use without feeling guilty because you know he'd do the same. I sat back down.

"You think you can stuff dessert into that big, fat gut of yours after what you just ate?"

"I left some room," he said, patting his stomach, which seemed to have expanded at least a couple of inches from when we walked into the joint. "And you know, I'm kind of sensitive about my weight."

"Jesus, Goldblatt, you never cease to amaze me."

"Stick around, Swann, there's more where that came from."

He couldn't make up his mind between the apple pie and the chocolate cake, so he ordered both. Me, I had nothing. Trying to watch my weight while Goldblatt increased his.

The deal was simple, or so he said. The next night, I'd go out to Long Beach and meet someone on the boardwalk at precisely 9 p.m., in front of one of the little huts that during the summer months was where the kids issued beach passes. The person, he didn't know if it would be a he or she, would hand me a package. In return, I'd hand over an envelope, which he'd give me when I agreed to the job. Then, I'd hop back on the train and deliver it to him the next morning in his office, which with Goldblatt meant some cheap, anonymous diner somewhere in the city.

"I can trust you not to open the package or the envelope, right?" he said, as he dug into the last piece of apple pie, then pushed that plate away and started in on the enormous slab of chocolate layer cake.

"I don't like the sound of this, Goldblatt," I said, doing my best to look away from the epicurean spectacle going on in front of me.

"What's not to like?"

"You want me to go to the deserted boardwalk, in the middle of the night, in the middle of winter, with no one else around, carrying God knows what, meeting God knows who, for God knows what reason."

"Well, if you put it that way . . ."

"What the fuck other way is there to put it? And the kicker is, you're not even paying me for this. Do I look like a moron to you?"

"You owe me, Swann."

"How do you figure?"

"How many times have you asked me to dig up information for you?"

"Three."

His face fell. "What're you, keeping count? I thought it was more."

"Three. And we're not exactly talking brain surgery here."

"I'm asking you for one favor and then I'll call it even."

I laughed. Because he was entertaining. And because he was persistent. Would it kill me to do a favor for him? No. Was I going to do one for him? Not a chance.

"Two-fifty plus expenses."

"You gotta be kidding."

"That's my bargain, friends and family rate. Take it or leave it."

"You're killing me, Swann."

"Tell you what, you explain to me what this is all about and what's in that package and maybe I'll knock off a few bucks."

He put down his fork, which was unusual for him, since there was still half a slice of cake left on his plate. Putting on his serious face, he lowered his voice and said, "I don't know if I can trust you."

I laughed. "And I can trust you? Maybe both of us ought to give it a try."

He was silent a moment, looked down at his cake, then whacked off another hunk with his fork and stuffed it into his mouth.

"The name Starr Faithfull mean anything to you?"

"It's got a familiar ring, but I can't quite place it."

"In June of 1931, a beachcomber found the body of this beautiful, twenty-five-year-old chick named Starr Faithfull."

"And this has what to do with you?"

"I've got a little something going."

"Like what?"

He leaned forward. "This is top secret, Swann."

"Yeah. I'm sure the fate of the free world rests on it. Cut the crap, Goldblatt. You know and I know it's got everything to do with . . ." I rubbed my fingers together, "and in that case, we're on the same page. You want me to get into something I need to know what it is. And I need to get paid for it."

"Okay, okay. Faithfull was a slut who was involved with a bunch of important people, and some of them might have wanted her dead. Even her own sister supposedly said, 'I'm not sorry she's dead. She's happier. Everybody's happier.' You know the kind of chick I mean. Anyway, the DA at the time admitted lots of people in high places would rest easier with her dead. They did an autopsy and found she was full of Veronal, the Ecstasy of its day. The coroner ruled it death by drowning, but the DA said it was 'brought about by someone interested in closing her lips.' Not long before she died she wrote a friend saying she was playing 'a dangerous game,' and that there was no 'telling where I'll land.' She was leading this double life, see. She went to the finest finishing schools, but she was also a wild child, like that Paris Hilton chick or one of the Kardashians, Khloe, Zoe, Shmoey, whatever. Shit, I can't keep straight one from the other. Can you? Anyway, she was heavy into drugs and sleeping around. One of her boyfriends was this guy, Andrew Peters, a former mayor, ex-congressman, and Woodrow Wilson's assistant secretary of the treasury. His wife was Starr's mother's first cousin."

"Get to the point, Goldblatt."

"Keep your shirt on, Swann. I'm getting there. Starr left a couple diaries along with a bunch of letters, some of them filled with suicidal thoughts. But her father claimed they were forgeries. One of the diaries told all about her fourteen years of sexual, shall we say, adventures, with close to twenty guys, including British aristocrats and well-heeled Manhattan playboys. A lot of them gave her money. Apparently, one of them was Peters. *The Daily News* did this investigation and found that Starr's stepfather was nearly broke and that a few days before Starr disappeared he'd traveled to Boston to get payoffs from Peters. The question is, for what?"

"I still don't know what all this has to do with you," I said, tapping the face of my watch.

He looked around to see if anyone was listening to us, which would have been quite a feat, since there were maybe two other people in the restaurant and neither of them was within twenty feet of us. "There's another diary," he whispered.

"So that's what's in the package."

"Yeah."

"And how did all this come to you?"

"I've got a lot of connections, Swann. That's why you come to me for help."

"I come to you for help?"

"Yeah. Three times. Remember?"

"Okay, so why is this diary important now, eighty years after the fact? Who the hell cares about Starr Faithfull?"

"There's interest, okay. That's all I'm gonna say and that's all you gotta know. You in or out?"

"I want a piece of your action, Goldblatt."

"You gotta be kidding."

"You wouldn't be doing this if it didn't mean you weren't getting something out of it. You make money I make money. That's what friends do for friends."

"One percent."

I laughed.

"Five percent."

I laughed harder.

"Ten percent. But that's it."

"Give me the damn envelope."

Just my luck, the next day the weather turned bad. Very bad. Okay, it was winter, first week in January, but what happened to the January thaw? It was raw. It was cold. It was windy. And it was depressing now that all the holiday lights across the city had been taken down. It was back to grim reality now, eleven months of it, and I didn't like it one damn bit. Life was grim enough without having the lights turned out. To make matters worse, by the time I made it to Penn Station there was the whiff of snow in the air.

I didn't trust Goldblatt. It's not that he's a bad guy, it's that he plays the angles. And the thing is, he's not even that good at it. That's why he's not a lawyer anymore. He dipped his hand into his clients' pockets once too often and got caught. But something told me he might be onto something here. A lost Starr Faithfull diary might be valuable, especially if it shed light on her death. Goldblatt wasn't above a little blackmail, but who was left to blackmail? Would the families of anyone named in Starr's diary care? Only if someone mentioned was very famous and revered. Someone like Joe Kennedy came to mind. But did anyone care anymore? Is there anyone left in the world who thinks Joe Kennedy was a good guy? It was possible Goldblatt had other fish to fry. I knew he had publishing and film connections, at least that's what he's told me. He claimed one of his childhood pals was this top Hollywood producer, another the head of some big-time publishing house. Maybe he was concocting a book or movie deal. Whatever it was, I was in for ten percent—plus a hundred-fifty and expenses—a day. I knocked off a C-note, just so he wouldn't think I'm the money-hungry, hard-nosed, sonuvabitch rat bastard I'd like to be. So any way you sliced it, I would come out with something, and that's the way I liked it.

It was a fifty-plus minute ride on the LIRR out to Long Beach, the last stop on the line. I made a 7:10 train, which would give me plenty of time to grab a bite, then walk the three or four blocks to the boardwalk. The heavy commute was over so I pretty much had the train to myself, which suited me fine. I took out the heavy-duty manila envelope, locked in by wide strips of transparent tape, and examined it. It felt like there was money inside. And plenty of it by the thickness of the envelope. I wondered how Goldblatt got his hands on so much cash, including the wad he waved in my face. No matter how he did, I suspected there was something funny about it. But that wasn't any of my business. My business was to pick up a package, hand over the envelope, and get back to my occasionally warm apartment in the East Village.

I knew Long Beach, or at least a good part of it, like the back of my hand. My father, who took a permanent hike before I hit puberty, was born and raised there and that's where his folks, my grandparents, lived until they died not long after he disappeared. My father didn't talk much, but my grandmother loved to regale me with stories of the town's checkered history.

Around the turn of the last century, a real estate developer named William Reynolds, who was behind Coney Island's Dreamland, the world's largest amusement park, bought up a bunch of oceanfront property so he could build a boardwalk, homes, and hotels. As a publicity stunt, Reynolds arranged for a herd of elephants to march from Dreamland to Long Beach, supposedly to help raise funds to build the boardwalk. Reynolds touted the area as "the Riviera of the East," and ordered every building he constructed to be built in an "eclectic Mediterranean style," with white stucco walls and red tile roofs. The catch was that these homes could only be occupied by white, Anglo-Saxon Protestants.

When Reynolds's company went bankrupt, these restrictions were lifted and the town began to attract wealthy businessmen and entertainers, many of whom my grandmother claimed to have seen at a theater Reynolds built called Castles by the Sea, which boasted the largest dance floor in the world, intended to showcase the talents of the famous hoofers, Vernon and Irene Castle. Later, in the forties, she claimed to have seen the likes of Zero Mostel, Mae West, and Jose Ferrer perform, while other notables, including Jack Dempsey, Cab Calloway, Bogart, Valentino, Flo Ziegfeld, Cagney, Clara Bow, and John Barrymore, resided in Long Beach. Later, the town was home to Billy Crystal, Joan Jett, Derek Jeter, and the infamous "Long Island Lolita," Amy Fisher.

But there was another, much darker side to Long Beach, one my grandfather, a local cop who supposedly picked up extra cash doing errands for the mob, was far more familiar with. In the early twenties, the legendary prohibition agents, Izzy and Moe, raided the Nassau Hotel and arrested three men for bootlegging. Police corruption ran rampant, to the point where an uncooperative mayor was shot by a police officer. In 1930, five Long Beach police officers were charged with offering a bribe to a U.S. Coast Guard office to allow liquor to be offloaded.

By the fifties, Long Beach had turned from a resort area to a bedroom community. The rundown boardwalk hotels turned into homes for welfare recipients and the elderly. A decade later, the town devolved into a drug haven, as kids from other towns in Long Island flocked to Long Beach to score dope.

Over the last couple of decades the town had undergone a renaissance. Most of the drug dealers had been run out of town and in summer the boardwalk and beach became a magnet to those who couldn't afford the Hamptons or Fire Island.

By the time the train arrived at the Long Beach station, the weather had changed and not for the better. A storm had blown in from the southwest and the bitter wind was whipping around large, wet flakes of snow that stung my face and battered my eyes. It was just after eight o'clock, and I could have waited in the warm, inviting station, but I was hungry so I crossed the boulevard and took shelter in the Five Guys burger joint on the corner.

I ordered a cheeseburger, fries, and a diet Coke, because when I die I want it to be a result of artificial substances in my body. The place was empty and I chose a table by the window. As I ate, I watched the streets and sidewalk fill with snow, wondering what the hell I was doing out there. I thought seriously about packing it in and heading back to the city, but ultimately dismissed that idea. It wasn't loyalty to Goldblatt that kept me there. I've long since given up the idea of being loyal to anyone or anything. Why should I? It only adds to the risk of disappointment. Instead, it was curiosity. I wanted to see this thing through, if only so I could figure out what was the twisted little scheme Goldblatt had hatched.

I looked at my watch. A quarter to nine. I waited five more minutes. I didn't want to be the first one to show up, preferring instead to have the advantage of seeing who was waiting for me.

I patted the inside pocket of my peacoat to make sure the envelope was there, buttoned up, turned up the collar, pulled my wool watch cap over my ears, and headed out into the storm, a lone figure in blue set out against the blanket of white, which covered the streets, shrubbery, lampposts, and houses. I wished I'd worn something more substantial on my feet, because my socks, exposed to the elements, were already damp and I knew it wasn't going to get any better.

I headed down Edwards Avenue toward the boardwalk, and for every three steps I took the wind blew me back one. I crossed Olive, then Beech, then Penn, till I finally reached Broadway. Only one block left. The only sound I could hear was the crunching noise my shoes made in the newly fallen snow and the howling wind. Before crossing the street, I looked back and my eyes traced the footsteps I'd imprinted in the snow. By morning, my footprints would be gone and the snow would have turned a shade of black unknown to nature.

Despite the illumination of a streetlight in front of me, I

could barely make out the wooden ramp leading to the boardwalk. I crossed Broadway, then made my way up the ramp. The whistling wind and the roaring of the waves drowned out all thoughts other than wondering how long I would have to wait under these god-awful conditions. A chill ran up my back and I pressed my arms closer to my body and lowered my head, as if to use it as a battering ram against the wind.

The boardwalk, bustling in the summer with joggers, bikers, and bikinied beachgoers, was empty. The hut was about 75 yards to my left. I squinted through the veil of falling snow in an attempt to see if anyone was waiting there. No one. I glanced at my watch. It was a few minutes past nine. Was this all a wild goose chase? Did the person I was supposed to meet have better sense than me and decide to blow it off?

I cursed Goldblatt, then myself, for taking this ridiculous job as I headed toward the hut, my hands jammed deep in my pockets. Maybe I should have brought a gun, if only I'd owned one. Why should I? That's not the kind of work I do. I used to own one, but that ended badly. Now, I leave that sort of thing up to the heroes, a group I most definitely do not belong to. I am not a character out of a novel or the movies. I do not look for trouble. I avoid conflict whenever I can. Boxing great Joe Louis once said about his opponent Billy Conn, "he can run but he can't hide." I can run and I can hide, and under the right circumstances I am capable of both at the same time. But keeping my hands in my pockets might make someone believe I was packing and that might give me a much needed edge.

About fifty feet from the hut, I veered right, toward the oceanfront railing. With both hands on the rail, I looked out toward the ocean, west then east, to see if anyone was on the beach, then bent over the rail and peered over and down, to see if anyone was hiding under the boardwalk. There was no one I could see, which didn't mean someone wasn't there, hidden in the shadows. But if so it would take a while for them to reach me, enough time for me to run and then hide.

I reached the wooden hut, which was boarded up for the winter, and rapped on the side.

"Hey, anyone in there?" I called out, loud enough to slice through the roaring surf and surging wind.

Nothing.

I checked my watch. Quarter past nine. I'd give it till nine-twenty then I was out of there.

Suddenly, the wind died down a bit, a breather, so to speak, giving me a little more visibility. I didn't need it. Not a soul around. To my left, about a hundred yards away, there was a series of high-rises, but in front of me and to my immediate right, there was nothing but a parking area and land waiting to be used for new co-ops or condos. I felt like I was at the end of the world. I thought about Starr Faithfull, as I looked out toward the ocean. On a ship. Fell or pushed. Floating up on shore. It was a good story. Knowing Goldblatt, whatever he was paying for would probably be worth it to him, which now meant to me, too.

I looked back at my watch. Time was up.

I patted the envelope in my pocket. Once I was back on the train I'd open it and take out what I was due. I wasn't about to trust Goldblatt to pay me when there were no results. The hell with him and his crazy deal, whatever it was. I was going home.

I got to the bottom of the ramp and was headed toward Broadway, when I heard a crunching sound behind me. Before I could turn around, I felt a sharp pain in my side, in the vicinity of my kidney. Someone had punched me. Hard. And then another one. I lost my balance and fell to one knee, gasping for breath, instinctively raising my right arm to protect myself from another blow.

"Stay down," a raspy voice ordered.

"Whatever you say," I said, raising both arms up in submission. I looked up. The guy was a giant. Or at least he looked that way from where I was. He was wearing an overcoat, a muffler, and a fedora, like he was someone out of the forties.

Another, much smaller, slimmer figure moved out from under the ramp and stood beside the giant.

"That's some punch you've got there," I managed, holding my side, trying to regain some of the breath that had abandoned me. My first thought was that he'd done some boxing. I didn't take it any further.

"I guess I'm supposed to thank you for the compliment," he said, with a growl.

"Look, I'm just a delivery boy. You've got something for me; I've got something for you. Am I right?"

He turned to the figure beside him, who was wearing jeans and a gray hoodie under a black leather jacket that was at least two sizes too large. By the build, I figured it was either a boy or a woman, but I couldn't quite tell which.

"Who are you?" asked the smaller person, whose high voice tipped me off to her gender.

"Henry Swann. I was hired by Goldblatt to make the exchange."

"Why didn't he do it himself?" asked the big man.

"Because he's a fuckin' coward," the woman answered.

The big man laughed. The woman shot him a look and he sobered up.

"You've got the envelope?" she asked.

"You've got the package?" I said.

"It looks to me like you're in no position to bargain. Sidney here," her hands in her pockets, she nodded in his direction, "could just take it from you."

"That would be robbery."

"Yes. It would. You gonna call the cops on us?"

23

"If you just gave me what I came for it would be a simple business exchange. Look, my pants are getting soaked. Mind if I get up?"

She nodded. I stood. I still couldn't catch my breath and the pain had me listing to one side.

"Search him, Sidney."

I raised my hands. "You won't find a weapon, if that's what you're looking for."

"Better safe than sorry," she said.

"Open your coat," Sidney ordered.

"It's friggin' cold out here, Sidney."

He raised his hand. "Just fuckin' open the coat or I'll open it for you."

I could tell he meant business, so I opened the coat, spreading apart the sides. He patted me down.

"See. Nothing. And nothing up my sleeves, either," I added, sliding my hands down the sleeves of my coat.

Sidney spotted the envelope in my coat pocket and pulled it out. "This it?" he asked.

"Yes."

He handed it over to the woman.

"Now what about what I'm supposed to bring back in exchange?"

She ripped open the envelope. It was filled with cash, and lots of it. Just like I thought. She unzipped her jacket halfway, stuck the envelope in, then zipped it back up.

"You're not going to give me anything, are you?"

"Nothing but a message for Goldblatt."

"What's that?"

"Tell him the next time he tries to fuck with people he should think twice. Oh, and you can also tell him that payback's a bitch."

"What's that supposed to mean?"

"You seem to be a smart guy, Mr. Swann, you figure it out."

"You wouldn't happen to be a disgruntled former client of his, would you?"

"Goldblatt has disgruntled clients? What a surprise," she said, waving the envelope in the air. "Sidney, did you know that Goldblatt has disgruntled clients? Clients he stole money from?"

"News to me," said Sidney, without cracking a smile.

"You mind telling me how much is in there?" I asked.

"He didn't tell you?"

"You'd be surprised what he doesn't tell me. I'm just his dumb-ass errand boy. But I've got to tell you, whoever came up with that Starr Faithfull story really knew how to bait the hook. I've got to hand it to you. And you know something, I couldn't care less what you're doing to him."

"Isn't he a friend of yours?"

"We're acquaintances who use each other when the occasion arises. He uses me and I use him. But I see that isn't going to work out this time around. For either of us."

She closed the envelope and stuffed it in the pocket of her jacket.

"I think we're finished here, Sidney. I'm just sorry Goldblatt didn't come here himself. We wanted to give him some interest on his money."

"I could give this dude one more shot . . . you know, interest. For the scumbag."

"No. I think we got what we came for."

"So, just out of curiosity, how much did you take him for?" I asked.

She smiled. "Let's say it was a lot more than he took from me. How about chalking it up to earning interest on my investment. I'm sorry you got into this, Mr. Swann, but that's life, I guess."

"Yes, it is." I would have sighed if I could have managed it.

"Especially mine."

Sidney and the woman disappeared under the boardwalk and I and my aching ribs headed back to the train station.

I should have been pissed, but I wasn't. Sure, I probably wasn't going to get paid, but the look on Goldblatt's face when I told him what happened might be a lot better than a lost $150 and the cost of a round-trip ticket to Long Beach.

2
SHAKE, RATTLE, AND ROLL

"So, listen, I got an idea. I been thinkin' about it a while now. You and me, we should team up and go into business together."

"Are you crazy? I just told you I lost five grand of your money," I said, as I sat across from Goldblatt in a Starbucks on East 60th Street within shouting distance of the Bridge Market, which considerably jazzed up the base of the Queensboro Bridge. By now, the snow that had fallen the night before had morphed into ugly puddles of gray slush laced with salt, creating small inert ponds of floating ice by the curbs. The more intrepid pedestrians waded right through, while the more circumspect found alternate routes, some of which took them far afield from the corner they were crossing. Me, I was somewhere in the middle, trying to find the shallow spot that wouldn't overrun my supposedly waterproof shoes. Sometimes I was right, sometimes I wasn't.

"Easy come, easy go," he said, forcing my attention back to Goldblatt, who hadn't even bothered taking off his coat, despite the fact he'd been waiting for me when I arrived. Cynical of me, I know, but I couldn't help wondering if he was hiding anything under that oversized down jacket. "Besides, it wasn't my money. Anyway, we should open up, like an agency, you know. We kinda complement each other, don't you think?"

"How do you figure?"

"You're the outside man, I'm the inside man."

"You mean I'd do all the work and you'd sit around on your

fat ass and collect the money. No thanks."

"It wouldn't be anything like that. One hand washes the other, Swann."

"When was the last time you washed your hands, Goldblatt?"

He laughed, which only encouraged me to insult him even more. "If I didn't know better, I'd think you didn't like me," he whined.

"Nothing could be further from the truth. I like you; I just don't trust you. And why would I want to partner up with someone I didn't trust? So, if it wasn't your money, whose was it?"

He shrugged. "That's inconsequential."

"Not to the people you're going to owe it to."

"That's my problem."

"Precisely. And that's why I don't think it would be a good idea if you and I teamed up. I don't want your problems to become my problems. I've got enough of my own, thank you very much."

"That's where you're wrong. You need me, Swann."

"Really? Remind me what you bring to the table, other than your elbows."

"I could be the rainmaker. You know, bring in the clients. I'm good that way. You wouldn't believe the kind of connections I have. And listen, there are plenty of people who could use our services."

"I'm still not clear on what 'our' services would be."

"Whatever's needed."

"I don't do whatever's needed. In fact, I try to do the least of what's needed. I think we share that philosophy and regardless of what you might think, two negatives do not necessarily make a positive."

"This could be a beautiful thing, Swann."

"I doubt it. Listen, why don't you take your coat off? You're making me nervous sitting there all bundled up. It's like you're expecting a blizzard to hit the inside of Starbucks."

"Too much trouble. Hey, guess how many layers I'm wearing."

"I don't think so."

"Come on. Guess."

"Three."

"Five," he announced proudly, as he opened his coat and lifted each one, counting them as he did. "It's the secret to staying warm, my friend. Layers."

"I'll try to remember that."

"Hey, how about I get you a chocolate chip cookie and maybe one of those fancy latte things while you think about my proposition?"

I smiled. If you didn't take Goldblatt seriously, and who could, he was damned amusing. "Do they have plain, old-fashioned coffee here?"

"Don't know. I'll check it out. Don't go anywhere."

He got up and moved, make that waddled, to the counter while I checked my phone for messages. Nothing. I never expect anything, but I check anyway. Once I got back into the business I realized I didn't really need an office anymore. With one of those smartphones you carry your office with you. That and a pocket full of business cards and you're all set. Of course, you do need somewhere to meet potential clients, assuming there are any, so that's why I "borrow" an office from a friend, Ross Klavan, a rare book dealer I met on a case I worked a year or so ago. Like Goldblatt, he's amusing, but in a very different way. He knows he's funny, the smart kind of funny, whereas Goldblatt is funny only when he's dead serious.

Goldblatt returned with my coffee, some fancy, high-caloric, foamy drink for himself and an assortment of cookies and Danishes.

"Everything looked good, so I got one of everything. Help yourself," he said, plopping them on the table while daintily lowering himself into his chair. It suddenly occurred to me that for such a big man he was surprisingly graceful except, of course, when he ate. Over the years, he's told me several stories about himself, none of which I necessarily believe, though I suppose in some alternate universe they could be true. That he was a boxer and had, in fact, gone a few rounds with Norman Mailer and Muhammad Ali, though not at the same time and before, I hoped, Ali came down with Parkinson's and Mailer's head got so big he was in danger of toppling over without being pushed. That he worked for the CIA and had been stationed in Southeast Asia. That he climbed Mount Everest, though he did allow that he never made it all the way to the top, having to turn back as a result of bad weather. That he was an Olympic quality skier, but fucked up his knee just before the trials. And so on. Over the years, I just listened and nodded because, in the end, who knows what the truth is and, even more important, who cares? It is what it is and that's all that it is.

Goldblatt broke off a piece of the Danish like he was snapping a twig and jammed it into his mouth. "It looks like shit, probably sitting there half the day, but it don't taste half-bad. Here," he said, shoving the other half in my direction.

"No, thanks. I've had my cholesterol fix for the day."

"So," he said, pulling back the Danish. "You think it over?"

"It doesn't take all that much thought, Goldblatt."

"Then we'll do it!"

"Not so fast. I just want to get things straight. You want us to be partners, but I'm still not sure what's in it for me and what exactly being partners means. I can get clients on my own," I lied. "I don't need you."

"Never bullshit a bullshitter, Swann. And don't make me ask you to pony up your wallet to show me what's inside. But the truth is, I offer more than just supplying *us* with clients. I can provide backup, if necessary."

"What kind of backup are you talking about?"

"Information. Sources. Muscle."

I laughed. "From where I sit, I see a lot of fat but very little muscle."

"In my time I was known as something of a badass," he said, puffing up his chest.

"Maybe you used to be a badass, but now you're just an ass."

"See, that's another service I bring to the table. I can be the butt of your hostile, puerile, juvenile jokes, which takes the edge off. It's better and much more convenient than going to the gym."

I took a sip of the coffee. It tasted burnt. For three, four bucks a shot you'd think they could provide a smooth cup of joe.

"What about an office?"

"We don't need no stinkin' office. This is our office," he said, swinging his arms out wide.

"What the hell are you talking about?"

"Starbucks, my friend. You can sit here for hours and no one bothers you. And I've got other places like this, all over town. It's the twenty-first century. We're mobile, my friend. We go where the clients are. So, whaddya say?"

I took a sip of my burnt coffee. I didn't have to look at my bank account to know I needed something to give me a cash infusion, because I certainly didn't want to go back to the cable company, or find myself another real job. Besides, what harm could there be partnering up with Goldblatt? It wouldn't be anything official. It wasn't like we were signing papers, or anything. I'd use him. He'd use me. Fair play, we both came to see.

"You're thinking about it, aren't you?" he said, his face widening with a smile.

" 'I do perceive here a dividing duty.' "

"Huh?"

"Shakespeare."

"Whatever. So, you are thinking about it, right?"

"Yeah. God help me, I am."

"You won't regret it, Swann."

"I already do."

He reached out his hand. "So, let's shake on it."

"Do we have to?"

"Not if you don't want to, partner."

But I did. I don't know why, I just did it. I closed my eyes and shook his sticky, stubby-fingered hand.

"This is great. By tomorrow, I'll have some work for us. You'll see."

"Yeah, sure. But there's one more thing before I leave you alone with your pastry."

"What's that?"

"You owe me a hundred and fifty bucks for last night."

"Oh, yeah." He took out his wallet and carefully counted out some bills and handed them to me.

"You're a little short here, Goldblatt. It's only seventy-five."

"We're partners now, Swann. Everything's fifty-fifty, so that's all I owe you. The other half is mine."

I could already see this was going to be a bumpy ride.

3
CHERCHEZ LA FEMM

The next morning, I woke up with a very bad c
remorse. What was I thinking? Partnering up w
was like getting drunk, hooking up with a stripp
her, then trying to get her into med school. Those
work out. If they did, I'd be out of a job and there
more strippers with medical degrees.

The saving grace was that no papers were sign
doubted Goldblatt would come up with anything o
terms of work. Besides, I still had the right to say no.
way. Nyet. Not on your life. Take your job and shove it.
ing various ways of making our agreement null and
headed off to Ross Klavan's for no other reason than to
believe I actually had a professional life outside my dea
the devil.

"You've got to be kidding," Klavan roared in his d
resonant, radio-ready voice, as he poured me a cup of real
fee. "You're not going to actually partner up with that door
are you?"

"What can I tell you? He's a good talker and the truth is, I'
got nothing on my plate."

"You're broke?"

"Pretty much," I said, as I pulled my pockets inside out to il-
lustrate the point.

"I can ask around."

I took a swig of coffee. It was pretty good. Strong enough so

ld immediately feel the caffeine hitting my bloodstream
making its way up to my brain. "No thanks. I'll be fine.
be I'll give Jake a call and see if he's got any jumpers for
And there's always Craigslist."

don't know how you can do this kind of work, Swann. It's
eath you."

I know, I know. I'm not living up to my potential. Never
e. Problem is, I've never been able to quite figure out what
t potential is. Wouldn't it be ironic if there wasn't any?"

"I'm gonna check out a book collection that just came on the
arket. American between the Wars. First editions of Twain and
ather. Wanna join me?"

"I'd say I have something better to do, but you'd know that
asn't true."

My back pocket started vibrating. I pulled out the phone. It
was Goldblatt. I was tempted to let it go to voicemail, but we
were partners now, so I decided to give him a little respect.

"What's up?"

"Say you're glad I talked you into going into business with
me."

"Why should I do that?"

"Because in less than twenty-four hours I've got us our first
gig."

I doubted the *us* part, but I let him continue. "Where are you
now?" he asked.

"At Klavan's."

"Okay. You need to be at the Silver Star Diner, 65th and
Second Avenue, as soon as you can. We're at a table in the
window."

"Why don't we show this client of yours that we have a little
class and meet him here at Klavan's." I looked up at Ross who
was smiling, while indicating with a wave that he had to take
off. I nodded and mouthed, "see you later."

"This is a very classy diner, Swann."

"Because it has the words *silver* and *star* in it?"

"Very funny. And between you and me, I'm not crazy about your friend, Klavan."

"That's okay, he's not crazy about you either."

"So, you gonna be here or not?" he said, with an edge in his voice that let me know he was serious.

"Yeah. I'll be there. Fifteen minutes."

"Make it ten. I just ordered."

" 'There is no armor against Fate,' " I thought, as I pulled on my coat and headed out the door.

As soon as I made it through the revolving door of the Silver Star, I spotted Goldblatt—still wearing the same ridiculous oversized coat he'd had on a day earlier, though today it was unbuttoned—sitting at a window table, facing the entrance. As usual, he was shoveling something into his mouth. The man facing him was wearing a baseball cap, so I couldn't tell whether he was young or old, white or black, Hispanic or Asian. When Goldblatt looked up and saw me his face morphed into a smile so wide the glare from his suddenly preternaturally white teeth almost blinded me. He put his fork down, got up, spread his arms out wide, and announced, "Here he is. The man of the hour."

"Someone's been to the dentist since yesterday," I said, as the man with Goldblatt swiveled in his seat to face me. He was white, in his early to mid-forties. He was wearing a plaid shirt under a blue, crew-neck sweater, rimless glasses, and he hadn't shaved in several days.

"You noticed."

"Hard not to. You planning on doing some TV work?"

"You never know. Dentist friend of mine owed me a favor, so I figured I'd collect. It's a new, super-fast working, whitening

35

method. I'm trying to get my act together. You know, in honor of our new partnership. Pretty good, huh?"

"Let's just hope your teeth don't fall out because of it."

"Why do you always have to go to the dark side? Anyway, let's get down to business. Henry Swann, this is Jack Kerowak."

"You're kidding."

"Why would he kid about my name?" said Jack who had a face made to be forgotten. No particular feature stood out. Medium-sized nose, washed-out blue eyes with dark circles under them, straight teeth that were nowhere near as white as Goldblatt's.

"He likes to kid, that's why. He means no harm. And sometimes his so-called jokes go right over everyone's . . ." he passed his hand over his head.

Jack smiled, stood up, took off his baseball cap and extended his hand. He was about my size, five-ten, medium build, with mousy brown hair. In fact, other than the hair color, he could have been me. "Like I don't get that at least twice a day," he said. "No relation. I spell it K-E-R-O-W-A-K. Funny thing is, my uncle used to hang around with those guys. He went to Columbia with Ginsberg, Carr, and Kerouac, so that makes it even weirder. A pleasure to meet you, Mr. Swann."

"Nice to meet you, too, Jack," I said, as I shook his hand and then slid into a chair next to my partner.

"Want to order something, Swann?" asked Goldblatt, ever the thoughtful host.

"No. I'm good."

"So, Jack here would like to hire us to help him out," said Goldblatt.

"He would, huh?"

"That's right. I've heard some very good things about you from Mr. Goldblatt."

"You shouldn't believe everything you hear. Especially from

. . ." I not so discreetly nodded toward Goldblatt, who was wearing one of his shit-eating grins. "Why don't you tell me about your situation."

"It's actually kind of embarrassing."

"Jack, and believe me, I'm not saying this to put you at ease because frankly, I don't know you so I don't give a shit about you and even if I did I probably wouldn't give a shit about you, but I've seen and heard just about everything. As a result, I'm way past embarrassment and deeply into contempt and disgust."

"Mr. Goldblatt thought you might be able to help me find my . . . my girlfriend."

"She's lost?" I cracked.

"Well, I'm sure she knows where she is, but I don't. And I want to find her."

First impressions are usually that, and they rarely pan out. In fact, sometimes the better the first impression the worse it is in the end. But I had an okay feeling about this guy. I'm not sure why. Maybe it was his eyes, that nonthreatening blue, gentle, serene, and his voice, which had a very soothing quality to it. Or maybe sitting next to Goldblatt was making him look good. At the very least, I thought he deserved some of my time and less of my sarcasm.

"How long's she been gone?"

"A little over a week."

"And you don't suspect foul play? Jeez, I'm sorry. I always wanted to say that."

"Well, now you have," said Goldblatt, obviously pissed at me because I wasn't taking this as seriously as he wanted me to.

"It's okay," said Jack, squirming a little in his seat. "No. I'm pretty sure she left of her own volition."

For once, Goldblatt was probably right. I had to take this more seriously. Matters of the heart deserved it. I might not be happy but that didn't mean that everyone else had to be as miserable as I was. I actually preferred being around happy people because then I could justify feeling sorry for myself. If everyone else is happy and I'm not, then the world is obviously against me and I *can* take it personally. But I could see in his face, which was hanging low, that this guy was miserable enough for both of us.

"You mean she skipped out on your relationship."

"Yes. I guess she did," he said, lowering his head. "But I'd like to think she didn't skip out *because* of our relationship . . ."

"Let's back up a little, Jack. How long have you and . . ."

"Donna. Her name's Donna Recco."

". . . Donna been together?"

"On and off, a little less than two years."

"Then there's been trouble before?"

"Not trouble, really."

"I think we need an explanation," I said, a not so subtle nod to Goldblatt that we were, in fact, still in business together.

"What I mean is, we didn't fight or not get along or anything like that. The thing is, Donna maybe has a bit of a problem with commitment. When things get close she tends to back off. And when things get really close, she, ah, runs away."

"So she's done this before."

He shook his head. "Not like this. I mean, she's cut off communication, but never for more than a few days."

"How is this time different?"

"This time she's moved."

"What do you mean, moved?"

"Her apartment is empty."

"Empty as in she isn't there?"

"Empty as in nothing was there. The apartment was totally cleaned out. No clothing, not a stick of furniture. Nothing. She's vanished. I even spoke to her landlord and he said she didn't give notice or leave a forwarding address. She didn't even ask for her rent deposit back."

"This happened in the space of a week?"

"Yes."

"Did you try to reach her by phone?"

"Of course. But she must have changed her cell phone number, because I get a message that says it's no longer in service."

"Email?"

"My message bounced back. Either she's blocked me or she's changed that, too."

"Jack, I've got to tell you, with all due respect, something sounds a little fishy." I wanted to say that I thought, no matter what, that he was well rid of her, but I knew that wouldn't go over well. No one in love wants to hear they're better off not being in love. It's like a drug, and it's both legal and lethal. There's no antidote and the side effects can be devastating. "Had you fought?"

"No. We never fought. Ever. Nothing was out of the normal. I thought things were going great, that we were getting closer than ever. And then this." He shook his head and cleared his throat. "I don't understand it."

"And you think that was the problem, that it was getting too close for her?"

"Maybe. Maybe that was it."

"I hate to say this, Jack, but how about another guy?"

"No. Absolutely not. She was never secretive about where she was, where she was going, who she was with." He paused for a moment, as if it were the first time he was considering the possibility of her two-timing him. "But if that's it, I'd want to know."

"You know, Jack, today you hear about people having affairs over the Internet, sometimes not even meeting, just communicating through emails or Facebook. Could that be the case with Donna? Could she have met someone on the Internet?"

He shook his head.

"I have to be honest with you, Jack, things like this rarely end well. Chances are, I can find her. It's what I do. But that doesn't mean I can put things back the way they were. She's a grown woman. She's got the right to get out of a relationship, no matter what her reasons are and no matter how she does it. Even if it's shitty, insensitive, and hurtful."

"I understand that. I just need you to find her so I can talk to her. I have to find out why she left and then maybe I can fix things. If not, at least I'll have had the chance to try. Please, Mr. Swann, I think I just need closure."

"I've heard that before, Jack, and it's never really about closure. That's shrink talk. The truth is, we want what we want . . . and what we really want is hope to stay alive so we can get what we want. That's really why you want me to find Donna, isn't it?"

He was silent a moment. So was I. And for a change, so was Goldblatt. I don't know why, but I felt for the guy and in the end, I knew I was going to take his case and maybe, just maybe, it wasn't only going to be because of the money.

Finally, he spoke. "I suppose it is. But is that so wrong? Mr. Goldblatt says if anyone can help me, it's you."

"Goldblatt is a humanitarian. He thinks he can help everybody." I didn't add, "for the right price." And why should I? We were partners now. What was good for Goldblatt was suddenly good for me.

"Swann, can't you see the guy's in pain and we can help him."

I knew this meant Goldblatt had already discussed money with Jack. And I knew Goldblatt well enough to know that he'd negotiated a pretty sweet deal for . . . us.

"What do you do for a living, Jack?"

"I'm a writer and a teacher."

"How much money do you make a year?"

"How is that relevant?"

"Yeah, how?" Goldblatt piped in.

"How much, Jack? Fifty, sixty grand."

"About that. Maybe a little more, if I've had a good year selling my work."

"You're not a very good liar, Jack, which actually makes you a little more appealing. I can read people pretty good and I don't read you as making that much dough. Where do you live?"

"Not far from here."

"A walk-up, right?"

"Yes."

"How long have you lived in the same place?"

"Since I got out of college. Twenty years, maybe."

"That means your rent is pretty low."

"Yes."

"No offense, but you certainly don't spend money on clothing."

He smiled.

"And I'm guessing you walked here."

He nodded.

"How much did Goldblatt say we charge?"

"Swann, let's discuss this later," Goldblatt said, squirming in his seat. He knew what was coming and he didn't like it.

"No, I think we'll discuss it now. How much, Jack?"

"He said your day rate was usually $1000, but that in special cases you gave a twenty-five percent discount."

I looked at Goldblatt and gave him a shame-on-you shake of my head. "A case like this could take a day, but it could also take a week or two. How did you expect to come up with that kind of money?"

"My mom died and left me a few bucks."

I felt a kick to the side of my leg, and it wasn't coming from Jack's direction.

"You're a lucky man, Jack. We're having our post-Christmas special this week. I'm going to give you a whole week's work for a thousand bucks, plus expenses, of course. And if I find Donna in less than three days, you're going to kick in an extra grand. If it takes me longer than that, five hundred dollars for the next week. So right now, why don't we start with a retainer of five hundred dollars."

"You're kidding?"

"If you get to know me better, Jack, you'll find out one thing I never kid about is money."

Goldblatt sunk his head into his hands. "Christmas was fuckin' three weeks ago," he muttered, through open fingers.

"It's always Christmas. Get in the holiday spirit, Goldblatt."

"Thank you so much, Mr. Swann, and you, too, Mr. Goldblatt. Would a check be all right?"

"We prefer cash," said Goldblatt.

"I can go to the ATM. There's a bank right across the street. I'll be right back."

As I watched Jack scurry across the street, hopping over slush puddles, I girded myself for Goldblatt's tirade. I wasn't disappointed.

"What the fuck do you think you're doing? We're in business, aren't we? We're not registered as a not-for-fuckin'-profit company. This isn't like you, Swann. As long as I've known you you've been a money-hungry, unsentimental, take-no-prisoners guy. That's one of the reasons I thought we'd make a good team. What the fuck is going on?"

"He touched my heart, Goldblatt."

"Bullshit. There's something else going on here. Or else you're just doing it to toast my ass. Well you know something, if that's what it is it's not going to work. You want to do this job for peanuts, fine. I'll take my fifty percent and go out and find another job for us, one that you can't fuck up by undercharging. But believe me, you're not going to pull this shit on me again," he said, his face turning redder by the second. "No sir, not on me you're not."

"Okay, Goldblatt, think what you want to think. But you're right. After this, I'll owe you one. But I don't know where you got the idea we were fifty-fifty partners. In that case, you'd do half the work and we know that's not going to happen. Twenty-five percent. That's more than fair."

"What about my expenses?"

"What expenses? Picking diners out of the phone book?"

"This is something we're going to have to talk about," he said, as Jack tumbled back into his seat, the smile still pasted to his face. Goldblatt was still grumbling as Jack counted twenty-five Jacksons and handed them over to me. I counted out six twenties, added another fiver from my pocket, and handed them to Goldblatt. "And here's an extra twenty for the meal," I said, handing him an extra twenty.

"This is not what I had in mind," he said, shaking his head as he tucked the bills into his wallet.

"You can always dissolve the partnership. No harm, no foul."

"Yeah, right. So you can find the chick, I mean Donna," he said, turning toward Jack, "in less than a week and keep the extra grand all to yourself. I don't think so. I'm going to make a list of our responsibilities and make a chart of who gets what. And I think I'll even draw up a legal partnership agreement . . ."

"You do that. But in the meantime, why don't you let Jack and me have a little alone time so I can get all the information I need to get this ball rolling."

"Okay. But screw the twenty dollars for the meal. I'm gonna get myself some lunch and put it on the tab that you're going to pay," he said, as he rose and zipped up his jacket.

"It would be my pleasure," I said.

I knew things would be fine with Goldblatt because, in the end, he needed me more than I needed him. But somewhere deep inside me, I knew I did need him because I realized that he represented the worst in me, my baser instincts, and so long as I had him in my life I had a negative role model that would force me, out of shame if nothing else, to be better than I am.

We were an odd pair, all right, but maybe this thing would work better than I could ever have imagined.

4
CRIMES OF THE HEART

Once a grumbling, disgruntled Goldblatt departed, with his belly full and a brown bag holding his lunch gripped firmly in hand, I pulled out my small reporter's notebook and began quizzing Jack about Donna, starting with how they met.

"We met at a reading down at KGB Bar, in the East Village. We hit it off and went out for something to eat. It turned out we had a lot in common. We both loved reading, going to movies and the theater. Donna was a freelance editor and writer. She'd been an actress before that. You know, all my friends warned me against dating an actress. They said they're flighty and self-involved, but that wasn't the case with Donna. She was really grounded and besides, I didn't really consider her an actor because she'd left that life out of frustration to write and do some editing. She was working on a one-woman show."

"So she still wanted to act."

"I guess it was in her blood but she was really more into the writing and directing aspect of it. She realized that the ship had pretty much sailed in terms of making it as an actress. She'd just turned forty, even though she looked much younger, and she was a woman. Not an ideal combination for making a splash on stage . . ."

As Jack continued to babble on with details about how perfect he and Donna were for each other, which made me all the more suspect about their relationship, I glanced out the window. The traffic, which had been backed up, had begun to move. Across the street, huddled in a doorway, I noticed a figure in a black leather jacket, collar turned up, a hoodie over his head, faded blue jeans, smoking a cigarette. He caught my eye only because in New York everyone, unless waiting in line for a movie, waiting for a bus, or to get into the latest "hot" club, is on the move. Not this guy. He was just standing there, in the bitter cold, occasionally looking up, his eyes pointed in our direction. Probably nothing, I decided, as I turned my attention back to Jack and the notebook in front of me.

". . . she was a very good writer and a very astute editor. I wasn't crazy about the idea at first, but I eventually let her read some of my stuff and she made a few terrific suggestions."

"How about you, Jack? How good are you?"

He smiled weakly and I detected a hint of pain in his face. I'd seen it before, probably in the mirror. The pain of lost expectations. The pain of time passing and dreams passing with it. The pain of pissing away a life. "I wanted to be the next Bellow or Roth, but it doesn't look like that's gonna happen. I had a novel published, a few good reviews, but sales sucked. It's an uphill battle, so I had to take on some ghostwriting projects. They pay pretty well but it's just a job and sometimes the people you're working for can be pretty disgusting. The worst are the ones who micromanage and then when you're finished actually think they did all the writing."

I couldn't help thinking that Jackie boy and I had a little too much in common. "What about the teaching?" I asked, trying to focus back on my client instead of falling into despair about my own pathetic existence.

"I kinda got into it by accident. I have a few writing classes around town. I enjoy it. I meet some interesting people. It keeps me busy and helps pay the rent. It also keeps me focused on writing, which is a good thing because like most writers I'll do just about anything to avoid actually writing."

"You working on something now?"

"Another novel. I think this might be my breakthrough." He crossed his fingers but I could read the doubt in his eyes.

"Why's that?"

"I don't want to talk about it, if you don't mind, but I think I've finally hooked into something commercial, something that might actually make me more than a few thousand bucks."

I looked back across the street expecting to see an empty doorway, but the guy was still standing there. The cigarette was gone and he was busily texting. A moment later, when I looked back, the doorway was empty. I turned my gaze a little and spotted him, his hands jammed in his pockets halfway across the street, headed toward the diner.

"Is something wrong?" Jack asked.

"No. I just . . . it doesn't matter. Where were we?"

"We were talking about my new book."

"Yeah," I said. Out of the corner of my eye, I saw the guy coming through the door of the Silver Star. He looked around, his eyes lingering on us a little too long, then headed past us, to a table behind and to my right.

"Where're you from?" I asked Jack, lowering my voice.

"Shouldn't this be about Donna?"

"I like to get everything in focus before I snap the shot."

"I grew up in New Jersey—no jokes, please."

"Jersey's no joke, Jack," I cracked, doing just what he'd asked me not to. But that's the way I've led my life and it's too late to change now. I never do what I'm supposed to do, and look where it's gotten me.

"I moved to the city as soon as I graduated college. Got my MFA from Columbia. I worked a couple odd jobs while I worked on the next Great American Novel no one wanted. It's still sitting in my desk drawer. I accidentally got into journalism, where I made a meager living writing for trade magazines."

He stopped. "I'm depressing myself, Mr. Swann, so is there anything else you need to know about me?" he asked, with a slight edge in his voice.

"You don't like talking about yourself, do you, Jack?"

"Not particularly. I lead a pretty boring life and so talking about it just reminds me how boring it is. It's why I don't write about myself and never will."

"How about people you know?"

He shook his head. "I'm much better making stuff up."

I made a mental note of that and moved on.

"Okay, let's get back to Donna. Where was she from?"

"Florida, originally, but her family moved a lot. Her mother and father divorced when she was nine and she didn't see much of him after that. They have no relationship now. She says she doesn't even know where he lives, or if he's even alive. She claims she didn't care."

"What about her mother?"

"She was living in Virginia, but she recently moved back down to Florida. West Palm Beach, I think."

"She work?"

"She's a therapist."

"You've contacted her about Donna?"

"No."

"Why not?"

"I don't know how to reach her."

"You're a smart man, Jack. You can look her up in the phone book. Or find her on the Internet."

"She remarried and she's using her husband's name and I don't know what that is. All I know is that her first name is Delores."

"You dated this woman for two years and she never mentioned her mother's married name?"

"No," he said. "It never occurred to me to ask. I guess I feel pretty stupid now."

"Do you know where she works?"

"Donna mentioned she's affiliated with an assisted living place down there. She counsels the residents and their families. Maybe she mentioned the name of the place, but if she did I don't remember what it is."

"Donna ever hold a full-time job?"

"No. She just picked up freelance work here and there. I seem to remember her saying she even did a little catering early on, when she first got here from L.A., which she really hated, by the way. She said it was soulless."

"Her last employer?"

"She was doing research for an author, some woman who was doing a book about the end of the world or something like that. I don't remember her name, but I can probably dig it up if you'd like."

"That would be good. Where's Donna's apartment?"

"Seventy-third, off First Avenue."

"How long did she live there?"

"A little less than a year. She moved there from New Jersey, about nine months after we started dating. It was easier on us, because we were closer geographically. I'd usually stay over there three or four nights a week, or she with me."

Something was bugging me about the guy sitting behind us and I just couldn't shake it. I had this feeling he was there because of either me or Jack or both of us. My gut isn't always right, but over the years I've learned to listen to it. I leaned forward and whispered, "Don't make it obvious, Jack, but the guy who sat down behind us. You know him?"

Jack picked up a napkin and wiped his mouth, his eyes focused behind me.

"Never saw him before. Why?"

"No reason. It's just that it's a big restaurant and it's almost empty and he chooses a table right behind us." I shrugged. "It's probably nothing more than the herd instinct. You're in this business long enough you start seeing things that sometimes aren't there. And vice versa." I leaned back and asked, still in a lowered voice, "What about her friends?"

"Mostly people she knew from her acting days. I'll email you their names and numbers, too."

"She ever married?"

"For a short time, when she was young."

"How young?"

"Early twenties."

"You have her ex-husband's name?"

He shook his head. "She didn't like talking about him. They were married less than six months. She met him when she was living in L.A., trying to make it as an actress. He was an actor, too. A bad one, she said. She referred to him as 'the asshole.' 'The biggest mistake of my life, and there were many,' she used to say. She lost touch with him years ago."

"Tell me about her intimacy problems, Jack."

"I'm sure it stemmed from her parents' divorce and the estrangement from her father, but she wouldn't talk about it. It's odd, because most women like to talk about stuff, about feelings, not Donna. It was fine with me because I'm not all that comfortable talking about that kind of stuff either and there didn't seem to be any problems we had to deal with. At least at first."

"What's that mean?"

"About three months after we started dating, out of the blue, she announced we had to break up because we were 'too different.' I didn't understand what she meant because we had so much in common. Besides, I told her different was fine. I didn't want to be with someone who was just like me. That would be a nightmare," he laughed. "I told her I needed someone with a different set of neuroses. That didn't seem to convince her. But the next night she called and asked if she could come over. She did and without any discussion, we were back together again. Nine months later, pretty much the same story. Two weeks passed, she called, she came back, and everything was fine again. It was like she had to blow off steam and once she did, everything was back to normal."

"Did you ask her reasons for breaking up?"

He turned his gaze from me. "I'm embarrassed to say I didn't. I was just so happy to have her back. Whatever the problem was, I figured she'd worked it out."

"Ever consider moving in together or getting married?"

"I thought about it, but everything was so good between us I didn't want to push my luck."

Jack checked his watch. "It's getting kind of late. I have some research to do at the library and then I teach tonight. Do you think you have enough to get started?"

"I will when you email me those names and anything else you can think of that might help. What's her best friend's name?"

"Allie Pearson."

"What's she do?"

"Advertising."

"I'll start with her."

"I really appreciate your taking this case, Mr. Swann. And lowering your fee. I mean this, if you can't track her down in a week, I want you to throw in the towel. It's just that . . .." he started to tear up. "I'm forty-seven years old and I'm embarrassed to admit that I've never found the right woman or rather she hasn't found me. I thought Donna was the one." He hesitated a moment. "I know Donna was the one. I just can't give up without a fight. Who knows if I'll ever get another chance like this. I just need to know what I did wrong, so I can fix it. Have you ever been in love, Mr. Swann?" he asked, his voice breaking.

"I was married," I said, avoiding the question. First off, it was none of his business; second, I didn't want to go there. Not now. Maybe not ever. Besides, this tearing up thing was making me uncomfortable. I don't like it when women cry and it's even worse when a man does it. I folded up my notebook, tucked my pen in my pocket, and started to get up, but Jack didn't want to let it go.

"Have you ever had your heart broken?"

"Who hasn't?" I said, dodging another bullet. I was beginning to feel very uncomfortable. I don't like feeling uncomfortable.

His head sunk. This was not my strong point, dealing with people and their feelings, and I squirmed a little in my seat as the words tumbled out of my mouth.

"The worst crimes are always the crimes of the heart, Jack. I'll do my best. But if I do find her, I just hope it's worth it. Because the truth is, in my experience it rarely is. Most times when it gets this far, things just can't be fixed. I'll do what I can but you can always call it off."

"I'm not going to do that. I want you to find her. I want her back."

"Your call, Jack. Why don't you get going and I'll take care of the check."

"Okay. Oh, and here's my card, in case you need to get in touch with me."

"I'll need a photo of Donna."

"I've got a few on my iPhone. I'll email them to you."

After Jack left, I dawdled a while, waiting to see what the guy behind me would do. Ten minutes later, I paid the check and left. As I passed the window, headed downtown, he was reading the paper over a cup of coffee, but I thought I saw him glance at me and smile.

I had to get a life.

5
BACK TO THE FUTURE

Goldblatt was waiting for me when I got back to Klavan's. For him this was a little like entering the Devil's Den, so I knew it must be important. I was prepared for the worst: him reaming me out for lowering our price without consulting him. Me not taking our partnership seriously. Me not taking him seriously. Blah, blah, blah. But he was surprisingly nice, which I knew meant trouble.

"Nice guy, huh?" he said, as he swiveled back and forth in my chair.

"Jack?"

"Yeah."

"I try not to jump to conclusions."

"You don't like him?"

"I didn't say that. I just said the verdict isn't in yet. There's something a little off about his story . . . and him. I don't pretend to know women, and I know they're unpredictable, but disappearing into thin air like that. That's something professional con-women do. But in this case, she didn't take him for anything, at least anything he's admitting to her having taken, so I'm stumped."

"Just his heart."

"Yeah, just his heart. Suddenly, I've turned into Miss Lonelyhearts," I said, as I made a subtle motion with my hand for him to get out of my damn chair. Somehow, he didn't get the message. "Would you please stop swiveling around like that. You're making me dizzy. Besides, shouldn't I be sitting in my own chair?"

"You want I should get up?"

"God forbid," I said, as I dragged a folding chair from the corner and sat down opposite him. "How'd you come up with this guy?"

"Through a friend of a friend."

"I must say, Goldblatt, I'm impressed with how many friends you have."

"I'm a friendly guy, Swann. Life is measured in how much you do for other people and that in turn sometimes translates into how much they do for you."

"Your version of what goes around comes around."

He thought for a moment. "Yeah. I guess that's right. Anything you need me to do on this case?"

"Not right now. I've got a few people to track down so I can learn a little bit more about this chick. Either she's got a good reason for leaving Dodge in such a hurry or she's a little," I twirled my finger by the side of my head. "Either way, he's probably better off with her gone. But he's not gonna see it that way. And you know something, I'm no Dr. Phil. He wants her back, that's his problem. Who am I to judge? What about you? What are you going to be doing while I'm working this one?"

"I've got a few other irons in the fire. But there is something else I wanted to talk to you about."

"I don't renegotiate. The split is the split."

"It's not that, although I think we are going to have to revisit that subject at some point in our relationship. We've got a little unfinished business I'd like you to take care of."

"It wouldn't be that Long Beach fiasco, would it?"

"Yeah. As it turns out, that money you lost is a little more important than I thought it would be."

"Quel surprise. And by the way, just for the record, I didn't lose it. It was taken from me. And it never would have happened if you'd warned me what was going on. You sent me in there like a lamb to the slaughter."

He started swiveling again. "Be that as it may, since you've significantly lowered my income stream with this Jack Kerowak deal, and our split, which is officially under protest, by the way, I need to ask you to do the right thing and help me get the dough back."

"So you did the right thing when you cheated those people out of their money?"

"Who says I cheated them?"

"They do."

"Swann, you've known me how long?"

"Ten, twelve years and now that I think of it, yes, you took the best years of my life."

"Have you ever known me to cheat anyone out of anything?"

"What did they disbar you for?"

"That was political."

"How's that?"

"I pissed off the wrong people because I wouldn't play ball. Sure, I play the angles, but that's what life's about. It's like shooting pool. Angles. I have never, ever stolen money or cheated anyone out of anything. Swear on . . ." He looked around for something he could swear on and the closest thing he could find was a copy of a book of poems I had lying around by e.e. cummings. "On this, which I know you hold dear."

". . . 'a salesman is an it that stinks.' "

"Huh?"

"cummings."

"Oh."

"So you didn't misappropriate funds from your clients?"

"Define misappropriate?"

"Taking something that doesn't belong to you."

"Bingo. That money was mine. They owed it to me and they wouldn't pay me so I had to get it any way I could."

"And what about those people out in Long Beach?"

"Gonifs."

"You're telling me they stole the money from you?"

"It didn't actually go down like that. They paid me to do a job, things didn't turn out the way they thought they should, which by the way is the case with the law, nothing is guaranteed, and suddenly I've stolen money from them. That's not the way it works."

"It's a blurry line with you, isn't it?"

"There are no straight lines in life, Swann. You of all people should know that."

I couldn't argue with him there, because he was right. And besides, even if I could argue with him I knew I wasn't going to win. He liked arguing. He thrived on it. He would argue until he wore you down. That's why Goldblatt was a lawyer and I was, well, I was whatever I was. I learned long ago that it was better to simply shut up and let him think he'd won.

"What did you have in mind?" I asked.

"I'd like you to make another trip out there and get my money back."

"You think if I show up and just ask for it they're going to hand it over?"

"I doubt that approach will work. I think you'll need another plan."

"I find people. I find things. I don't even scores. There are other kinds of people who do that," I said, squashing my nose with my thumb.

"Then find my damn money and bring it back to me," he said, pounding my desk. "Because if you don't, or if I don't find another way to come up with five grand, some very pissed-off investors are going to take it out of my hide. And I know you wouldn't want that to happen, even if we weren't partners."

My true feelings for Goldblatt were rising to the top—I really didn't want him to get hurt, even though he might deserve it. I didn't believe half his bullshit but I didn't think he was an out and out crook. It wasn't a case of right and wrong. He saw things a certain way, his way, and he acted accordingly.

"Okay. Give me the damn name and the address of the chick behind this and I'll see what I can do. But I'm telling you, Goldblatt, this is back burner to Jack's situation."

"I understand that. But not too back burner, because I promised my investors I'd get it back to them within a couple weeks. Oh, and see what you can find out about that lost diary, too, because if that thing is real they can keep the damn five thousand, but I want that book."

"You really don't believe there is one, do you?"

"Yes. I do. But if there isn't, I want to know for sure. I know I can count on you, Swann. I have your back and you have mine."

I smiled. Not because I didn't believe him, but because, God help me, I did.

6
BFFs

True to his word, Jack sent me a detailed email with contacts for three of Donna's friends as well as a few more details of Donna's life, including where she went to college and what town she grew up in. He also attached a few photos of her. One was a head shot, which meant it had been touched up, perhaps considerably. Dark hair, pretty, slightly round face, big, brown eyes, pale skin, straight white teeth, inviting smile. Another, taken outside in front of what looked like a baseball stadium, showed her with her arms high above her head, almost like she was cheering, wearing a baseball cap and big sunglasses, big smile, red sweater raised just high enough to see her flat belly. A third was a close-up, in profile, showing her eating a corndog, while smiling guiltily into the camera. It was summer, because she was wearing a tank top, and in the background was Nathan's Famous, meaning it was taken at Coney Island. Taken together, they gave me a pretty good idea of what she looked like.

I always take the easiest route first, so I contacted Allie Pearson, who Jack claimed was Donna's best friend. As expected, she wasn't anxious to talk to me, but I convinced her to meet me for a cup of coffee at a Starbucks near where she lived on the Upper West Side, a block north of a recently abandoned Barnes and Noble.

"I'll be the one without the laptop," I said, eliciting a somewhat tentative throaty laugh.

"I'll be the bleached blonde carrying a fake Louis Vuitton

bag," she said, which considering the neighborhood wouldn't be much help.

She was as true to her word as I was to mine. About five-seven, full-figured, with golden-blonde streaked, shoulder-length hair, she arrived carrying the bag and wearing what I assumed was a fake fur coat, a dark skirt, and knee-length, black boots. She had a winter tan, from skiing or a trip to the tropics, I assumed, and her face had angular features and a prominent nose, and piercing blue eyes, all of which somehow worked to make her striking looking. She looked around, spotted me staring at her, and approached. I stood up.

"A gentleman," she said, "so rare in New York."

"I give a pretty good first impression, but don't hold me to it," I said, as I pointed to a small table I'd saved in the back.

"Would you like something?"

"You paying?"

"At the risk of being mistaken for a gentleman again, yes, I am."

"I'll have a double-latte, skim milk, and maybe one of those biscotti," she said in a sexy, raspy voice, pointing to a glass jar on top of the counter. "Chocolate, please. It's my weakness. Make it two. I skipped lunch today and I'll go to the gym in the morning."

When I returned, she'd made herself comfortable, her coat tossed casually over the back of an adjacent chair. She was wearing a low-cut, light blue sweater and a gold chain dangled from her neck, both of which drew attention to her ample breasts. I tried to look away but, like an accident on the highway, it was impossible. She didn't seem to mind, though. And she was enough of a lady not to call attention to where my eyes wandered every so often. I suspected she liked it. And, on occasion, I had no doubt that she used it to her advantage.

"Thank you," she said. "Aren't you having something?"

"If I want burnt coffee I'll burn it myself."

She laughed. It was a laugh that filled the room, a laugh that wafted through the air and took on a life of its own, a laugh you wanted to take to bed with you. "It's not burnt, it's strong." She took a sip of her latte. "We might as well cut to the chase. You wanted to talk to me about Donna."

"I'm looking for her."

"Tell me why I should help you. I don't even know who you are, other than your name and the cock-and-bull story you expected me to believe about being hired to find her because she's come into some money. Please," she said, rolling her eyes.

"Sometimes it works."

"On morons, maybe. Who even says she's lost?"

"Her boyfriend."

"Jack?"

"That's the one. Unless there are others?"

She smiled, took a sip of her coffee, and said, "Not that I know of, honey. But then Donna's always been one who keeps things close to her," she cast her eyes down slightly, "chest."

I didn't know if she was playing games with me or trying to tell me something. Either way, I decided I would just enjoy the ride.

"Do you happen to know where she is?"

She lowered her biscotti into the latte, swirled it around, pulled it out, took a bite, then followed it with another sip of the latte. She looked down, then slowly back up until she'd locked onto my eyes. "Assuming I did know, why should I tell you?"

"Because Jack is worried about her. According to him, she disappeared. Her apartment's cleaned out and he has no idea where she is."

"Donna's a grown woman. She doesn't need permission from anyone to move, or to do anything else, for that matter."

"So you do know where she is."

She smiled. "If I did know I wouldn't tell you, and I certainly wouldn't tell you just for a latte and a couple of chocolate biscotti."

"Understood. Let's back up a little. What do you think about Jack?"

"I don't know him all that well enough to think all that much, but he seems nice."

"Supposedly, you're her best friend. You mean you didn't hang out with him and Donna?"

"Once or twice. But you can't tell much from that. He was okay. Smart, kind, gentle, generous—he always picked up the check. Just like you. But you know, when you get right down to it you never know. Appearances can be," she dunked her biscotti, took a bite, smiled, "deceiving."

"You're preaching to the choir, baby. But best friends talk. Especially women. At least that's what I've learned when I was home sick watching Oprah."

She laughed. "Yeah, like I believe that. That dumb as a rock thing doesn't work with me, honey. I know the real thing when I see it—and I've gone out with plenty of rocks to know the difference."

"Unmasked for the genius I am. So, what did Donna think of him?"

"She wouldn't be with him for a year and a half if she didn't like him."

"Did she love him?"

"That's something you'd have to ask Donna."

"I'm asking you."

"There are all kinds of love, Swann. You don't mind me calling you Swann, do you?" she purred.

"That's my name, feel free to use it. So, did she love him?"

She smiled again, even batting her sky blue eyes. Yes, she

actually batted them. It would have been comical if it wasn't so sexy.

"I love steak and I love diamonds, but that's not the kind of love we're talking about, is it?"

I shook my head.

"Yes. I think she loved him. But I'm not about to rate it on a scale of 1 to 10, if that's what you're looking for."

"If she loved him anywhere on that scale, why would she just take off?"

She shrugged. "Sometimes Donna does things that are inexplicable. She's never been one to stay in one place too long. I've known her fifteen years and in that time she's moved more than a dozen times. I've even lost touch with her for a year or two at a time. But she always comes back into my life, so I'm assuming at some point Jack will hear from her again. Tell him he shouldn't be worried."

"Have you heard from her?"

"Not recently."

"Aren't you worried about her?"

"Not especially. Are you?"

"Not yet. But if you really haven't heard from her and you really don't know where she is, then maybe we both ought to be worried about her. When was the last time you spoke to her?"

"A couple weeks ago."

"You are her best friend, aren't you?"

"I hate that term. I don't even know what it means. I've known her a long time, we've been through a lot together, does that mean we're best friends?"

"How often do you usually talk to her?"

"Several times a week. But like I said, we've had times where we haven't been in touch for a year or more."

"So, it's not unusual that you haven't spoken to her in a couple weeks."

"Like I said, it's happened before. We each have our own lives. It's not like we have to check in on each other. And I certainly don't GPS her."

I shuffled in my seat. This wasn't going to be easy. Allie wasn't telling me everything she knew and there wasn no way I was going to get it out of her. But I was good at this and I figured I'd get something if I kept at it. It was just about how long I could keep her attention.

"Look, Allie, the fact that you're not worried about her tells me you know where she is or at least the reason she disappeared. All Jack's looking for is closure. The poor guy is a wreck. The woman he loves disappears on him. Wouldn't you be upset, confused, distraught, if you were in his shoes?"

She sighed. Yes, she sighed, and a more insincere reaction I cannot imagine. I knew that what came out of her mouth after that sigh wasn't going to be the truth. Oh, parts of it might be, but that would only make it that much more effective. This was a woman who knew how to manipulate men—most women do, but she was especially good at it. I could tell because even though I knew she was doing it I was still falling for it.

"I know you're just doing your job, Swann, but this is personal. I'm not surprised Jack's worried, but you can tell him that Donna's fine, that she just needed some time to work things out."

"So you have spoken with her."

"I didn't say that. I just know Donna."

"Someone who needs time doesn't empty out their apartment and disappear without a word. Someone who needs to figure things out packs a bag and heads to a yoga retreat for a weekend. Something's not right here and I think you know what's going on. And if you don't, then you should want to know."

She stared into her cup of latte as she spun a half-eaten piece of biscotti into it. I didn't say anything. She was thinking. Of another lie or the truth. I didn't know which but I wasn't stupid enough to think it was the latter. But it was okay. I knew that silence was not a sign that the truth was forthcoming. Lies are swirling around, forming, taking full shape. I let the process unfold. Finally, after maybe thirty seconds, she looked up. She stared at me a few seconds more before she said, "I really shouldn't be talking about this."

The truth.

"I honestly don't know where she is."

A lie.

"I didn't know about the cleaning out of the apartment thing."

Possibly the truth, possibly a lie.

She took a sip of her latte.

"She called me a few weeks ago and said things were getting a little too intense with Jack. She was afraid she was going to hurt him. She needed time away from him. A couple of weeks, she said. I asked her what that meant and she said she was going away. I asked her where and she said she didn't know. She just needed time by herself. Donna can be a very private person. Like I said, I've known her fifteen years and sometimes she'd disappear without saying a word. And when I did hear from her she'd moved from where she'd been living. She always had a good explanation. A new job. The apartment she was in wasn't good enough. A love affair gone bad. She was going back to school."

This had the ring of truth.

"She's a runner," I said.

"I guess she is."

"The question is, what was she running from this time? Was it Jack? Or was it something else?"

"You'd have to ask her," she said, with an edge in her voice that again told me she knew more than she was going to spill to me.

"Where would she be most likely to go?"

"I wish I could help you, but I can't. She might still be in the city; she might be in another city, or another state. Or even another country."

"But you aren't worried about her?"

"Donna can take care of herself. She always has." She stopped for a moment and there was a slight change in her tone. "You don't think I should be, do you?"

"Right now, this is just a domestic case and it might stay that way. I was hired to find her, not bring her back, and that's what I'm going to do. If she wants to stay lost, that's fine with me."

"I think we're finished, Swann. I have to get back to work and the truth is, I've probably violated my friendship with Donna simply by meeting with you. I've said all I'm going to say. It's nothing personal, you understand."

"As much as I keep trying, I understand very little, Miss Pearson. But somehow that seems to make me better at my job. I appreciate your meeting with me and when I find Donna, if there is anything wrong, I'll let you know. But one more thing, before you leave. I'd like to speak to Donna's mother. Maybe she knows where her daughter is."

"Sorry. Can't help you there."

"Huh?"

"I don't know how to get in touch with her."

"How about her married name?"

She shook her head.

"Are you toying with me, Miss Pearson? Would a package of chocolate biscottis make a difference?"

"They might make a difference, Swann, but not the way you think. I really have to go." She got up and started putting on her coat. "Good luck finding Donna. And if you do, tell her to get in touch with me. Oh, and if I think of anything I'll get in touch with you."

"You don't know how."

"Oh, Mr. Swann, I'm a resourceful woman. I'm sure I can find you."

7

A Fork in the Road

I was back at my desk fooling around on the Internet, trying to find Donna's mother, when my phone dinged. A text message from Goldblatt. "Call me. ASAP!!!" I rarely do what people want me to do, especially when it's formed as an order, and it's even less likely when exclamation points are involved, especially multiple exclamation points. But for some reason I thought this time I'd do what Goldblatt wanted. But not right away. Just punishment, I thought, for those three damn exclamation points. I put down my phone and continued my search for Florida assisted living communities, and there were plenty of them. Fortunately, there were only half a dozen or so in the vicinity of West Palm Beach. With her first name, and what might have been her second married name, I had enough to start with. I made a list of the six with phone numbers and addresses, then printed it out. Only then did I call Goldblatt, who picked up before the first ring was finished.

"What took you so long?" he said, breathless.

"Your text was fifteen minutes ago."

"Yeah. That's what I mean. What took you so long?"

"Are you running a marathon?"

"Huh?"

"You're out of breath. Even you have to be moving to sound that way."

"I just got out of the subway. Those stairs are a bitch."

"Maybe you ought to expand your workout regime beyond

pushing yourself away from the table after a three-course meal."

"You're hi-hi-larious, Swann," he wheezed.

"What do you want, Goldblatt? I'm busy. Working. For us."

"That's what I wanted to talk to you about. I need you to take care of this Long Beach thing. ASAP. And there's something else."

"I hate when people do that."

"Do what?"

"Use initials. And while we're at it, put a lid on the exclamation marks. Besides, I'm working on a case."

"Yeah. I know. A case that brings in bubkes. You have to get your priorities straight, my friend."

"*Your* problem is not *my* priority."

"Listen, you're responsible for me losing that five grand."

"How do you figure?"

"You're the one who wasn't watching his back. You're the one who let that goon coldcock you. You're the one who handed the money over to that thieving little bitch . . ."

I would have let him go on, I was actually enjoying it, but I had things to do and Klavan had just popped his head in my office to announce his arrival, which meant he probably wanted me to shoot the breeze with him. I much preferred chewing the fat with him than with the fatty on the line.

"All right, Goldblatt, I give up. I'm responsible for your borrowing money from someone to pursue some harebrained scheme, then losing the dough, even though I had no idea what I was getting into. Maybe if you'd warned me I might have been more careful. But that's history, so why rehash it. What the fuck do you want from me?"

"I want you to go out to Long Beach and get my fuckin' money back, that's what I want. Or find that fuckin' diary."

"There is no diary."

"What makes you so sure?"

"Because if there was they would have done something with it, besides holding it over your head to get their money back."

"I told you. It wasn't their money. It was mine."

"Okay. You win. I'll go out to Long Beach. But I need direction. Who are these people you . . . who beat you out of the dough?"

"I'm way ahead of you. I've got all the deets written down. What are you doing this evening?"

I wanted to say, "anything but seeing you," but I knew that would be unnecessarily mean. It wasn't that I wasn't capable of being mean because I am, but he was, God help me, my partner—at least for now—so I owed him at least a modicum of respect. It was either that or cut him loose, and for some reason I wasn't ready to do that. Not yet.

"Meeting you."

"That's the spirit. There's a diner on . . ."

"Uh-uh. What say we celebrate our partnership by meeting at a step up from a greasy spoon."

"I don't see them that way."

"I know. You see them as floating offices. But how about humoring me. There's a pasta joint near me, on First and Fifth Avenue, Three of Cups. Meet me there at seven."

"So long as this isn't a precedent."

I hung up before I could give him a smart-ass answer.

After half an hour of phone calls, I finally got the lead I was looking for. There was a Delores Wren who worked as a part-time social worker/therapist at the Sunnydale Residential Home not far outside West Palm Beach. Being as it was the middle of winter, and a particularly bad one, at that, I figured I might as well take a business trip down there. So I booked a flight for Saturday morning, returning Sunday early afternoon, which meant only a one-night stay at a cheap motel I found not far from Sunnydale. That, with a weekend car rental, would probably eat up a good chunk of what Jack was paying, but somehow I got a perverse pleasure out of eating into Goldblatt's profit margin. I knew I couldn't keep this kind of torture up if I wanted to continue paying my bills, but I did have a couple outstanding pre-partnership payoffs due me, which would float me a couple weeks.

Goldblatt was fifteen minutes late, which didn't surprise me. I was catching up on a three-week-old *New Yorker* when he appeared, still wearing the same coat he'd been wearing the last two times I saw him. Having never seen where he actually resided, I was beginning to suspect that he lived on the streets. Or maybe he slept in diners. Or maybe he never slept.

"Sorry I'm late," he said, removing his Yankee baseball cap and stuffing it in his pocket. "Got a call just as I was running out. I've got something else cooking. Word of mouth is awesome."

He started to sit down. "Take off the damn coat, will ya. You're making me nervous."

"Oh, yeah." He took it off, revealing one of those insulated vests over a plaid, flannel shirt over a dark turtleneck.

"Now the vest."

"You want a striptease act, try Sapphire's."

"Just take it off, will you. I don't feel like sharing a meal with a homeless person."

"Mind if I leave on the shirts?"

"Be my guest." I couldn't help but wonder if he was wearing his entire wardrobe.

He sat and grabbed the menu, studying it for a moment. "Is it dark in here or are my eyes fading?"

"Both."

He returned to the menu, holding it closer. Another moment passed, as I dipped pieces of warm bread into the spicy olive oil concoction. He peeked over the menu. "Good bread. This is a business expense, right?"

"Whatever you say."

The waiter arrived. I ordered a puttanesca pizza. After announcing he was trying to watch his weight, Goldblatt ordered fried calamari, meatball and sausage pasta, and a glass of Merlot. I didn't ask him exactly what he was watching it do.

Once the order was in, Goldblatt got down to business. He pulled a small notebook from his pocket, tore out a sheet of blue-lined paper, and handed it to me.

"That's her. Claudia Bennett. The address is where she works. Her father was my client."

"Why did he hire you?"

"It was a malpractice thing."

"What do you know about malpractice? I thought you were a criminal attorney."

"I'm a generalist. I do a little of this, a little of that. And if I don't do it, I refer it to someone who does."

I made a face. He knew what that meant.

"Don't look at me like that. It's called referrals. It happens all the time. I listened to his problem and then I referred him to someone. The guy dropped the case because it wasn't worth his while. That's not my problem and it's no reason for me to return my fee."

I shook my head. "And what was that referral fee?"

"Two grand."

I whistled. "Pretty steep."

"That's my going rate, Swann. And I'm worth every penny."

"Evidently not."

"You're always going to have disgruntled clients, people who don't think they're getting their money's worth. But quality costs. You set your fees too low, people don't think they're getting quality. This is a business lesson 101, for you."

"How much is this lesson costing me?"

"Very funny. I try to help you straighten out your life and this is the thanks I get." He picked up another piece of bread, broke it in half, and dipped one half in the olive oil while holding onto the other, as if I might steal it from him if he put it down.

"Before we go any further I ought to tell you that there's a little change of plan."

"What's that supposed to mean?"

"I've got another case for us."

"Does it having anything to do with this mythical Starr Faithfull diary?"

"No, it does not."

"You're confusing me, Goldblatt. I thought you wanted me to get your money back or get the diary, if there is one."

"I do. But that should take half a day, tops. You run out there tomorrow and get it done. Besides, about the diary thing, after giving it some thought, I don't think that's going anywhere."

"Since when did you become a genius?"

He ignored my crack or maybe he didn't hear it. He was on a mission and nothing I said was going to deter him. So I kept my mouth shut and let him talk.

"Ever hear of a photographer named Ed Feingersh?"

"Can't say I have."

"Well, he's not exactly a household name, but he did have a moment in the sun that made him kinda famous."

"What was that?"

"He was this guy who specialized in taking action photos in the late forties and early fifties. Evidently, he was quite the daredevil. Came up with all kinds of dangerous stunts, just to get some good shots. But his big assignment was following Marilyn Monroe around for a week while she was in New York trying to become a serious actress. She'd had some fracas with the studio heads and she was kinda on strike. Feingersh got this assignment from *Redbook* to get a series of unglamorized, un-staged shots of her in ordinary places. They traveled incognito in the subway, went to costume fittings, the premiere of *Cat on a Hot Tin Roof,* sitting around in her hotel suite, dressing for various events, and putting on her makeup. The big climax was her appearing riding a pink elephant at a benefit performance of Ringling Brothers and Barnum & Bailey Circus at Madison Square Garden. He turned in these beautiful black-and-white photos during this crazy week of hers."

"So?"

"So a bunch of photographs appeared in the magazine, but the negatives and tear sheets of a lot of other shots disappeared. Feingersh only lived a few more years, but after he died no one knew where those negatives were because he was kind of an oddball recluse. Finally, years after he died, I think maybe it was in the late eighties, several rolls of film were discovered in a garage somewhere, including a lot of shots that were never published. They've been exhibited now and they go for a small fortune."

"The ship has pulled out of the harbor on that one, so I'm still not seeing where you're going with this."

"Well, the thing is, no one knows whatever happened to any of his other negatives or tear sheets. They've vanished. And evidently they include some pretty incredible photos. But they've got to be somewhere, right? And if they're found, what with the state of the art photo market today, they'd be worth a fortune."

"I'm not interested on going on any half-assed treasure hunt, Goldblatt. What's next, Blackbeard's treasure?"

"You haven't let me finish. This is a no-brainer for us, because we're being hired to find it. That is, like in being paid. There's absolutely no risk. We find 'em we get paid. We don't find 'em we get paid. Am I a fuckin' genius, or what?"

"Someone's hiring us to find lost negatives and photos?"

"That's right."

"And it doesn't matter if we find them or not?"

"That's right."

"Who's the idiot who's hiring us?"

"Some collector who prefers to remain anonymous."

"I like to see who I'm working for."

He shook his head. Obviously, I was frustrating him . . . for a change. "Think of it this way, I'm the one you're working for. And at a grand a day, that's not bad work. One week guaranteed."

"Minus your twenty-five percent."

"No, you don't get it. We're getting paid fifteen hundred dollars a day. Your cut is a grand. My cut is five hundred. Plus we get five percent of anything you find. This makes up for that virtual freebie you got us into."

"I was never great in math, but I'm pretty sure that works out to thirty-three percent for you."

"Take it or leave it."

"So you're amending our contract?"

"Just this once, okay. To make up for the freebie you're giving Jack."

"It's not a freebie."

"Pretty close."

I'd never juggled three cases at once, but the money on this one, if it was real, was awfully tempting. In my head, while Goldblatt rattled on, I tried to organize how I'd handle it. This was Wednesday. If I went out to Long Beach Thursday morning, I could take care of that. Friday, I could start the ball rolling on the Feingersh case. Florida, Saturday morning, take care of that. I wasn't used to working that hard, but I could do it, especially if the motivating color was green.

Goldblatt was saying something about our actually getting an office when I interrupted him. "Okay, I'll do it."

"You will?"

"Yes. But I want to know how much you got up front and I want my two-thirds of it, right away. And this is generous of me, because I'm not forgetting that our deal was twenty-five percent, not one third. And I want it on the record that this is a one-time thing, no precedent."

"Give me a break, Swann, and stop busting my chops. I worked my ass off to get it. I deserve that one-third."

"It's our deal now because (a) I'm getting nothing out of getting your money back on the Long Beach thing, and (b) I'm getting practically nothing out of working Jack's case . . ."

"That's your doing, not mine, pal."

"You brought Jack in, you take the consequences, and there's a (c). I'm going to be doing more than two-thirds of the work on this case. And just so you know, whatever figure you quote me on the advance you got from this anonymous collector, I'm adding ten percent to it, just because I don't think you're telling me the truth. Unless, of course, you've got a signed contract . . ."

"For your information, it was seven and a half grand. That's for a week's work. You don't believe me, I'll show you the check."

"I need to know who this person is. I want to talk to him or her to see what they know, to see if I can get any leads."

He shook his head. "No can do. The person wants to remain anonymous. I never met him or her. I was contacted by email. I agreed by email. The money came as a bank check. What the hell difference does it make? The check was good, that's all we should care about."

He reached behind him, into his coat pocket, and pulled out a sheaf of papers, thumbed through it, and handed me two pages, stapled together.

"I'm a lawyer, my friend, it's what I do. This is our new office agreement. And I was going to present you with a copy, as soon as I made it over to Kinko's. Now maybe you'll have a little faith in me."

I took the papers from him, while muttering, "as little as possible."

I scanned the contract. It was concise. It was well written. It covered all bases. It even had this one-time two-thirds/one-third split. I looked up to see him smiling.

"I know my stuff, don't I? All you have to do is sign on top of your name, date it, and we're good to go. And you'll notice it's just for the first six months of our partnership. After that, the option is up for renewal and renegotiation."

I grunted. He had a point, and he was holding up his part of the bargain by bringing in new business. "You haven't signed yet," I said.

"That can be remedied very easily." He pulled out a pen, took the contract from me and signed it, then handed it over to me. What could I do? The thought of all that money to be made clouded what little judgment I had. So, I signed.

He picked up the paper, waved it in the air, as if he were drying the ink, folded it neatly, and put it back in his pocket. From his other pocket, he removed a checkbook.

"And just because I want to foment good relations with my partner, I'm going to post-date a check to you. Just to show you I trust you."

I was starting to think that perhaps going into business with Goldblatt might not be so bad after all. He gave me the check. Five thousand dollars. I stared at it to make sure it was real, that it wasn't written in disappearing ink.

"Not so sorry we partnered up now, are you?"

"We'll see. Tell me what you know about this Feingersh thing."

"I already told you what I was told. But I do have a name for you. Julia Scully. She was his girlfriend, back in the fifties. She's close to eighty now, but I'm told she's got all her marbles and she's here in NYC. She's even listed in the phone book. Here's her number."

He handed me a piece of lined paper, torn from a notebook, with her name and number on it.

"Has anyone already spoken to her?"

"Not that I'm aware of."

I folded up the paper and put it in my wallet. "Lost diaries, lost photographs, lost money, lost girlfriends, I don't know about all this . . ."

"It's what you do, Swann. Find things. Now go find them."

8
I Won't Dance, You Can't Make Me

The irony that I was back in Long Beach twice within a week, a place I hadn't visited in over twenty-five years, did not escape me. And the truth was, with two other cases to work on I certainly could have begged off this one. Sure, Goldblatt would have screamed bloody murder, and I actually held the moral high ground for a change, but I figured I could take care of it in a few hours, get the ever-expanding Goldblatt off my back, then get back to real business.

According to Goldblatt, who'd done a little research on his own, Claudia Bennett could be found at an address on Park Avenue, not far from the public library, only a couple blocks from the Long Beach police station. I made sure to alter my appearance somewhat from the other night—this time, I wore a leather flight jacket instead of my well-worn peacoat, a heavy blue, white, and maroon scarf, faded jeans, and a pair of Camper boots that mimicked football shoes from the 1930s.

When I got to the address, there was a frozen yogurt store on the ground level and above it, a dance studio called *Dance Heaven*, only the e was missing from Heaven, so it read *Dance H aven*, which I suppose could also have been the case.

I checked the address I'd scribbled on the back of an old movie ticket stub, to make sure I was in the right place. When it seemed I was, I called Goldblatt and slowly repeated the address I'd written down.

"Yeah, that's it."

"All that's here is a frozen yogurt place and a dance studio."

"My guess is the dance studio."

"You get one shot at this, Goldblatt. If Claudia Bennett isn't there, I'm back on the next train."

"Do what you have to do," he sang merrily. I knew why. The faster I finished in Long Beach the quicker I'd get back to the Feingersh case, which was where the real money was.

I climbed the double flight of stairs, remembering with every step why I made the decision to leave the cable business and rejoin the real world.

On the door, it read:

> Dance Heaven,
> Home of the Dance
> Ballet, Ballroom, Swing & Jazz.
> Claudia Bennett
> Sid Glitz

I rang the bell. No answer. I knocked. No answer. I knocked again. Still no answer. I pressed my ear to the door and heard the faint sound of music. Someone was home. I twisted the doorknob and walked into a small waiting room. Facing me was a desk with a phone, computer screen, a few papers, and a vase holding an array of colorful, what looked suspiciously like artificial, flowers. Above me was a gently whirring electric ceiling fan, circulating the faint aroma of perspiration and air freshener. Folding metal chairs lined both sides of the room. There was a series of dance-related posters on the walls—Gene Kelly jauntily swinging from a lamp post; a white-suited John Travolta, arms raised to the heavens, or perhaps to the havens, lit by the colored strobes of a disco ball; *Dancing With the Stars;* Baryshnikov, his legs spread wide, his arms outstretched, seemingly defying gravity as he sailed through the air.

I sat down next to a small table with a stack of magazines on it. I picked up a few. *Entertainment Weekly. People. Teen Voices. Girls' Life. Teen Vogue. Seventeen. Rolling Stone.* Nothing of interest to me, but it told a lot about the studio's clientele. I put them down and stared at the two doors on either side of the desk. I'd give it ten minutes. If no one showed, I would be back on the next train to Manhattan.

Only a few moments had passed when one of the doors opened and an older woman, gray hair, pink-framed glasses dangling from a chain around her neck, and dressed in a pink tracksuit, emerged.

She squinted at me. "Can I help you?"

Before I had a chance to answer, she added, "Had to make a visit to the little girl's room." She smiled. "TMI, right?"

"I think that qualifies."

"Yeah, I've been told I sometimes say inappropriate things at the wrong time. Maybe it's the meds. Oops, there I go again. Name's Helen. So, what's your story, handsome?" she asked, as she plopped down on a chair behind the desk.

"Sweetheart, you haven't got enough time to hear my story."

"Well, I get off at five," she winked. "And there's a nice, little bar up the street. Half-price drinks till seven."

"I'm afraid I'll be long gone by then. I'm looking for Claudia Bennett."

"You're in the right place. She's in there with a group of bratty kids, most of 'em with two left feet. But you can't tell that to their parents. They all think their kid's the next Ginger Rogers, not that they've ever heard of her. You heard of her, handsome?"

"I have."

"I thought so. You look like you been around the block a couple times."

"I've traveled my share. How about Sidney?"

"He's in the other studio, giving a mambo lesson. The

women, 'specially the older ones, love to dance with Sid. He's got charisma. And plenty of it."

I smiled. Ripped off by two dance teachers. *I could have danced all night . . .*

"That's not a bad thing to have."

"It looks like you've got a nice dose of it yourself, babycakes. So, what did you want to see them about?"

"I've got a kid. He's a little shy. Girls scare the hell out of him. I think he should have dance lessons. I'm hoping it'll open him up a little. You know, have an excuse to get his arms around a girl."

"Married, huh?" she said, her face scrunching up.

"Not anymore. But don't get your hopes up. If I were straight, though, I'd be all over you like white on rice."

"You're a gay boy?"

"Just came out of the closet. But you know, if I gave it a chance, I think you could have me right back in that closet."

"Ain't you sweet."

"Mind if I take a peek in there, just to see how things work around here?"

"Be my guest, Sweetie. That door," she said, gesturing to the one on her right, "is where Claudia's got the girls. That one," she gestured to her left, "is where Sid's giving his mambo lesson. You know," her voice dropped to a whisper, "I wouldn't tell him 'cause his head's big enough as it is, but he's dynamite on the dance floor. He could be on that TV dancing show," she pointed to the *Dancing With the Stars* poster on the wall, "only he ain't famous."

"Maybe he will be one day. That his real name?"

"You mean, Glitz? Who knows? But it kinda fits him. You'll see what I mean."

I opened the door on the left a few inches and peeked in. There, in front of a gaggle of little girls, all dressed daintily in their brightly colored spandex ballerina outfits, spinning, turning, their arms outstretched in time to yes, *Swan Lake*, was a very attractive, slim young woman with dark hair pulled back in a ponytail, wearing a gray tank top and black tights. I couldn't tell for sure, but that certainly could have been the woman who'd come out of the shadows beneath the boardwalk.

I closed the door as quietly as I could, crossed past Helen's desk, and opened the other door slightly. Sure enough, there was Señor Glitz, dressed in tight pants and a black, silk shirt, his arms around an elderly woman, towering over her, leading her deftly through the steps of a mambo to the strains of a Tito Puente song I recognized as one that was played regularly on the jukebox at the now defunct Paradise Bar and Grill. Helen was right. On the dance floor, he was definitely, and there was no other word for it, charismatic. He reminded me of that guy who played Ray Romano's brother in that sit-com. Of course, in the dark on a cold, snowy night near the boardwalk, he was something else altogether.

I couldn't help but think of the William Carlos William poem, one of my favorites, "The Artist," where the bareheaded guy in a soiled undershirt, hair awry, stands on his toes, heels together, his arms gracefully above his head.

I shut the door.

"How long till they finish?" I asked, nodding toward Claudia's door.

She looked up at the clock on the wall behind me. "They should be breaking in about five minutes."

"And Sidney?"

"Half an hour, longer if the ladies have anything to say about it."

Perfect, I thought, as I sat back down and began thumbing through a copy of *People* that I had absolutely no interest in. Reality TV shows were evidently the rage, with one more outrageous than the next. As if the words *reality* and *TV* should ever occupy the same space. Life is lived. TV is observed. Were people really so gullible that they thought the reality on TV in any way had any resemblance to real life? Probably.

A few minutes passed, the door swung open, and a tsunami of more than a dozen little girls suddenly flooded the room, jabbering away, grasping backpacks and athletic bags, pulling on their heavy, winter jackets. I stood and they brushed by me, as if I didn't exist.

When I made my way into the surprisingly large rehearsal space, Claudia Bennett was in a corner, crouching over a large tote bag, pulling on a white, cable-knit sweater. She looked up when she heard me approach. She was even prettier up close, favoring a young Audrey Hepburn.

"Can I help you?"

"I guess you don't recognize me."

She squinted, her head tilted to one side. "Should I?"

"It was dark. I wouldn't recognize you either. Especially in that outfit."

"I'm sorry, I have no idea what you're talking about."

I pointed to a row of folding chairs lined up against the back of the room. "Why don't we sit down and talk."

She looked around nervously.

"I'm not going to hurt you. Look," I said, backing up toward the door. I pushed it open. "See, you can call for help, if you need to. And Sidney's right next door. He's already proven he can handle me."

I could see from the look on her face that now she knew exactly who I was. She bent down and removed her cell phone from her bag.

"And yes, you can hold onto that, just in case."

"What do you want?" she asked, taking a step toward me, the cell phone clenched in her hand, as if it were a weapon.

I headed toward the row of chairs and she followed. I sat down. Tentatively, she did too, keeping one chair vacant between us.

"We met the other night. Under the boardwalk."

"I know."

"I wasn't expecting that. You and Sidney did a good job."

"It wasn't personal," she said, trying to defuse what she thought might be a situation.

"I know. But when you get right down to it in the end it was personal, because I was the one who lost the money. I was the one who got his ass kicked. I was the one who had my feelings hurt. I was the one who was made to look like a fool. The thing of it is, I need that money back. Well, it's not me who needs it. As you know, it wasn't mine and personally, I don't give a damn. Besides, the chances are Goldblatt deserved it. But he needs it back and so I need it back."

"He did deserve it."

I shrugged. "Maybe yes, maybe no. But I got in the middle of it and I'm the one who lost the money."

"I'm sorry about that. Sidney got a little carried away. He's not like that, you know. He wouldn't hurt a fly. He was playing a part and he was just trying to help me."

"I'm sure that's true, but it doesn't change what happened. I saw him in there mamboing away. He's not bad, by the way. I don't hold a grudge. I just want to make things whole. So about that money."

"It's ours. Goldblatt stole it from us."

"Goldblatt is many things, and sure, he stretches the truth, but he doesn't out and out lie. Or steal, though I'm sure there are some who would disagree. He explained to me why he took that money and on some level, it makes sense. There are no guarantees in life, Claudia. Your father paid him that money in good faith and I believe he recommended you to another lawyer in good faith. The fact that your father didn't have a case, well, that's life. But it doesn't give you the right to rip someone else off."

"Two wrongs don't make a right and all that bullshit?"

"As much as I hate clichés, I'm afraid that's the way it is. Now if you'll just give me the money back, I'll be out of your life."

"And if I don't."

"I hope it doesn't come to that."

"But if it does?"

"I'll have no other choice."

She backed away.

I smiled. "Don't worry, Claudia, I'm not the physical type. I'll just have to report you to the police."

She laughed.

"You think I'm kidding?"

"You don't have any proof."

"You think?"

"It's your word against mine . . . and Sidney's."

"And you think because we're in Long Beach and because you know the cops personally they're going to believe you and not me."

"That's right."

"Maybe. But you ought to know that my father was born here. His father, my grandfather, was on the force. I might have some contacts myself."

"Mine might be better," she said, her back straightening, as if we were in a tennis match and she'd just served an ace.

"True. But what if I had proof?"

"What kind of proof could you possibly have?"

"A tape recording of what happened."

Her eyes opened wide. "You don't."

"You think?"

"How could you?"

"Maybe I had a tape recorder in my pocket and maybe I flipped it on as soon as Sidney coldcocked me."

"Prove it."

"Claudia, honey, I don't have to prove anything to anyone but the cops. You want to take that chance? You've got a nice little operation here. The kids really seem to like you. And Sidney, well he really seems to be into that dance lesson thing. I've heard he's a real favorite with the ladies. How do you think it would go down if this matter went to the police? You think parents would keep sending their kids here? You think the ladies would sign up for lessons with someone who's been charged with assault? I'm just saying, is it worth the chance?"

She put her head down. I kept my mouth shut. I wanted to give it time to sink in.

"It's our money . . . my father's money."

"That's not for me to decide, Claudia. But if you really feel that way you ought to take it to small claims."

She was silent, staring down at the floor.

"You know, I don't believe you."

"Then don't give back the money."

She looked up at me. She had extremely pretty, bright blue eyes. I could see tears forming in them. I looked away. There's nothing worse than a woman crying. It's an unfair advantage, not that it was going to work on me. You have to have heart-strings to have them tugged. But I have to admit they were vibrating a little.

"Would you take a check?"

I smiled and shook my head.

"I don't have that kind of cash on me."

"I would hope not. Tell you what . . ." I looked at my watch. "I can make the 4:17 train, and I noticed there's a bank down the block. Why don't we take a walk . . ."

"I have another class . . ."

"Claudia. We're going to get this done, so why not just do it now and be done with it? I'm out of your hair, Goldblatt's out of mine. Your class can wait fifteen minutes, I'm sure."

She paused a second, surveying her options. I knew she didn't have any and I was betting she felt the same way. "Okay."

I heard someone at the door. I looked up and there was Sidney, a look of surprise on his face. He recognized me and moved forward, on cat's feet.

Claudia raised her hand. "It's all right, Sid."

"You sure?"

"I'm sure."

"He's not going to try anything, is he? You're not going to try anything, are you?" he asked, his fists balling up at his sides. Actually, he looked kind of ridiculous standing there trying to look menacing in his mambo dance outfit. But I wasn't going to let him know that.

"No, Sidney, I'm not going to try anything."

Five minutes later, we were in the bank. Two minutes after that, I had Goldblatt's five grand, fifty C-notes, in my hand. I peeled off ten of them and gave them back to Claudia.

"What's this?"

"You deserve something."

"But what about Goldblatt?"

"Don't worry, I'll take care of Goldblatt. Trust me, I know him well and I'm pretty sure he doesn't have completely clean hands in all this. He probably overcharged you, at the very least. Maybe losing a grand will teach him a lesson, though I doubt it."

"Did you really have a tape?"

"Does it matter?"

"I guess not."

"Let me ask you something, Claudia. That was a pretty clever scheme you came up with about the lost diary. Was it true?"

She smiled. "Does it matter?"

"Probably not, but I'm curious."

"I guess you'll have to come back to Long Beach to find out."

"Is that an invitation?"

"Does it matter?"

I smiled. I couldn't help myself. She was flirting with me and she was pretty good at it. I know she was good at it because I couldn't help thinking that maybe I would make a trip back to Long Beach some day.

She dug into her bag, which was slung over her shoulder, and pulled out her wallet. She opened it and handed me a card. "It's for a free dance lesson."

"What makes you think I don't know how to dance?"

"I'm sure I could teach you something. Unless, of course, you'd rather have Sidney show you a few steps."

"I like to keep my options open," I said, as I stashed the card in my pocket. You never knew. Maybe I would make it back to Long Beach. If not for the diary at least for the free dance lesson.

9

You Oughtta Be
in Pictures

I was in no hurry to give Goldblatt his money back, so I ignored his calls that night. The next morning, I rang up Julia Scully and asked if I could stop by to talk to her about Ed Feingersh. I told her I was a journalist doing a story on him and though she proclaimed she really didn't know much, that it was a long time ago, she was amenable to meeting with me. She invited me over to her apartment on the Upper West Side. "If you can make it around noon," she said, "I can offer you lunch."

"That won't be necessary," I said. But she insisted and I, never one to turn down a free meal, let her win that argument.

I made it through security of the large high-rise and headed up to the seventeenth floor. I rang the doorbell once, expecting to find a doddering old woman greeting me. Instead, I was surprised to find the door answered by someone who looked remarkably good for a woman pushing eighty. She had a beautiful face, sparkling blue eyes, a Roman nose, and high cheekbones; her hair, pulled back, was a pale blonde, only a couple shades away from gray. She was fit looking enough so that I suspected she worked out, even at her advanced age. She was wearing a well-pressed pair of beige slacks and a white blouse, covered by a camel's hair cardigan.

"Mr. Swann, I presume."

"Ms. Scully, I presume."

"May I take your coat?"

"You may, but I'm happy to put it in the closet myself."

"That's not the way we do things here. I'm the host, you're the guest." I removed my coat and she took it from me, hanging it in a closet just to the right of the doorway. "Come. I'm sure you're hungry. I certainly am. I have to eat every few hours or else my blood sugar drops and you wouldn't want to be around me if that happens. Fortunately, I have the metabolism of a hummingbird."

I followed her through the living room, past a wall of beautiful, black-and-white photographs, one of which was a startling print of a submarine sliding into the sea, shot as if the photographer was submerging with it. I couldn't help wondering how that possibly could have been taken. Lagging behind, I found her standing in front of a dining table in an alcove that obviously served as a dining area.

"Terrific photographs."

"Thank you. I rescued most of them from the trash bin."

"I don't understand."

"I was a photo magazine editor, well before photos were considered art and photographers considered artists. The photographers who later became world famous and their work collectible would give us their photographs to be reproduced and then, when we were finished, they'd be tossed away. I thought many of them were too beautiful to be trashed, so I took them home, framed them, and there they are. I've got them all throughout the apartment."

"They must be very valuable."

"Some are, some aren't. Those that are, well, I like to think of them as my annuity. Whenever I run low of funds, I sell off one of them. It's not easy, they're like my children, but you do what you have to in order to survive, don't you? I'm afraid I'm running rather low now. Unfortunately, the cost of living in this city keeps going up. Please. Sit."

The table was set beautifully with what looked like expensive china and real silverware. The chairs, lushly padded, were obviously expensive, too. This was a woman who knew how to live well but not ostentatiously.

"I hope you didn't go to any trouble."

"I'm afraid I'm well past the age where I go to any trouble for anything, Mr. Swann . . ."

"Henry."

"All right. Henry. I just stopped by Zabar's and ordered anything that looked good. I enjoy having visitors, especially journalists."

"We'll see about that," I said, as I sunk into one of the plush dining room chairs.

She served me a variety of salads, sliced turkey, and smoked salmon, all of which was delicious. I felt guilty, milking her for information while she fed me, but I overcame that pretty quickly when I thought about how much money Goldblatt and I were making.

"So," she said, as she nibbled on some chicken salad, "you wanted to know about Ed."

"Yes."

"I'm surprised anyone's interested. That was a long time ago and Ed's been dead almost, well I guess it's close to fifty years now. It's surprising to hear that number of years come out of my mouth. I look in the mirror and ask myself, 'who is that person?' because the truth is up here," she tapped her head, "I'm still twenty-two. It's down here," she said, tapping her chest, "that I know I'm not."

"It's more his work that I'm interested in, but first maybe you can tell me about your relationship with him."

"I met Eddie while I was working at *Argosy*, a men's magazine. I'd just moved to New York from out west and I stumbled onto this job as an editorial assistant in the photography department. I didn't know anything about photography, but that didn't stop me from applying or, thankfully, them from hiring me. Eddie was one of the steady stream of young freelancers pitching photo story ideas. As I recall, he was already one of the top magazine photojournalists, but he certainly wasn't much to look at. He was slight and scrawny, with a narrow face, a crooked nose, and bulging eyes. He always had a cigarette dangling from his lips and wore a stained, crumpled raincoat. I remember the first thing he tried to pitch my boss, who was the ultimate New York cosmopolitan. He called it 'Hell Drivers,' daredevil performers who entertained crowds by racing cars through burning walls, over hurdles, and into thunderous crashes. He wound up on a racetrack with Irish Horan's Lucky Hell Drivers, crouching between boards tented at a forty-five-degree angle with the speeding cars whipping by so close he could see the ply marks on their tires. He was always proposing crazy, dangerous stories like jumping from a plane with paratroops."

She stopped to take a sip of white wine. "I'd never met anyone like Eddie before. How could I? I grew up in the wilds of Alaska and went to school at Stanford. Anyway, one day Ed asked me if I'd like to join him for a drink at Costello's—that's where he hung out, with all the other journalists."

"The name is familiar. Is it still around?"

She laughed. "I'm lucky I'm still around. No, I believe it closed down years ago. It was on Third Avenue and 44th Street."

"So you started to date?"

"Yes. Like I said, he wasn't much to look at, but he was engaging and very charming, at least when he wasn't talking about photography, which according to him had to be totally free of bullshit. His idol was Henri Cartier-Bresson. He used only available light, no cropping, and he wouldn't let anyone else develop or print his pictures. Besides being my boyfriend, my first in New York, he became my mentor. He gave me my first camera—a Yashica twin lens reflex, one of the inexpensive models they were beginning to produce in Japan. I started taking pictures and he said, 'Hey, you've got an eye.' He convinced me to sign up for Alexey Brodovitch's class at the New School, whose mantra was, 'surprise me!' And believe me, I tried."

"How long did you date?"

"Only about a year. I'm not even sure why we broke up. I was only twenty-two or twenty-three, and probably fickle. I have some photographs, if you'd like to see them."

"I would."

She returned with an album and flipped open a few pages. "This is Eddie," she said, showing me a black-and-white photo that looked remarkably like her description of him, leaning against something, wearing a shabby raincoat, a cigarette dangling from his lips. "I took it."

"Very interesting-looking man."

She flipped to some others. "He was a tragic man. He drank too much and he suffered from deep bouts of depression."

"What happened to him after you stopped dating?"

"We remained friendly. We bumped into each other every so often. But I was young. I was juggling work with a social life. We drifted apart to the point where I hardly saw him, though I used to hear about him every so often. He had an up-and-down career until those Monroe photographs. You know about them, I'm sure."

"I do."

"There was a point in his career where he became blocked. And then a friend, Bob Stein, who was the editor at *Redbook*, offered him a job as photo editor and he took it. But he refused to take any photo assignments. Probably due to his depression. He married for a short time—they actually lived a few blocks from me in the Village—then divorced. A short time after that he was found dead. I don't recall exactly what happened but it was probably due to a combination of alcoholism and deep depression."

"What happened to his work?"

"That's a good question. Eddie insisted on holding onto everything. He was what we'd now call a control freak. He was also very mysterious. I don't think I ever knew where he lived—I know I never went back to his apartment. In fact, if you asked most of his friends they'd probably say he lived at Costello's."

"So no one knew where he kept his work?"

She shook her head. "I do know they found the Marilyn negatives sometime in the eighties—time gets away from you when you get older, so I can't tell you exactly when—in some storage place somewhere. I suppose it's possible his agency, PIX, had some of them. Why do you ask?"

"It seems like a good angle for the story."

"You'd like to find them, wouldn't you?"

"It would be quite the scoop."

"And they'd be very valuable."

"You would know that better than I."

She smiled. "You'd like me to help you find them, wouldn't you?"

"If I could."

"I'm afraid the only thing I could do would be to point you in a direction that would probably wind up in a dead end."

"At least I'd have a direction."

"Well, if it were me looking for them, I'd probably try to find some of the fellow photographers he hung out with, though that would be difficult, since most of them have passed on. Or, I might speak to Bob Stein. I believe he's still alive. Or, I might try to contact the agency that took over PIX. I'll write down the name of a few people who might be able to help you with your search."

"You're pretty good at this."

"You forget, I was a journalist, too, Mr. Swann." She winked. She knew exactly who and what I was, and yet she was still playing along. Somehow, that made me feel okay.

Before I left, I asked, "Do you mind if I get back to you if I have any other questions?"

"Of course," she said. "But if I'm out, just leave a message. Tomorrow night, for instance, I've got my weekly poker game with the boys."

"You play poker with the boys?"

"Sure do. And I'm damn good at it. Most of them have trouble keeping their eyes open when it gets late. And that's when I pounce."

"Remind me never to play poker with you, Julia."

"For some reason, Mr. Swann, I don't think you'd be falling asleep on me."

★ ★ ★ ★ ★

WEST PALM BEACH, FLORIDA

★ ★ ★ ★ ★

"There is a reason that all things are as they are."

Bram Stoker, *Dracula*

10
Birds of a Feather

While New Yorkers were slogging their way through ice and slush, Floridians were in the grip of a tropical heat wave. Knowing this before I left—like the Boy Scout I never was—I did my best to be prepared. I dressed light and packed even lighter, stuffing everything I needed into a well-worn, khaki-colored knapsack I used when I took my son hiking in upstate New York. I hadn't used it in almost a decade and when I opened the side pocket to pack a notebook, I found a parking receipt from Harriman State Park. Part of me, the part that hates remembering, the part of me that wants to think only of tomorrow and the infinite possibilities for success and happiness open to me, wanted to toss it in the trash. The other part of me, the part that feels it is sometimes necessary to go to the dark side, to feel the pain, if only for a moment, to know that I have suffered and will suffer again, that the future is only filled with failure, needed to hold onto it. This time, the dark side won out and I folded and refolded till it was hardly visible, then tucked it into the not-so-secret, zippered compartment of my wallet.

Outside, as I headed toward the parking lot to pick up my rental, the heat pounded at me even harder than Sidney's unexpected punch in the gut. It wasn't until the cool air had kicked in as I headed down I-95 toward the address I had for the Sunnydale Residential Home that I was able to breathe a little easier.

I may not be master of the bluff, but I know when and how

to use it. When I first started in the business, in those early days when I was a small-time reporter aspiring to be the next Woodward *and* Bernstein, people weren't as suspicious as they are now. You could just about sell them any cock-and-bull story and they'd buy it, because they wanted to believe it. Now, after decades of TV news shows, exposing frauds and con men, and reality shows that encourage lies and deceit, it isn't so easy. But if you sound like you know what you're talking about and you say it with authority, people are, amazingly, still inclined to trust you. But you can only take that so far, and to pull it off you have to have a relatively honest face. Somehow, I was blessed (or cursed) with that. God knows why. I've been told it's the eyes. And the nonthreatening smile behind which lurks anger and cynicism. But I don't care. Whatever it is, it usually works. But only if you have a good, believable story and you stick to it as long as you have to.

I didn't think I could just waltz into Sunnydale and ask for Delores, without even knowing her last name. I had to have a reason. So I did what I do best, I made one up. I walked right into the administration office and found a young, pretty blonde at the front desk. When I saw she was reading a copy of *Entertainment Weekly,* I knew it wouldn't be much of a challenge.

"Excuse me," I said, in that tone that is supposed to communicate how fragile and vulnerable you are. "I wonder if you could help me."

"That depends," she said, raising her eyes only slightly from the magazine, which had a half-naked Lady Gaga on the cover.

"On what?" I said, with the sincerest nonthreatening smile I could muster.

"You're not from around here, are you?"

"If you mean, am I a resident, what do you think?"

"I think you're a little young to be living here," she said, her cheeks flushing with embarrassment.

"Thank you for that, whatever your name is."

"Tiffany."

"Like the store."

"Huh?"

"The store. Tiffany's."

"There's a store called Tiffany's?"

"There is."

"Oh . . ."

"Well, you know, Tiffany," I said, with a wink, "I don't live here but sometimes I sure could use some assistance in living. But, I'm afraid I'm not here for that. A year or so ago, my mom resided at Sunnydale for a bit, but she passed away a few months ago."

"Oh, I'm so sorry."

I leaned forward and lowered my voice, "It was her time, and frankly, she was ready to go. All kinds of things were breaking down. I'm sure you don't want to hear about all her complaints, because I sure didn't. Hell, I'm guessing you get plenty of those. Anyway, when she was here she mentioned she had a wonderful relationship with a woman named Delores. Evidently, Delores helped her through some pretty tough times. She said that when she passed she wanted to do something for her and that's why I'm here. Do you think you could possibly tell me her last name and how to get in touch with her?"

"Like what?"

"Like what?" I echoed quizzically.

"Like what did she want you to do for her? Like, is Delores in the will?"

Her eyes lit up. I could see the wheels turning. If I said yes, obviously the residents of Sunnydale would get much better treatment and service from Tiffany. But I have learned to keep my lies vague. "Well, you know, Tiffany, I think that's really between Delores and me. It is kind of personal, don't you think?"

"I guess," she said, her face turning into that annoying yet surprisingly sweet frown left over from her teenage years, which weren't that far behind her. I reckoned there wasn't much to talk about at Sunnydale and any gossip, no matter how slight, was appreciated.

"So you know who I'm talking about."

"Sure. Delores Wren. She's a sweetheart. And I guess it's your lucky day. She's like usually not in on Saturdays, but she's here this morning because she said she needed to catch up on some paperwork. You can probably find her in her office."

"Where would that be?"

She stood up and walked to the door. She was wearing a very short, white skirt, and I could make out the outline of her panties. "See that building over there?" she said, pointing across the courtyard, bending forward so I couldn't possibly miss her well-shaped ass. Pilates? Yoga? Plenty of gym time? Running? Sex?

"I do."

"Walk into the building, take a left, walk down the hall, and it's like the second office on the right. I'd take you there myself, but I can't leave the office unattended."

"Wouldn't want anyone breaking in and stealing paperwork, would we? That's okay. I'm pretty good at finding things." I took a couple steps toward the door. "You wouldn't be married by any chance, would you Tiffany?" I don't know why I asked it. She was way too young and uninteresting for me. But she was hot and maybe it was just reflex action. Or maybe it was because at that moment I needed some kind of human connection.

Her face reddened. "No. Not yet."

"Got a boyfriend?"

She hesitated a moment, as if contemplating the pros and

cons of her answer. "Yeah."

I shook my head. "Too bad. Guess I'll have to eat alone tonight." But it wasn't too bad. It was good. I felt better having asked the question, but I was satisfied with the answer. And in the end, it was probably best that I'd be eating alone that night. I would have used her and then felt bad about it. I feel bad about enough things.

I walked across the courtyard and entered a small, three-story building, followed directions, and wound up in front of a door that read,

Social Services
Delores Wren
Sharyn Wolf

I knocked on the door. "Come in," came a sweet voice with what sounded like a slight southern tinge to it.

The office was small, yet airy and pleasant. The wallpaper was white with blue and yellow flowers scattered throughout. The colorfully printed matching love seat and rattan chairs made the place look like it had been decorated by a Laura Ashley wannabe. I assumed it was to keep the tenants of the Sunnydale Residential Home happy, as if anything can make being that much closer to death a happy occasion. There were two small, glass and chrome desks, tables really, because neither had drawers. One was empty. Behind the other was none other than Delores Wren. I knew that not because I am any great detective, but because the nameplate placed discreetly in front of her announced that fact.

"May I help you?" she asked, with what appeared to be a mildly surprised look on her face. I suspected it was because she didn't recognize me and because most of her clients had ten to fifteen or more years on me. She was a very pretty blonde, in her early to mid-fifties, though she looked younger. She was lightly tanned, her hair was cut short, so that it fell just over her ears and halfway down her forehead. I couldn't help but be reminded of a Delta flight attendant named Jody, who I dated a couple times before I was married.

"That's what I'm hoping."

"Please, sit down," she said, pointing to the small, paisley print couch. "Who are you, would be my first question."

I remained standing because I thought it gave me a slight advantage putting myself in a superior position. "My name's Henry Swann and I'm here on personal business, Ms. Wren."

"What kind of personal business?" she asked, warily.

"Ever hear of someone named Jack Kerowak?"

"You mean the writer?"

"No. Another Jack Kerowak."

"I don't believe I have," she replied in that social worker's voice that's supposed to calm the inner beast. I could sense she was a little wary of me and that was a good start. She would be so busy trying to protect herself that information about someone else would be easier to get.

"That's odd, because from what I understand he's your daughter's boyfriend."

She hesitated a moment. "I . . . I didn't know that . . . I really don't know anything about my daughter's boyfriends."

Her body became rigid. I had put her in defensive mode. I liked that. I wanted her on edge. She would try to restore her balance and in doing so she'd inevitably say something she wouldn't necessarily want to reveal. The thing of it is, most people want to be helpful, they want to please. And if you give them the opportunity, if you create a safe environment, if you bond with them, you can pretty much get them to tell you anything you want to know. With women, though, it's tougher. Here's what I've found to be the difference. Men will lie, they will cheat, they will steal. But they usually aren't that good at it.

They have a tell because they're used to telling the truth. They're not smart enough to lie well. They give themselves away. With women, it's different. They spend their lives revealing truth. When a man says something he means it. "I'm bad for you, baby." He's telling you the truth, but most women don't believe it. The reason they don't is because when a woman tells you something she doesn't necessarily mean what she says. "Honey, I don't want anything for my birthday. Really." Guys, stupid guys, believe that, and they don't get a gift. What the woman really means is, "You'd damn well better get me a gift and it damn well better be a good one."

It was now time for me to put Delores Wren more at ease, which I did by sitting down.

"Listen, Delores. May I call you Delores?" She nodded her head. "Good. Well, Delores, I just flew down here from New York City where the weather really sucks. I'm only here for a day and I'd like to take advantage of it. The grounds are awfully pretty. What say we take a little walk and we can talk."

"I . . . I guess I could take a break."

"That's great."

She shuffled some papers on her desk, then stepped away from her desk and led the way out of the building. She was wearing a short, tight-fitting tan skirt cut just above the knees, and a short-sleeve, white blouse. Despite the fact that she was wearing flats, her legs were still shapely and well toned. I imagined she did some running. Or maybe walking the Sunnydale golf course we could see not far in the distance from the main buildings.

As we walked out the door she spun on her heels, faced me, and said, "I know just the spot." The smile was back on her face and I knew she was a little more comfortable, probably feeling that now she was back in control.

We walked past a complex of two-storied buildings, past a

pool, and four shuffleboard courts.

"It's a beautiful day, but it doesn't seem many people are taking advantage of it," I said, trying to make meaningless conversation, something I'm not particularly good at.

"It's lunch time. Most of our residents are in the dining room. This afternoon, they'll be out by the pool or if it gets too hot, inside playing cards."

"Looks like there's plenty to do here."

"We try to keep our residents busy. It's one of the reasons they're so happy here."

"Not much need for a social worker, you'd think."

"You'd think wrong," she said, as we reached the edge of a pond, with benches facing the water. "You don't think the elderly have problems? You don't stop living when you reach fifty-five, Mr. Swann. And when you see the end in sight, well, it's a very unsettling feeling. I'm here to help people deal with that inevitability. Old age is not a sentence, Mr. Swann, it's a privilege. And you'd be surprised at how happy these people can be if they accept the limitations that come with age. They've actually done studies that show as we age we actually get happier, more content. But this only comes with acceptance."

"Very interesting, Delores," I said, purposely using her name to help cement the bond I was trying to create.

"Would this bench do?" she asked, pointing toward a slatted wooden bench that faced the pond.

"Of course."

She sat down. I sat down next to her. We stared out on the water for a moment or two. It was a beautiful, bucolic view. If I weren't me I might have been calmed by it. But it takes a lot to quiet the demons running through my mind.

"I don't understand why you're here to see me. Has something happened to Donna?"

"I hope not."

"You're frightening me, Mr. Swann."

"I don't want to do that. I'm sure she's fine." I looked out across the pond. A foursome had just teed up. "Kind of funny, isn't it?"

"What?"

"Two birds, Swann and Wren, sitting by a pond."

She smiled and primly folded her hands in her lap. "So my daughter has a boyfriend."

"Yes," punctuated by the thwack of a golf club hitting a ball.

"You know him?"

"We've met."

"Is he . . ."

"Seems like he's okay. But in my business jumping to conclusions can lead to trouble. As André Gide said, 'Please don't understand me too quickly.' "

"What is your business?"

Another thwack.

"I find lost people, which isn't as easy as it sounds. People who want to get lost usually have something to hide, or they're running from something. That's why they're lost."

"Donna isn't lost."

"Then you know where she is."

She hesitated a moment. "No."

"Jack doesn't know either. According to him she packed up all her things and left without a word."

"Donna does have a history of running away."

"Without telling anyone?"

Another thwack. I looked up just in time to see the little white ball get launched into the air.

"Some people are lost because they can't find themselves," she said, softly.

I watched the ball soar through the air and land with a dull thud just a few feet from the green, then watched as the foursome moved toward the hole. They were making progress, moving through the course one stroke at a time. That's the beauty of golf. Steady progress. Eighteen holes, one at a time. You know the beginning and you know the end. You just don't know how long or how many strokes it's going to take you to get there. I didn't feel as if I were doing the same. But I took another swing, anyway.

"Those are the people you're supposed to help, aren't they?" She nodded.

"And those are the people I'm hired to find. I've been hired by Jack to find Donna. Do you know where she is?"

"You're probably not going to believe this but I haven't a clue."

"You're right. I don't believe you."

"I told you so."

"You don't seem particularly worried?"

"In the past ten years, Donna's moved more than a dozen times. Sooner or later, when she's ready to tell me, I find out where."

"Maybe she's in trouble."

"Donna's made a life's work out of being in trouble. I suspect it's probably because she has me for a mother."

"Why's that?"

"Because I do what I do and I am what I am. All her life, I've tried to get her to face herself, but that's not something she wants to do. It frightens her, so she runs."

"When was the last time you saw her?" I asked, as the cracking sound of an iron hitting the ball cut through the air.

"I honestly can't remember. A year or so, perhaps. I think it was just after I got remarried."

"Would you say your relationship was . . ."

"Contentious. But I don't want you to get the wrong impression. I love my daughter. I always will."

"Tell me about her."

"What's to tell?" she said, removing a pack of cigarettes and a lighter from her purse. "I hope you don't mind. I'll blow the smoke away from you."

"We're all gonna die sometime and somehow. I doubt I'm going to go from secondhand smoke."

"It's an ugly, dangerous habit and I'm trying to quit. Down to four a day," she said, lighting up, then putting the lighter back into her purse.

"You don't need to explain anything to me."

She lit up, took a long drag, turned her head away, and exhaled. I didn't want to tell her I had a pack a day habit that I quit the day my wife died. My son lost one parent and I wasn't about to be the cause of him losing another. Ironic, since he wound up losing the other one anyway.

"Why don't you tell me what's going on, then maybe I'll tell you what you think I know," she said, holding the cigarette down and away from me. I could tell she was in the right job, sensitive to people around her.

"Jack comes to me. He's heartbroken. He's been with Donna almost two years. Things seem like they're going pretty good. He wakes up one morning and she's gone. Without a word. Without a sign. Without a trace. As if she'd disappeared from the planet. He's worried. He's confused. He wants answers. He wants closure. And frankly, I think he'd like an opportunity to get her back. But none of that is my business. My business is to find her. That's why I'm here. I'm hoping you can point me in the right direction."

"I don't see how I can help you, since I don't know where she is. She won't even give me her cell number."

"Why's that?"

"She said I abused the privilege, as if it's a privilege to speak to your own daughter," she said, crushing the cigarette against the seat of the bench. "She was always a difficult, headstrong child."

"When was the last time you heard from her?"

She hesitated a moment. "About a month ago. She called. In the middle of the night. She made it sound like it was just one of those 'it's about time we touch base calls,' but I could sense it was more than that."

"More how?"

"She wanted to talk to me about something."

"What?"

"I don't know. I started to ask some innocuous questions, like how she was doing, what she was doing, and she got upset. She accused me of prying into her life. I tried to explain that I was just interested, as a mother, as someone who loved her, but it was too late. She said she had to go and that she'd call again. I still haven't heard from her."

"If you had to reach her, how would you do it?"

"I guess I'd contact Allie Pearson, her best friend. Allie's the only constant in her life."

"I've already gone that route. She said she couldn't help me. Do you believe that?"

She shrugged. "I don't know. I just don't know. But I'm afraid I can't either."

"No one disappears without a trace," I said, my voice hardening, staring her in the eyes.

"You think I'm lying?"

"Someone is."

"Well, it's not me." Her voice took on an edge that hadn't been there before. "Besides, if Donna wants to disappear, that's her business. She hasn't done anything wrong. And if she didn't tell this so-called boyfriend of hers maybe she had a good reason. Tell him he's probably better off without her. Better a runaway girlfriend than a runaway wife. Why can't you just let sleeping dogs lie?"

"Because it's in my nature to poke them till they wake up."

"You could get bitten."

"I sometimes do. You'd think I'd learn my lesson, wouldn't you? But somehow that stick always seems to make its appearance and once it's there I tend to use it."

I looked over to the pond. Several geese had flown in and they were sailing in our direction. I watched their progress as Delores Wren lit up another cigarette and continued her lethal ritual of inhaling, turning away from me, then exhaling the smoke. I watched it trail upwards, disappearing into the bright blue sky.

"I'm surprised you aren't worried about her."

"I've done all the worrying I can. Donna can take care of herself. She's made that quite clear to me."

"So there's nothing else you want to tell me."

"Nothing I can think of." She looked at me and smiled. "I'm sorry you came all the way down here for nothing, but at least you got away from that terrible weather for a couple days."

★ ★ ★ ★ ★

NEW YORK CITY

★ ★ ★ ★ ★

"It is better for you not to know this than to know it."
Aeschylus, *Prometheus Bound*

11
FOCUSING IN

Monday morning, I was back in Klavan's—much larger than my own—office, shooting the breeze with him. He was spewing jealous nonsense about my one-nighter in warmer climes, and offering his dream choices of where he'd like to spend the winter—Bali, the Canary Islands, the French Riviera, Costa Rica, the list seemed to be endless—when Goldblatt barged in. I say barged without prejudice, because he truly has no other way of entering a room.

"Morning, Goldblatt," said Klavan who sitting at his desk facing the door was the first to see the big man enter.

"Yeah, it's morning but that doesn't mean there's anything good about it."

"Turn down the lights, will ya, Ross, Goldblatt's presence is more than enough to brighten any room."

"Very funny. You disappear for two days, you don't answer my calls, what am I supposed to think?"

"Does that mean you were worried about me?"

He hesitated a moment. "Yeah. I was worried about you. Anything wrong with that?"

"I think it's sweet," said Klavan. "Why don't you take off your coat and stay a while?"

"You might consider planting a GPS device on me," I said, as Goldblatt peeled off his coat to reveal a brand-new down vest. It pleased me to see that he was spending some of our money on upgrading his wardrobe.

"Nice vest," I noted.

"Thanks. The old one was kinda ratty looking."

"You think?" said Klavan.

Goldblatt sneered and directed his gaze back at me. "You got my money?" he asked in a voice that held both hope and desperation.

I patted my pocket. "Yes, I do."

His face brightened like a teenager finding out his parents are leaving him alone for the night with the alcohol cabinet unlocked.

"How about some coffee, Goldblatt?" Klavan offered, in what I thought was a conciliatory effort to make peace, though I knew it wouldn't work. "I think there's still some in the pot."

"No thanks. I'm off the stuff. It's the caffeine. It makes me jumpy. I'm trying to calm down. Look at me," he said, offering his jittery hand, palm down. He glared back at me. "If certain people will stop aggravating the hell out of me, I might be all right. You gonna make me beg?"

"That would be entertaining, but no, I am not going to make you beg." I reached into my pocket and handed him the envelope of dough. I was anxious to see his expression when he realized it was a little short. Without saying thanks, he ripped open the envelope, his eyes expanded to twice their size, and then he counted it, bill by bill, as Klavan and I watched in amusement.

"Hey, this is a grand short," he said, waving the bills in the air after he'd finished counting.

"I know. Expenses."

"A grand in expenses. Are you crazy? Do you think I'm stupid? You took the fuckin' train out to Long Beach. What's that, twenty bucks? And maybe a cab to and from Penn Station, twenty more, tops, though I don't see why you can't take the subway like everyone else . . ."

"That's all I could get back and you know, you're lucky you got that much. You're going to have to make up the other grand yourself. You think it was easy going out there and dealing with those thugs?"

I could see the wheels turning. He was wondering where he was going to get the extra grand. Or, even more, if there was vig involved.

It didn't take him long to come up with the answer. "How are you doing on that Feingersh thing?"

"Making progress."

"You do understand that you find those negatives or the prints, we're in for a nice piece of cash?"

"I'm aware of that."

He plunked himself down in a chair in the corner, leaning back and spreading his legs out. "So where were you this weekend?"

"Florida."

"In the middle of this fuckin' job you're taking a vacation?"

"Who said it was a vacation?"

"What, you were visiting relatives? Oh, Jesus, it wasn't this Kevorkian thing, was it?"

"Kerowak."

"Whatever the fuck his name is. That's a dead-end case for us. You gotta get smart, Swann. You put those kinds of cases on the back burner. This is A, number one."

"Don't worry, I was just discussing it with Ross when you came in and ruined the mood."

"What's he got to do with this? Suddenly we got a third partner?" he said, as Ross looked on with amusement.

"He's a friend. You know what that is, Goldblatt. It's someone who helps out . . . for nothing . . . when you need them. It's someone who gives advice and guidance without charging for it." I looked over at Klavan. He was smiling. It egged me on.

117

Sometimes I hate myself when I do these things. Sometimes, not. This was one of the latter times.

"Ross here happens to know something about the collectible markets, okay. He's willing to share his expertise for nothing, nada, niente."

That seemed to shut Goldblatt up. But only for a moment.

"Well, thanks, then . . . but Swann, when you go out of town, you've got to let me know. I need to know your whereabouts at all times."

"That's not going to happen."

If looks could kill, I would have been a dead man.

"Did you speak to the old broad?"

"If you mean Julia Scully, the answer is yes."

"She give you anything good?"

"Maybe."

"What's that supposed to mean?"

"It means what it means. Listen, Goldblatt, we ought to get something straight. I work the way I work. I don't share information. I don't share plans. I don't call. I don't write. No hugs. No kisses. I just do things. I don't need anything or anyone holding me back. I make my own schedule. I work on cases my own way. I need my space," I added, trying hard to suppress a smile. "If you don't like that, we can just dissolve this partnership right here and now."

"No. No. I don't want that. We're in this together, Swann. You and me, we're in a learning curve. You're learning how I work, I'm learning how you work. We're going to make this thing we got a well-oiled machine. All you gotta do is communicate with me. You know, every once in a while."

"I'm communicating now, so back off."

"That's not exactly what I meant."

I could see Goldblatt was on the ropes, so I softened a bit.

"Okay, how's this for a compromise. We've got two cases going at once: Kerowak and Feingersh. I'm going to put Feingersh on the top of the list and when there's a lull, I'll work on Jack's case. How does that sound?" I didn't mention the Faithfull thing, because I was sure it was a load of shit and I didn't want to give Goldblatt even the least possibility that there really was a lost diary out there and that someone had it. If I had, I never would have heard the end of it.

He smiled, baring his newly whitened teeth. "That's all I ask for."

"Then that's all you'll get."

Once Goldblatt left and Klavan and I finished discussing his pros and cons as a partner—for the time being, the pros won out—we got down to the subject of Feingersh's negatives.

"You understand, Swann, the chances of those negatives or original prints existing is infinitesimally small."

"I do. But they did find those Monroe negatives, so there's a chance the rest of his work is still around, that either someone has them or they're stored in an attic or a basement somewhere. Let's just say, for the sake of discussion, someone has them, why wouldn't they have made that known and cash in on them?"

"The only reasons I can think of is that they want them to remain private or they're waiting for the right moment to expose them to the market."

"What's that mean?"

"Markets for art and collectibles go up and down, just like the stock market. When an artist or writer dies, the demand for their work, if they were good, if they were collectible, goes up, because the supply is now limited. Also, artists and writers go in and out of favor. A particular artist might be out of favor now, but something happens and bam! There's a big demand. The market for photography has been on the upswing for years, so I don't know why they wouldn't already have offered them for sale, so that's why my money is on their either having been destroyed or they're just sitting somewhere without the person who has them either knowing what they are or that they even have them. It happens sometimes with books. They turn up in an attic somewhere with the owner having no idea what they are or what they're worth. But by this time almost everyone in the country has cleaned out their house, had a yard sale, and brought things of value to be sold or auctioned. The days of finding buried treasure in the attic or basement are coming to an end. They've got that *Antiques Roadshow* program that's made everyone loot grandma and grandpa's attics. My question is, how do you expect to track them down, if they still exist?"

"There are three possibilities. One, they're sitting in a file somewhere in a photo agency. Two, someone he knew has them, maybe without even knowing they have them. Three, he used to hang out at Costello's, on 44th Street, maybe they're there."

"Costello's. Man, that place is legendary. When I was in my early twenties, I used to hang out there. Used to be a watering hole and hangout for *Daily News* and *New York* magazine people, when they were still on 41st and 42nd. Place has quite a history. Know anything about it?"

"Not really. Give."

I had put Klavan in his element. His true calling was to be a teacher. His head was crammed with all kinds of useful and useless information. All I had to do was turn him on, which is exactly what I'd done.

"There are hundreds of stories. When James Thurber ran up an enormous bar tab, the owner, Tim Costello, gave him the keys to the joint and asked him to draw some art. Thurber wound up creating his famous 'Battle of the Sexes' drawings on eleven beaver wood panels that were there for something like fifty years. No one knows where they are now, but the best guess is the Costello family has them. Am I boring you?"

"Hell, no. I love this stuff. It's like I'm back at Columbia, only without the coeds and asshole professors. Only you."

"Okay, so Hemingway, John Hersey, and John O'Hara used to hang there. Story goes that one night O'Hara was pounded hard on the back by Hemingway who was just leaving the bar. O'Hara propped his blackthorn walking stick up on the bar and Hemingway asked, 'When did you start carrying a walking stick?' O'Hara said something like, 'That's the best piece of blackthorn in New York City.' Never to turn his back on what he thought of as a challenge, Hemingway said, 'Is it? I bet I can break it with my bare hands.' O'Hara bet him fifty bucks that he couldn't, so Hemingway took the bet, then broke the walking stick over his head, took the money, and walked out. That busted walking stick hung over the bar for many years. But Costello's closed a long time ago, sometime in the seventies, I think. I don't even know if the building it was in is still there."

"I'll head over there and find out. If that doesn't pan out, then I'll try to track down people who hung out there. If I can find anyone still alive, they might know something. Meanwhile, Julia Scully gave me a couple leads of people who used to know Feingersh, including his ex-wife."

"Listen, I've got nothing going at the moment, what say I do a little legwork for you and check out the photo agencies? I know a couple guys over there and I always wanted to be a gumshoe."

"I love it when you go all noir on me, Klavan. Well, since it would break Goldblatt's heart that you were helping me, us, out, the answer's, yes."

"I'll have my assistant, Angela, do a little preliminary research on the Internet—she's always looking for things to do and telling me how savvy she is—then I'll take it from there."

"I appreciate it, Ross, and no matter what Goldblatt says, you'll get a piece of the action if we find anything."

"I wouldn't say no, but on one condition. You have to pay me, in cash, in front of Goldblatt. The idea of him watching me getting paid out of his pocket would be worth four times as much as anything you'd pay me."

The image of that exchange made me laugh. I couldn't help myself. Later, I knew I'd feel a little guilty, but at that moment, well, it just felt right.

I was slowly making my way up to 44th Street, sidestepping slippery patches where melted snow had turned to ice, when I felt my cell phone vibrating in my back pocket. I pulled it out and saw the name Jack Kerowak. I was tempted to ignore it because I didn't want to speak to him since I had nothing new on Donna. I hate telling that to clients because it makes them feel like I'm not earning my dough. I don't much like looking like a failure in someone else's eyes. I can do that to myself any time, thank you very much. But instead of letting it go to voice-mail and feeling obligated to call him back, I bit the bullet and answered it.

He got right to the point. "Mr. Swann, I'm calling to see if there's anything new?" he asked in a voice tinged with a combination of hope and despair, turning me into a minor league seer.

"So far, I'm afraid I'm drawing blanks, Jack," I said, in my most solicitous tone, a voice I use when I'm pissed off but don't want anyone to know it. After years of practice, I've gotten pretty good at faking sincerity and concern. "I've been to see Allie Pearson and I just got back from Florida where I tracked down Donna's mother. Both of them claim to have had no contact with her lately. And both say they have no idea where she is."

"Do you believe them?"

I was losing a little breath, talking and walking while trying to keep my balance against the wind and ice, all at the same time, so I stopped and leaned against a building. "Not necessarily. But I can't go all Guantanamo on them and besides, I couldn't get my lead pipe through the metal detector."

"What do you do when you know someone knows something and you can't get them to talk?"

"I find another way to get the information I'm looking for." The sun had come out and some of the ice on the window ledges was beginning to melt, sending large, heavy drops of water onto my head and shoulders. I moved away from the building, back into pedestrian traffic.

"How's that work?"

I was starting to feel a little annoyed. Two things I don't like being quizzed too closely about, if at all: my work methods and my personal life. I was starting to wonder about Jack. Why was he so curious about how I was working? Why wasn't he just let-ting me do my job? Maybe it was because he was a writer and writers ask questions. They like to know how things work. They like to take things apart and put them back together again. I tried to convince myself that that's what Jack was doing, and that I shouldn't let it get to me. Still, I didn't feel like giving him a blueprint of how I work because then he'd hold me to it and that would only wind up inhibiting me.

"I improvise and I haven't come up with a new plan yet. But I will, Jack. You have to be patient. I think I might be able to get something out of Allie, but I want to give her a little time. She's either protecting Donna or she really doesn't know. But even if she doesn't know where Donna is, I think she can help point me in the right direction."

"I could talk to her."

"No. Don't do that. You'll only get in the way. Just let me do my job."

"I'm having a hard time, Swann."

"You'll have to deal with it, Jack," I said, hoping the impatience in my voice didn't seep through. I sensed he was on an emotional ledge and I didn't want him to fall . . . or jump. I wanted to tell him no woman was worth it, but that's not something he wanted to hear. "I'm doing my best, but you have to understand there's a chance I won't be able to find her."

"I don't want to think about that."

I was tempted to suggest he see a therapist or maybe get some kind of prescription medication, but sometimes I'm able to censor myself before the words fly out of my mouth like machine gun bullets, only potentially more lethal. This was one of those times.

"Suit yourself. But you've got to give me time. These things don't solve themselves overnight. This wasn't a spur of the moment thing, Jack. She cleaned the place out in one day. That takes intent and planning."

"I'll try," he said, and I could hear the exasperation in his voice.

"Tell you what. Today's Monday. I'll give you an update Friday. In the meantime, get back to writing whatever you're writing. Or hang out in your favorite bar with some friends. Just do anything you can to get your mind off Donna."

"I've tried that."

"Well, try again. And Jack . . ."

"Yes?"

"Don't call me till then and don't do any investigating of your own. You'll only mess things up."

"Okay."

Once he hung up, I pulled out my notebook and scribbled, "check with super to see about moving van." When I got time, I'd go back to Donna's place and see if anyone remembered her stuff being moved out. Then I might be able to find out where her belongings were shipped, which might lead to where she was. But I knew I wouldn't get to that till the middle or end of the week. I owed Goldblatt that much.

I hadn't walked another two blocks before the phone buzzed again. Dammit, I thought, as I wondered if I'd ever get to my destination. If it was Jack again, I was just going to let it go to voicemail, but it was a number I didn't recognize, so I answered. A slightly familiar woman's voice asked, "Whatcha doin'?"

"Who is this?"

"I'm hurt that you don't recognize my voice. Especially after all we've been through."

"You'll get over it. I'll ask one more time, before I hang up. Who is this?"

"Claudia."

"Claudia who?"

"Claudia Bennett. From Long Beach. The chick who was responsible for you getting your ass kicked last week."

"Oh, that Claudia. You calling to apologize again?"

"Not exactly."

"I'm kinda busy. What can I do for you?"

"It's what I'm gonna do for you."

"What's that?"

"I'm gonna let you take me out to dinner tonight. It's kind of like, if the mountain won't come to Long Beach, Long Beach will come to the mountain. I'm gonna be in Manhattan. Gotta give a private dance lesson this afternoon, so I thought you and me could hook up for a meal. I figure you owe me at least that much."

"How's that?"

"I let you sweet-talk me into giving back four thousand dollars."

"Four thousand dollars that wasn't yours."

"That's debatable. So, you free or not?"

Of course I was free. When wasn't I free? And there was

something about this chick that I liked. So, why not spend some time with her?

"Yeah, I'm free."

"I like Mexican food. Good Mexican food. Not that taco and burrito crap. So no Chipotles. Or Italian. Same deal. None of that Ronzoni out of a can style food or doughy pizza, that I'm sure you exist on. And seven's a good time. All that work for you?"

Of course it did, but I wasn't going to let her call all the shots. "Seven-thirty," I said, not because seven wasn't good but because I wanted to establish myself as someone who couldn't be pushed around. "There's a restaurant called Dos Caminos on 50th and Third Avenue. That work for you?"

"Make a reservation and I'll see you there, bud. And Swann, wear something nice, okay? Make like you give a shit."

"What if I don't give a shit?"

"Fake it."

"What is this, some kind of date?"

"If you're lucky."

The building that housed Costello's was no more. In its place was one of those large, nondescript office buildings. I ducked into the lobby to avoid the sharp wind, which was picking up, pulled out my smartphone, Googled the joint, and found out that Tim Costello, Jr., son of one of the owners, had moved the bar to 225 East 44th Street, where he opened the second Costello's. That closed in 1990, and reopened as the Turtle Bay Cafe. When that closed down, it was replaced by the Overlook Lounge, which was evidently still up and running. I didn't really think I'd find anything, but I was only half a block away and I was hungry, so I figured I might as well drop in and see if I could pick up any information and maybe a quick bite to eat.

The Overlook was housed in a three-story, yellow tenement.

Inside, I immediately saw that it was a long way from the Paradise Bar and Grill, up in Spanish Harlem, where I used to hang out. For one thing, it was spotlessly clean. For another, there was actually some thought put into the décor, the floor didn't crunch from scattered peanut shells when you walked on it, and la cucarachas were nowhere to be seen. There was a long bar on my right and booths on my left. Above the booths, the walls were covered with cartoon characters, many of which I recognized from my childhood. It was only 11:30 in the morning, so the place was empty.

"Can I help you?" asked the bartender, a kid, no more than his late twenties who, his elbows on the bar, was reading the sports pages of the *Post*.

"You serving yet?"

He looked at his watch. "Kitchen's open. Take a seat and Gracie should be out in a sec to give you a menu."

"I don't mind sitting at the bar."

"Why not?" he shrugged. "Anything to drink?"

"Coke'll be fine."

"You got it."

He picked up a tall glass, filled it with ice, hosed my drink into it, and handed it to me.

"Nice place."

"Hadn't noticed," he said, picking the newspaper back up. I could see he was in no mood to talk, but I was.

"Worked here long?"

"Couple years."

"Did you know this place has a history?"

"You mean the cartoons?" he said, pointing his shoulder toward the wall.

"Further back than that. Used to be a place called Costello's."

" 'Fraid I don't know anything about that."

"You think there might be anyone around here who would know something about it?"

"Maybe the owner."

"He around?"

"Nope. Doesn't come in till later. You some kind of historian or something?"

"Amateur urbanist."

"What's that?"

"Someone who's interested in the history of the city."

He seemed unimpressed. "The building's old, but this place isn't. You want urban history, you ought to speak to Elliot."

"Who's that?"

"This old guy hangs around here from time to time. I think he used to be a newspaperman."

"Last name?"

"I don't think he ever mentioned it."

"Know how I can get in touch with him?"

"He's kind of erratic about coming in. This kind of weather, you never know when he might show up. He told me he breaks easily. You meet him you'll see what he means."

I took out my wallet, pulled out my business card, wrapped it in a twenty, and slid it across the bar. "You'd be doing me a big favor you give me a call if he comes in. Then, give him my card and ask him to get in touch with me, or get his contact information. I'd really appreciate it."

He took it and slipped it into his shirt pocket.

"How about something to eat?" he asked.

"Burger, medium rare," I said.

"No problem. And it's on me," he said, reminding me of an old trick I learned back in my days hanging out at the Paradise Bar and Grill. Tip the bartender big and he'll comp you drinks, lowering the bar tab considerably. When you're broke, as I usually am, that comes in pretty handy.

12
MOVING RIGHT ALONG

I had a few hours to kill, so I took the subway up to Donna Recco's apartment building. As a result of my unfortunate stint working for one of the local cable companies, I knew that in smaller buildings the super was almost always housed in the least desirable apartment, which meant either in the basement or in the front on the first floor. Donna's building was no different. First try, Apartment 1A.

"Whatcha want?" asked a lanky, dark-haired, middle-aged man with a hangdog expression, dressed in jeans and a work shirt, who came to the door only seconds after I rang.

"You the super here?"

"Yeah. What's the problem?" He squinted at me. "You ain't no tenant."

"No. But Donna Recco was."

"Yeah. But she ain't here no more. Moved out a couple, three weeks ago."

"Did she tell you why she was leaving or where she went?"

"Bad idea to make friends with tenants. They think you're their friend they call you in to fix every damn thing that goes wrong. Tenants have to be a little afraid of the super. Just call in an emergency, I tell 'em. Otherwise, bother the front office with it."

"I'll take that as a no."

"Take it any way you wanna take it, friend."

"Were you here when she moved out?"

"Yeah. She moved out middle of the night. Woke me the hell up."

"She must have been in a hurry."

"You could say that."

"Did you know she was going to move?"

"Like I said, I don't make friends with my tenants. None of my business what they do, none of their business what I do. Ask the office. Maybe they knew. Why you so interested in Donna? She skip on a bill or something?"

Images of one of my other former professions, skip-tracer, raced through my mind. Back then, I never would have admitted why I was looking for someone, but now I thought I could make it work for me.

"Other way around. I work for an attorney and Donna has inherited some money from an uncle. The letter we sent her bounced back, so I was hired to find her so we could give her the inheritance."

He looked at me with his squinty eyes. Like I've said, New Yorkers believe nothing . . . unless you can back it up with enough lies so that it seems like it's the truth. "You got any I.D.?"

"You mean like a driver's license?"

He thought a moment. "Anybody can have a driver's license. You got something that shows me you work for a lawyer?"

"What did you have in mind? A note from my employer . . ."

"Yeah. That might work."

"You think lawyers give letters to guys like me? All I've got is my card. It'll tell you who I am and then maybe we can finish this conversation." I pulled my wallet from my back pocket, went through it, and picked out a card, making sure it was the right one.

"Here," I said, handing it to him.

He took it. He read it. I knew that because I watched his lips move. He looked up at me, handing back the card.

"Good enough?"

"I guess. But I told you all I know. She just up and left."

"She woke you with the moving, right?"

"Yeah."

"Did you get out of bed to find out what was going on?"

"For about a second and a half. Didn't concern me, so I went back to bed."

"What did you see?"

"A couple guys lugging down her stuff."

"Did they have shirts or sweatshirts on with the name of the moving company?"

"Don't remember."

"How did you know they weren't burglars?"

" 'Cause I looked outside and saw the truck."

"What was the company name on the truck?"

"How the hell am I supposed to remember that? I was half-asleep."

I went back to my wallet and pulled out a twenty.

"Think hard," I said.

"It had a picture of a bunch of furniture on the side of the truck."

"What else?"

He thought for a moment. I knew that, because he crinkled his forehead. "A picture of Abraham Lincoln."

"It had a name, too, right?"

"Yeah. Lemme think. Yeah. Yeah. Yeah. It had a name. Honest Abe Movers."

"You're kidding."

"No. I remember it, 'cause I thought it was funny."

I didn't even bother to jot down the name because I knew I'd remember it.

"Thanks," I said, and handed him the sawbuck.

"I liked her," he said, as I turned to leave.

"Yeah."

"She was a good kid."

"What about her boyfriend? Ever run into him?"

"Which one?"

"You mean there was more than one?"

"It's not like there were dozens, but I saw her with a couple guys."

"How many?"

"Hey, don't get the wrong idea, man. She had a few male friends. How'm I supposed to know which ones were her boyfriend. She had female friends, too. You think I sit at the window all day keeping track of who goes in and out of the building? I don't have no spy cam up there, you know."

When he said this, his eyes lit up, like maybe he had some installation work to do in the future.

"You ever talk to any of them?"

"Why would I?"

"I don't know. Just to be sociable."

"Do I look like the sociable type?"

"Good point. Look, why don't you hold onto that card and if you think of anything else, or you spot anyone coming back looking for Donna, let me know."

"Why would I do that?"

"Because I'm a good judge of character and my nose," I tapped it with my finger, "tells me you're one greedy son-of-a-bitch who doesn't get tipped particularly well during the holidays. And one of my many vices," I said, in a bald-faced lie, "is that I'm a good tipper."

From the greedy look on his face, I knew I didn't have to say any more.

★ ★ ★ ★ ★

The problem with Honest Abe Movers is that they weren't honest enough to make it easy to find their headquarters. There was only a phone number listed and when I called I was told to leave a message and that someone would get back to me. This led me to believe that it was an amateur operation, probably a few enterprising, muscle-bound guys with a truck. It would take a little more work than I wanted to put into it, but it wouldn't be impossible to track them down.

When I got back to Klavan's, I put in a call to the Better Business Bureau and found that there hadn't been any complaints lodged against Honest Abe's, which did something to build my faith in this hard-to-find moving company. Finally, using the Internet, I was able to track down an address, which was in the Greenpoint section of Brooklyn. It was too late to make it out there and back before my dinner with Claudia, so I put it on the to-do list to take care of in the next day or two, depending on what happened with the information Klavan came up with regarding the photo agencies. For now, Jack would have to be on the back burner while I dealt with Jill.

13
THE LAST SEDUCTION

She was fifteen minutes late. I suspected it was on purpose. To make me anxious. To throw me off-balance. To piss me off. Maybe all of the above. But the fact that it did none of those things gave me the advantage.

I took a booth downstairs, in the back. It was dark and it was cozy and it was private. I waited while nursing a Dos Equis.

The hooded waif I'd "met" a week earlier, under circumstances I preferred to forget, had morphed into a femme fatale, and it was not, I knew, unplanned. She was wearing a skintight, low-cut, just over the knee black dress, and her curly, brown shoulder-length hair was down. She wore a silver chain around her neck with a turquoise fish hanging from it, had three silver studs in each ear, and I stopped counting at six silver rings on her fingers. And when she reached out her hand toward mine, I noticed a small tattoo of a Chinese symbol on the inside of her wrist.

"Sorry, I'm late," she purred, as I stood to greet her. I'm not one for formalities or doing the right thing, even if I know what the right thing is, but for some reason getting up and pulling her chair out for her seemed to be the right thing to do. So, I did it.

"No problem," I muttered, as the aroma of her perfume, a scent I could not identify, made the quick journey from my nose to my brain. This, I said to myself, is a chick on a mission.

I didn't know what the mission was, but I was sure I was going to find out.

"Hope this place suits you," I said, retaking my chair.

She looked around and smiled. "You did good."

"I did my best."

The waiter, dressed in a white, button-down shirt and black slacks, his fair hair cropped close, appeared, introduced himself as Craig, and handed us both menus, along with a single wine list, which I handed to Claudia.

"Would you like something to drink," Craig asked, "or do you need a moment?"

Claudia glanced at the wine list, handed it back, and said, "I think I'll have a margarita. On the rocks, salt, please."

Craig turned his attention to me. For a moment, I wondered if I should copy Claudia's order or go out on my own. I chose to set the tone for the evening early on.

"I'll have the same as her, without the salt," I said.

"Blood pressure problem?" she purred.

"Not yet."

"I love margaritas. It's like having dessert at the beginning of the meal," said Claudia.

"You like turning things upside down?"

She thought a moment, as if the answer was significant enough to change the world. "Yes. I guess sometimes, I do. There's nothing wrong with that, is there?"

"Not a thing," I said, knowing full well that no matter what we do the world turns upside down on its own.

"Let's check the menu, decide on what we want, and then we can talk," she said, taking charge rather early, I thought.

I didn't ask her what we would talk about. I just looked at the menu and chose what I wanted, going with a shrimp dish. She took longer, and I could practically see her weighing the choices in her mind.

Craig brought our drinks. "Are you ready to order?" he asked.

Claudia looked up, smiling, and said, "I think I just need a minute or two more, if that's okay?"

"You checking out the left side or the right?" I asked, taking my first sip of my margarita.

"That's a pretty rude question."

"I like to know where I stand, Claudia. You ought to know that right up front. I don't know whether this is business or a date. The way I see it, you invited me. In most circles, that would mean that you pay."

"What makes you think it could possibly be a date?"

"Look at yourself in the mirror."

She smiled. "Sometimes, I like to get out of Long Beach and dress up. And maybe you shouldn't read too much into appearances."

"I never read anything into appearances. That's why I'm so good at what I do. So is it?"

"Is it what?"

"One of those times. Or is it something else?"

She took a slow sip of her margarita, and when she was finished, her tongue remained seductively on the rim of the glass, slowly licking the salt off one side of it. She looked up and smiled. I knew what she was doing. She knew I knew what she was doing. It was cute. It was provocative. It was working. But I wasn't going to tell her that.

"Maybe it's both," she said.

"Let's strike the word *maybe* from our conversation. How about we be straight with each other. Just for tonight. I'm tired of trying to read signals and when it comes to women, I'm not very good at it."

"I'm not giving any signals."

"Right."

"Be honest, Swann, you're having fun, aren't you?"

"Sitting here in a nice, warm restaurant with a prickly pear margarita and a beautiful woman, sure I'm having fun. But there's subtext here, you know it and I know it, and I'd like to get to it so I can enjoy my drink while sitting across from a beautiful woman. So, is this a date or is it business?"

"You're a very cynical man, aren't you?"

"I won't argue with that. I've earned it. But that keen observation doesn't answer my question."

"Like I said, maybe it's both."

"I warned you about those maybes."

She took another sip of her margarita. "This is good."

"Glad you like it, but you still haven't answered my question, and stalling, as charming as you may think it is, is ruining the possibility of my having a fun evening."

"Every question doesn't have to be answered, you know."

"That's true, and that's why I'm frustrated and pissed off most of the time."

"So if I answer your question you won't be frustrated and pissed off and we can just enjoy a nice dinner?"

"I'll certainly enjoy mine a lot better."

"Okay, I do have a proposition for you," she purred sweetly, "and depending on how things turn out, there might be another one."

"I'm intrigued, yet wary."

"Let's wait till our food arrives. Besides, I'd like another margarita. This was delicious." She licked her lips slowly, then looked up at me and smiled playfully.

I ordered her another margarita and she talked me into getting another one for myself. She was right. It was good. I could feel myself getting a little tipsy so I slowed down. The last thing I wanted to do with this chick was lose control.

"What's the story behind that tattoo on your wrist?" I asked, as the runner set our food on the table, along with small bowls of steaming rice and beans.

She turned the inside of her wrist, so I could get a better look. It appeared to be some kind of Chinese inscription.

"Pretty, huh?"

"What's it mean?"

She laughed. "It was supposed to be the Chinese symbol for love, but evidently I was misinformed."

"So what's it really mean?"

"It's a little embarrassing."

"Believe me, Claudia, I'm no stranger to being embarrassed, so lay it on me."

" 'Woman of easy virtue.' And no cracks, please."

"Too easy. I've got a theory about people who get tattooed."

"What's that?"

"They're the kind of people who live in the moment. The kind of people who don't have regrets, because if they did they wouldn't be putting something on their body that was there forever, that will fade, that will sag, that will inevitably embarrass them later on. Life changes. We change. Better to go into those changes with as little baggage as possible. You know the story about Johnny Depp and Winona Ryder, don't you?"

"I'm afraid I don't."

"When they were together he got a tattoo that read, 'Winona Forever.' They broke up and he had it changed to 'Wino Forever.' Fortunately, he was able to fix it."

"And the lesson there is?"

"Don't put anyone's name on your body. Me, I can't understand someone putting something permanent on their arm that they have to look at the rest of their lives. Would I wear the same shirt every day for the rest of my life?"

"So no tattoos for you, I'm guessing."

"You'd be guessing right. Got any others on you?"

"That's a very personal question and since I'm not, despite

what it might say on my wrist, a woman of easy virtue, I'll refrain from answering it." She paused a moment, smiled that winning smile of hers, then added, "for now."

Obviously, I was not as far ahead of myself as she was ahead of herself.

"I'm starving," she said. "Let's eat." She dove in, as if she hadn't been fed in days. Her body was taut, not an ounce of fat on her, so I could only guess that she either worked out a lot, or made frequent visits to the bathroom. But since she was a dancer, I preferred to think it was exercise and a particularly healthy metabolism that kept her so fit.

I watched her eat, as she shoveled in three forkfuls for every one of mine. When she finished, she dug hungrily into the bowls of rice and beans. I thought about entering her into an eating contest with Goldblatt, but the mere thought of it, though somewhat amusing, also turned my stomach.

"This is delicious. Aren't you hungry?"

"Slow down, kiddo, the food's not going anywhere."

She looked up, sheepishly. "Sorry. Can't help it. When we were kids my mom would put the bowls of food on the table and yell, 'dig in.' If you weren't quick, you wouldn't get enough to eat."

"So eating was a competitive sport in your house."

"I guess."

"How many siblings?"

"Two brothers and a sister. I was the baby."

"If you're still hungry, we can order something else."

"No. I'm fine. Really," she said, as I thought I caught her eyeing what was left of my enchiladas.

She put her fork down, and I took it as an opportunity to find out what was really going on.

"You want to tell me what that proposition was?"

"Oh, yeah. Okay," she said, leaning back from the table

slightly, as she knit her fingers together in front of her. I counted them. Four rings on each finger, including one on each thumb. It was very sexy, but I tried to turn my mind back to what she was going to tell me. "Well, you know that diary that got you out to Long Beach."

"I do."

"Well, it's real."

"You mean there really is a Starr Faithfull diary?"

"Yes."

"And you've got it?"

"Not exactly."

I cradled my head in one hand. "What's that supposed to mean, Claudia?"

"It's not what you think."

"You have no idea what I'm thinking, other than I'm going to hear something I don't want to hear."

"Just listen to me."

"I'm listening."

"With an open mind?"

"As open as it ever is."

"Okay, so here's the story. A few months ago, Sid and I were sitting around the studio, waiting for the next class, when he tells me this story about Starr Faithfull. It's a good story, right? So, I ask him what he thinks happened and he tells me he knows what happened. I say, 'how do you know?' He says, 'because a friend of mine has this diary and it's hers and in it she says she's scared to death of this particular person, who's from a very important family, and that she's sure he's going to kill her because of what she knows about him.' "

"What person?"

"That's the thing. Sid didn't know. He never actually read the diary, he just heard about it."

"I still don't understand what's so important about this,

Claudia. It's a seventy-five-year-old case. Who gives a shit?"

"Goldblatt did."

"Yeah, well, Goldblatt is Goldblatt. I'm sure he saw a way to make a buck out of it, but it's probably all just pie in the sky. Take my advice, just drop it."

"It's kinda too late."

"Why?"

"Because Sid says the guy who has the diary let it be known to the 'right people,'" she air quoted, "that he has it and one day he gets a visit from some guy who says he'll pay twenty grand for it. The guy asks why. The other guy says it's because he's Starr Faithfull's great nephew and he'd like the diary back because it's part of the family heritage. The guy who has it smells more money, so he says he'll sell it back for fifty grand. The other guy says he'll get back to him. And he does. But it's not the way he thinks. One day, he comes home and he finds his house has been broken into and torn apart. Fortunately, he'd stashed the diary in a safe place outside the house. Now, he's scared. He tells Sid because he figures Sid is connected and can get him off the hook. He says he'll take $5,000 from Sid and be done with it. Then Sid says he can get $30,000 from this other party."

"This is sounding a little too complicated for my feeble, slightly inebriated brain to process."

"It's really not that complicated. Really."

"What do you mean, Sid is 'connected'?" I air quoted, something I'd never done before and promised myself I'd never do again.

"I mean he knows people."

"What kind of people, Claudia?"

"People who . . . do this kind of stuff?"

"I'm getting a bad feeling here. I'm not crazy about getting involved with people who are connected, or with people who are the connections."

"It's fine. Sid is cool. He's been part of my family for years. He just looks out for me and he happens to know some people who can also look out for me."

I didn't like the sound of that, but I figured as long as Sid was just looking out for Claudia, I was fine. But it meant that I had to look out for Sid.

"So you really were going to use Goldblatt's money to help you get the diary."

"Sort of. I mean, I was going to use it, but not because it was Goldblatt's money but because it was mine, because he cheated . . ."

"Let's not go there, Claudia. There are three sides to every story and Goldblatt's got one of them. He's got his quirks and he doesn't always do things totally on the up and up, but I've never known him to lie. But frankly, I don't give a fuck about any of that. This whole thing is crazy. I don't see what makes it valuable and I don't care. You want my advice, drop it. You've got a nice little dance business there, stick to it."

"I need the money."

"Why?"

"I just do. It has to do with my family. My father."

"Please don't tell me he's in the hospital and he needs a very expensive operation or he's going to . . ."

"He's got a gambling problem, okay?"

"So your plan is to get the diary, sell it to whoever wanted it, pay the other guy the five grand, pocket the rest of the money, and pay off your dad's debts."

"Exactly."

I shook my head slowly. "Claudia, this sounds very sticky to me. Not to mention, risky."

"That's why I want to hire you."

"To do what?"

"To get the diary from the guy, then hold onto it until we get in touch with the other guy, then make the exchange, the money for the diary."

"He's already shown that he doesn't want to pay fifty grand for it, what makes you think he'll pay thirty?"

"Because he was willing to ransack the guy's house and he didn't find it. And we're only asking a little more than he initially agreed to pay. That's all I need to get my dad off the hook."

"And what am I going to get out of this? Because I have to tell you, honey, I do not work for free. Never have, never will."

She looked thoughtful for a moment, as if this matter of payment had never occurred to her. "Would ten percent work?"

"Ten percent of what?"

"Ten percent of the thirty thousand dollars we get when we resell the diary."

I shook my head. "I've got a partner and it costs a lot to feed him."

"Twenty percent?"

"What about the dough for your father?"

"It'll be enough, even after your cut."

"I gotta tell ya, Claudia, I don't like what I'm hearing."

And I didn't. Something didn't sound right. For one thing, I still couldn't figure out why this diary was so important. Important enough to pay all that money. Important enough to break into someone's house. The other thing is, with that kind of money always comes the threat of violence. I don't like violence. I avoid it at all costs. For one thing, someone can get hurt. For another, that someone can be me.

"Please, Swann. What do you have to lose?"

"How about it could be dangerous?"

"You're not afraid, are you?"

"Claudia, honey, I've spent my entire life in various states of fear, some of it so debilitating I could hardly get out of bed. If I think about something too long, I can work up fear about it, especially when it involves the possible threat of physical violence. And anything else that might get me fearing the next moment."

"You're better than that. I can sense it." She reached across and touched my arm, gently. It felt good. It felt intimate. I don't have that feeling very often and when I do, I don't trust that it's honest or that it will last. But it was nice. At least for the moment. She was going to get her way. I knew it and she knew it. But I knew something else she didn't know. I wasn't going to sleep with her. At least not yet.

When dinner was over, I tipped Craig well and outside I grabbed a cab and escorted Claudia to Penn Station. I even waited with her till her train back to Long Beach was called. She gave me a hug, then kissed me gently on the mouth. She slipped her hand into mine and squeezed it gently.

"After I speak with Sid, I'll give you a call tomorrow with details," she said.

"I haven't said yes."

"Of course, you have, darling," she said, kissing me again, this time letting her lips linger a bit longer.

She knew whom she was dealing with. But although I could have whisked her off the platform and taken her home, I did not. For one thing, my apartment was a mess.

Outside, bundling up against the cold—the temperature was supposed to dip into the teens and it felt as if it already had—I decided to walk a bit, to clear my head. I headed east, toward the Lexington IRT, which I would hop down to Astor Place. The streets were filled with people—a Ranger game had just let out, and I became one of the crowd, rushing to a parking garage or bus stop. But once I crossed Sixth Avenue, the crowd had dimmed and I was pretty much alone. I walked faster, to keep warm. For some reason, I sensed someone was following me. I don't know why. Maybe it's the business I'm in, as I have certainly done my fair share of following. Or perhaps it's just a healthy sense of paranoia that helps get me through the day, that reassures me that yes, I must exist.

I decided to amuse myself. I sped up, then slowed down, then ducked into a doorway and pulled out my phone, making believe I was calling someone. A man in a heavy down coat passed by. He was built like Sidney. Could it be him, I wondered? Was he "looking out" for Claudia? I tucked my phone back in my pocket and looked up the street for him. Whoever it was had disappeared. I waited a few moments more, then took off again.

Once I got home, I called Goldblatt. It was late, but I knew he'd be up. He never sleeps. At least, it doesn't seem that way.

"What's up, partner," he said cheerily, before I could even manage a hello. With caller I.D., there are no surprises anymore, and that saddens me. Part of the fun, and sometimes the anxiety, of getting a phone call was wondering who it was on the other end of the line.

"I have something to discuss with you."

"I like the sound of that unless, of course, it's bad news."

"No. In fact, it might be right up your alley."

"It's kinda late now, but I could come over."

"No. Let's meet for breakfast."

"Just you and me?"

"Yes."

"Great."

"Early, though, I've got a lot of things to do."

"Early's fine. There's this new diner I been wanting to try, The Barking Dog, on 34th and . . ."

"No. Let's do the diner near me. Sixth and Second Avenue."

"You mean where all the gay boys meet on Saturday night."

"That's the one. Be there at eight-thirty."

"Roger!" he said eagerly. Somehow, although I certainly hadn't meant to, I had made Goldblatt's day.

14
PARTNERS FOREVER, FOREVER PARTNERS

"So, what's the scoop?" Goldblatt asked, as he slid his ample body into the booth across from me. He had a bit of a hard time fitting himself in, despite the fact that this time he'd hung his humongous down coat on a rack behind the restaurant entrance.

"Don't you want to order first?"

"Sure. But I'm curious. And I'm excited. I could hardly sleep last night. It's the first business meeting you've called."

"It doesn't take much to get you excited, does it?"

The waiter took our order. Scrambled eggs and toast for me, practically everything on the menu for Goldblatt.

"You gonna make me wait all day for the reason why we're having this meeting?" he said, unfolding the napkin and tucking it neatly under his chin. He knew how he ate, and it wasn't pretty.

"No." I paused, trying to figure out a way to formulate what I was going to say so Goldblatt wouldn't take it the wrong way. And then I realized there was no way Goldblatt wouldn't take it the wrong way, so I just said it.

"I met with Claudia Bennett last night."

"The chick from Long Beach?"

"Yeah."

"Why?"

"She wanted to have dinner with me."

"You're fuckin' irresistible, Swann."

"Right. Anyway, she had a proposition for me."

"I'm guessing since you're here with me so early in the morning, it wasn't sexual."

"That's right. It was business."

"What kind of business? Wait. It was about the friggin' diary, wasn't it?"

"Yes."

He leaned forward. Now I knew I had his attention.

"So there is one!"

"Supposedly."

"Wait a minute. She paid back the money, or most of it, and she's got the diary and I don't. What the hell does she want from us?"

"She doesn't exactly have the diary. That's where I, we, come in."

He leaned back, and as he did our order arrived, the waiter juggling one plate for me, three for Goldblatt. He expertly set them down on the table but, uncharacteristically, instead of just digging in Goldblatt let his sit there, his mouth slightly ajar, waiting for me to finish.

"Come on, come on, I'm all ears. What's the story?"

I told him. Only I left out the part about why Claudia needed the money. It wasn't relevant and I wasn't even sure it was true. I just made it sound like a straight business deal. And it was only toward the end of my story that Goldblatt finally acknowledged the breakfast in front of him, by slathering butter on the top, then pouring an obscene amount of syrup on his pancakes. I watched in awe, as the syrup dripped down the sides of the stack, making a sticky puddle that enveloped the sausages and bacon that surrounded them. I could almost taste the sweetness and it was making me a little queasy. And yet, there was something oddly appealing about those syrup-soaked pancakes. Perhaps, they were a metaphor for Goldblatt, but I quickly dismissed that unpleasant thought from my mind.

"How much?" were the first words out of his mouth.

"Thirty grand, and I negotiated twenty percent for us."

"I would have gotten us more," he said, bringing a forkful of syrup-soaked pancake up to his mouth.

"You would have gotten us nothing, because somehow you would have screwed up the deal. Besides, there was no way she was going to deal with you."

"Well, six grand isn't too bad for just being a middleman. So what do you think we should do?" he asked, between neatly cutout bites of his flapjacks, each bite almost a perfect one-inch wedge.

"That's the reason for this meeting. I need your advice."

"Well, as I live and breathe. I knew this day would come, I just didn't think it would come this soon. Swann asking Goldblatt for advice. I love it."

"Cut the shit."

"You're not going to let me enjoy this, are you?"

"No. I'm not."

"Okay, okay. So what's the problem?"

"My first question is, who rightfully owns this diary and my second question is, what are we getting into if we act as a broker in what might be an illegal deal?"

"Two very good questions, my friend." He sliced off half the sausage with his fork, twirled it around in the syrup, then started it on its journey to his mouth. "And this is the perfect example of why we make a good team."

"So what's the answer?"

"The answer is, technically the diary probably belongs to the family, especially if it was stolen. On the other hand, if the diary was given to the person who has it, that would be a different story. If it was just found, well, that's something else again. It's a really murky area and I'd have to consult an intellectual property expert. Years ago, as I recall, J. D. Salinger sued an author for using letters of his that were written to someone else. You'd think they would be the property of the recipient, but the court ruled that they belonged to Salinger, because they contained his words."

"I'm not sure all that's relevant here because evidently it was found in someone's attic or basement or garage. Who knows how it got there? Whether it was stolen or lost. And the diary is over seventy-five years old. By the way, what the hell did you want it for?"

He shifted his plate of pancakes to the left and brought in reinforcements—his scrambled eggs and toast from the right. "Hollywood, my friend. They love making movies based on true stories. They change the hell out of them, but it's a terrific story and if they can say they've got their hands on a diary that sheds light on it, well, that's quite a selling point for a movie. Think of it—they keep the ending a secret and they base it on what's in the diary, that's quite a potential marketing tool. Trust me, it was a steal at five grand. And I wasn't doing anything wrong, anything that isn't done every, single damn day."

He grabbed a bottle of ketchup and poured it liberally over his scrambled eggs.

I shook my head. In his own, slightly sleazy way, Goldblatt was a genius. But now, of course, this latest turn of events would never get him to the Oscars.

"Okay, I know why you wanted it, now I have to figure out why someone else would want it."

"Some families will go a long way to make sure their ancestors were squeaky clean, you know, that family pride thing, even if the rest of us don't give a shit anymore. But my guess is it's more practical than that. Maybe there were payoffs made and it affected an election. Or a big business deal. Or maybe someone was cheated out of something because of her death . . . and life.

It could be anything. But one thing we know for sure, someone besides me wants that diary and they're willing to pay for it. I think we ought to ask for more than the chick is asking."

I shook my head.

"Why not?"

"Because I don't want to raise the stakes. I don't want any trouble—and neither do you. How about just once lowering your expectations a little? And how about just once, thinking about how we can help someone."

"What do you mean?"

Damn. The minute I said it I knew Goldblatt would catch it. He wasn't stupid. Far from it. And now the cat was half out of the bag. I might as well put it all out there, so I told him.

He laughed. "Jesus, you don't believe that bullshit sob story of hers, do you?"

"Why shouldn't I?"

"Because she coldcocked you and because she tried to cheat me out of my money. Wait, she did cheat me out of my money. A thousand dollars of it, thanks to you. The bitch is cold as ice. I wouldn't trust her far as I could throw her."

"First of all, she didn't coldcock me, Sidney did. Second of all, she thinks you cheated her father. That's why she did it."

"That so?" He swept up the last of his eggs in his fork, using his last piece of toast as a shovel. "She's a looker, isn't she?"

"What does that have to do with it?"

He smiled.

"That's not why."

"It's because you've got a fuckin' heart of gold, that's why, not because you want to bang her."

"I'm not continuing with this conversation, because it's going nowhere. Are you going to help or not?"

He shifted plates again and took another two big bites of the last of his pancakes, followed by half a sausage, before he answered.

"You're my partner. Partners stick together. So, what's the plan, partner?"

"Say that word one more time and I'm going to make you pay the check, which I should do anyway since you're eating enough for three people."

"Gotcha, part . . ." he stopped himself and smiled, "Swann."

"Claudia was going to set up a meet. I'll wait to hear from her and then we'll take it from there. But wherever it is, I'm going to want you there for backup."

"I love it."

"Don't get too excited, Kojak. This is going to be a simple operation."

"How do you know?"

"Because I'm going to make it simple, that's how."

"In the meantime, anything you want me to do?"

"Yes. I want you to check on the legal aspect of this and I want you to do as much research as you can on the Faithfull case, all the people involved with it."

"No problem."

"And Goldblatt . . ." I hesitated.

"Yes?"

"I don't want you to go overboard on this. Just do what I tell you. No more, no less. I want to take this very, very slowly. If I see anything that looks odd, we're pulling out."

"Why?"

"Because I don't trust anyone or anything. This sounds like it could be the real thing, but we've been fooled before and I want to be prepared."

"Just like the Boy Scouts."

"Just like the Boy Scouts. And no funny business. Remember, 'what is ordered must sooner or later arrive.' "

He looked at me with confusion in his eye, but that didn't stop him from continuing to eat, until his plate was sparkling clean.

I handed Goldblatt a twenty, told him he'd have to make up the rest if the check was more, and left him there as I slogged over to Klavan's. Earlier, the sun had been out, but now the sky was filled with dark clouds and the air smelled like snow. Again. It was only mid-January, but I longed for summer. Maybe it was that brief touch of it I'd had down in Florida.

"Winter is still icumen in," I repeated over and over again as I hiked uptown, too lazy to go down into the subway and remove my Metro card from my wallet.

By the time I reached Klavan's, it had started to snow again. I shook the recalcitrant flakes from my shoes and coat outside his apartment, and entered the large outer area, lined with books. For some reason, this always calmed me down, making me feel all warm and fuzzy. I loved walking into that room as much as I loved walking into libraries. Maybe even more.

I ducked my head into his office, but he wasn't there. Next, I tried his assistant, who occupied a small room next to her boss. Angela, a heavyset girl with thick glasses, was an NYU grad student who'd worked with Klavan since her undergraduate days. She was smart and savvy and always willing to help out in whatever way Klavan and now me, who had unofficially inherited her on a part-time basis, asked. Her services were gratis to me, so I tried not to overdo it. But she was always willing, even anxious, to help. I was under the impression that she got a kick out of telling her friends she was working part-time for a P.I., even though I tried to disabuse her of that, insisting that she understand that I was a former skip-tracer who did not have a P.I. license. I don't think it mattered and I certainly didn't make a point of it now. I just thought of her as part of my professional family.

"Angie," I said, as I stood in the doorway. Her eyes were glued to the computer, as usual, a coffee maker bubbling on a small table beside her. She was plugged into earphones and her iPod sat on the desk. I once asked her what she listened to and she just answered, "oh, all kinds of things." I didn't push it because the truth is, I didn't care.

"Mr. Swann," she said looking up, smiling at me. "I was just finishing up on that project Mr. Klavan gave me for you."

"Have I told you how much I hate being called Mr. Swann?"

"Only about two dozen times. I can't help myself. It just doesn't seem right to call you Henry."

"Thank goodness for that. I hate that name. Swann will do fine."

"You know I can't do that. It seems so . . ."

"Oh, the hell with it. Call me whatever you want."

She blushed and I was sorry I'd brought it up.

"Were you able to track down the photo agencies?"

"Yes. But it wasn't easy. Back then, there was PIX but it was purchased by Getty Images. Mr. Klavan went down there this morning, to see what he could find out." She looked at her watch. "He should be back soon."

"Thanks, Angie. You're a doll. I'll be in my office making a few calls. Just let me know when he gets back, okay?" I said, as I headed out the door.

"Sure thing, Henry," she said, and I couldn't stop myself from smiling.

15
DEAD PRESIDENTS

There was nothing I could do on the Faithfull case until I heard back from Claudia, and nothing I could do on the Feingersh case until Klavan returned, so the only thing left for me to do was see if I could turn up any leads on Donna Recco. Before I trudged out to Brooklyn, where the moving company was located, I figured I'd see if I could set up another appointment with Allie Pearson. I knew she was holding out on me, but if I turned up something from the moving guys, I might be able to use that to pry some information loose from Pearson.

I could tell from the tone of her voice that Pearson was not thrilled I called. She insisted she knew nothing more than she'd told me when we met earlier. It was only when I played the fear card that I made some progress.

"What if something bad has happened to her?" I said.

"That's ridiculous. She's fine."

"How can you be so sure, since you say you haven't heard from her in weeks?"

The line went dead for a moment. She knew she was trapped. If she insisted Donna was fine, then she was admitting she knew where she was. She had to see me, if only to show her concern for her best friend.

"Okay," she agreed weakly.

I made a plan to meet with her after work, near her office in midtown.

★ ★ ★ ★ ★

Back in the day, meaning just a few years ago, Brooklyn was like a second home to me. When I worked as a skip-tracer a large proportion of deadbeats and miscreants seemed to come from that illustrious borough, or at least they ended up out there, and so it became a popular destination for me. And so, the impression I had of the borough was dark, a place filled with people who lived on the margins of society, much like I did. It was a place that naturally led itself to be written about in books like *Brooklyn Noir* and *Motherless Brooklyn.* Maybe that's why I was so uncomfortable there. Yet, there was a familiarity that frightened me, giving me a sense that that's where I ought to be.

As I avoided icy patches by walking gingerly down the steps to the L train at 14th and First Avenue, which would then take me east, into Williamsburg, and then to the G train, which would then take me north out to Greenpoint, I had flashbacks to those times when I would make a similar journey out to Greenpoint or Williamsburg or Bushwick or Bed-Stuy, to find a wandering husband, or a bail jumper, or to do my least favorite thing in the world, repo a car. Repoing was too much like outright stealing for me and as a result it came with all the anxiety associated with that criminal act. The difference between me and a true criminal is that they think they're getting away with it, while I always knew I'd eventually be caught.

The offices of Honest Abe Movers turned out to be only steps from the waterfront, a treacherous several block walk from the train station, considering the streets hadn't been cleared and I couldn't avoid all the patches of ice in my path. The snow was still falling on and off once I got off at Manhattan Avenue and trudged down Noble Street, toward the water. Once there, I was confronted with a number of deserted buildings, warehouses, and small bodegas. Finding the office wasn't all that easy, as all that announced its presence was a small, makeshift sign made from what looked like a cardboard moving box. I wondered how many people would actually use their services if they could see what their headquarters looked like. It did not inspire the kind of confidence needed to move valuable or fragile items.

The buzzer didn't work, so I banged on the metal door a few times. No response. I stepped to the side and peered into a grimy, water-stained window that hadn't been washed in who knew how long. After wiping away some of the grime with the sleeve of my coat, I saw a figure step into the room. I went back to the door and banged again.

"Yeah, yeah, I'm coming," was the response. An elderly man, dressed in a heavy wool, holiday sweater, with a bright red muffler tied tightly around his neck, opened the door.

"Help you?" he asked.

"Yeah. I have some questions about . . ."

"Step in, sonny. It's cold out there and the heat ain't workin' too good."

I stepped inside and he quickly slammed the door behind me.

"I was out there a while, banging on the door, didn't you hear me?"

"In the john," he said, pointing to a half-open door behind him. "Hearing ain't too good. Don't get many visitors here."

Three explanations when none was really necessary.

"You Honest Abe?" I asked sarcastically, but I could see he didn't get the joke.

"There ain't no Honest Abe. That's just some goddamned cute name one of the bosses cooked up. Like I'm gonna trust someone to move my stuff just because his name's Abe," he added under his breath. "But people are that stupid."

"One of them around?"

"One of who?"

"The bosses."

He shook his head and laughed. "The big boss spends the winter in Arizona, sonny. He ain't no dumbass like me, still workin' up here in the fuckin' freezing cold."

"So, who's in charge?"

"His son, Jackie, but he hardly ever comes in. Why should he? Only thing has to be done is book the moves and then assign the movers. That's me, pal. And that answering machine over there. I guess you could say I'm the Abe in Honest Abe, only my name's George."

"As in Washington."

"You some kind of comedian?"

I shook my head. "I'm much too serious for that. Anyone else work here with you?"

"Just me and Margie, the bookkeeper, but she's only in twice a week. And this ain't one of those twice. So, what can I do you for?"

"I'd like some information about a move you guys did a month or so ago."

"You got a problem, sonny, take it up with the insurance company. You signed a waiver remember. And part of our contract is that you pay for insurance."

"It's not my move I'm interested in."

"You ain't a lawyer, are you?"

"Not in this life."

"Then whose move are we talking about and why the hell are you interested?"

"A woman named Donna Recco."

"Recco. Recco." He scratched his head, like that was going to help him remember. "Rings a bell . . . maybe."

"You have records, right?"

"You maybe think this is some rip-off, fly-by-night moving

operation. You ain't from one of those 20-20 shows are you?" he said, closing one eye.

"Yeah. I've got the camera hidden in this coat button."

"Wiseass. Well, you never know. Anyway, what's the story?"

"I need some information about that move."

"Like what?"

"Like where you moved her to?"

"Why you so interested? I know you're not the cops, 'cause if you were you would have identified yourself up front and helped yourself to that coffee and Danish over there," he indicated toward a makeshift kitchen area at the back of the room.

"The woman disappeared and I've been hired to find her. I thought a good start might be tracking where her belongings ended up."

He sucked in one cheek, let it go, then sucked in the other. "You're good at what you do, ain't you?"

"Good enough. You got those records?"

"Yup."

"Can I see them?"

"Not sure I can do that without authorization."

"From who?"

"From the boss."

"Honest Abe or Honest Jackie?"

"Very funny."

"You gonna help me out or what?"

"You're probably waiting for me to say, 'what's in it for me?' "

"Is that what you're saying?"

He looked at me, his eyes twinkling. I looked down and at one side his fingers were rubbing together rapidly. I pulled out my wallet, removed a twenty, and handed it to him. He stuffed it in his pants pocket and moved toward the desk. He sat down at the computer screen and asked, "What'd you say the name was?"

"Donna Recco."

"Wanna spell that for me, sonny?"

I wanted to grab him by the neck and wring it, but I didn't. "R-E-C-C-O."

I could see his lips move, reiterating the letters, as he typed them with two fingers on the keyboard.

"Yeah. We got a Donna Recco. Moved her just before Christmas. Usually, people don't move then, so I remember thinking it was kind of weird. We gave her a pretty good deal, though. You know, on account of we were kinda slow."

"What was the date?"

"December 20th."

"Does it say when she booked the move?"

He looked back at the screen. "December 18th."

"Is that short notice common?"

"There is no common in this business, but yeah, that's kinda outta the box. People usually book at least a couple weeks in advance."

"Where did you deliver the stuff?"

He looked up. "That's pretty private information."

"Got those fingers working again?"

"Maybe."

I pulled out another twenty and threw it on the desk. He grabbed it and stuffed it in his pants pocket.

He looked back at the screen. "Two destinations. One was a storage area in Hoboken. The other was a storage area Austin, Texas. Hey, this is kinda strange. The move took place at night. Usually, we don't do that kinda thing. She musta paid extra."

"Can I have the addresses?"

He looked up. "That could be confidential."

"You don't look like a priest or a doctor."

He grinned. I opened my wallet again and gave him another twenty. That was sixty bucks. My profit margin was shrinking quickly. He stopped grinning and wrote down the addresses for me. Our business was almost over.

"One more thing."

"Yeah."

"How did she pay?"

He looked at the screen. "Musta been cash, because there's no credit card information here."

"You can book a move without giving any credit card information?"

"She mighta gave it to book the move and then it was removed when she paid in cash."

"What do you mean maybe? You're the one entering the information, aren't you?"

"Sometimes yes, sometimes no. I don't live here, y'know. Sometimes we have temps come in, sometimes Margie does it."

I was finished and I turned to leave.

"Hey, you won't tell anyone I told you about this, will ya?"

"My lips are sealed. Honest, they are, Abe."

I was baffled by the two addresses. Who sends belongings to two separate cities, unless they're trying to throw someone off their trail. Someone who doesn't want to be found? Another thought ran through my mind: since the move was paid for in cash, how could I be sure that it was actually Donna who paid for it?

Pearson suggested we meet at a midtown Irish bar called Pig 'n Whistle, across from Rockefeller Center. Weeks earlier, the area would have been thick with tourists, but by now the tree was down and at six-thirty, when most of the few tourists still in town were at dinner before taking in a show, and workers had long since headed home, it had a much more deserted look. I was early so I spent the time watching the skaters glide across the small rink. The snow had stopped falling and it was, I had to admit, a pretty sight, watching them do their figure eights, axels, and a number of other cool moves they'd probably picked up watching the Winter Olympics. I don't skate. I tried once, but the first time I fell, I knew it wasn't for me. I like to stay on my feet. I like to minimize damage. I like to be in control. I like to know the footing ahead of me is solid. And so, moving across a slippery surface, real or metaphorical, is not my thing.

I looked at my watch. It was a quarter to seven. I headed past the bustling bar, and found a small quiet table in the back, away from the crowded bar.

At precisely seven o'clock, Pearson arrived, looking as if she'd just stepped from the pages of a fashion magazine. She was wearing black, knee-high boots and a faux fur coat, and a pair of large gold earrings dangled from her ears.

"Right on time," I said, standing because I knew it was the proper thing to do and because I knew it would make the right impression.

"I see you've started without me," she said, nodding at the drink in front of me.

"Wanted to be at my best when you arrived. What'll you have?"

"Merlot."

I motioned to the waitress. She came over and I ordered for Pearson.

First, I engaged her in some small talk, to get her comfortable enough so that maybe she'd lower her guard. I asked about her job. I asked a little about her personal life, starting with where she grew up. Where she went to school. How she got into the kind of work she was doing. Half an hour and three Merlots later, I could see she was warming to me. She liked talking about herself. She liked having someone listen. What woman doesn't?

"I was down in Florida this past weekend," I finally offered, figuring it was time to strike.

"Did you have a good time?"

"I haven't had a good time in years. I was down there on business."

"Oh," she said, taking a sip of her drink. She wasn't stupid. She knew playtime was over.

"I was looking for Donna's mother."

Her eyes widened, then shut slowly, her eyelids fluttering slightly. For the first time I noticed she had added a little glitter to her cheeks. She cleared her glass of the last of the wine. Finally, her eyes glued to the table, she asked, "Did you find her?"

"I did."

"Does she know where Donna is?"

"She claims she doesn't know. Claims she hasn't spoken to her in weeks. Does that sound right to you, Allie?"

She nodded slightly. "I don't want you to think I'm a lush, but could I possibly get another glass of wine?"

It was just what I wanted.

"Of course." I got the waitress's attention, pointed to Allie's glass, then said, "So you're not worried Donna's disappeared without telling you or her mother."

"Donna's a troubled soul. She sometimes does things that don't make sense."

"Like moving out in the middle of the night without telling the two people closest to her?"

The wine came. Allie took another sip and, without looking up, said, "That doesn't surprise me."

"Let me tell you something, Allie. I'm a failure at many things or else I wouldn't be doing this, but finding people is something I do well. Sooner or later, I will find her."

"I hope you do. She's my best friend."

"And yet you have no clue as to where she went."

"I told you before, no. I swear."

Maybe it was the three and a half glasses of wine, maybe it was the look in her eyes or her body language, but whatever it was I was beginning to believe her. And if she were lying, I knew she wasn't going to crack. She'd taken it too far to give in now.

"Why do you think she did this? Why did she sneak out in the middle of the night?"

For the first time in several minutes, Allie looked me in the eyes. "The only thing I can think of is that she was scared."

"Of what? Of who? Jack? Someone else? Is she in some kind of trouble?"

There was a long pause. I watched Allie slowly turn the wine glass, as the contents swirled inside. "You'd have to ask Donna."

"I'm asking you."

Her voice lowered to a whisper. She said something but through the din of the bar I couldn't hear her. I leaned closer and asked, "Who was she afraid of, Allie?"

Her voice raised slightly. "Of herself."

16
THE SEARCH CONTINUES

The next morning, Klavan gave me the bad news. He'd checked out Getty and they claimed they didn't have the images. "It's not surprising," explained Klavan. "One agency swallows up another and the photographs and negatives are moved. That agency is swallowed by another, and there's more moving and more cleaning out. Those photographs might be there some-place, but they're not willing to search out all their files, and I don't blame them. Or they could have been mislabeled, if they weren't trashed. The guy wasn't all that famous and his work was relevant over fifty years ago, so it's possible, even probable, they were trashed."

"So you think that's a dead end?"

"At least for now, unless you're willing to head over there and convince them to let you rummage through their archives by yourself . . . for the next ten years. So, what's next?"

"The guy was pretty much a loner, but he did have a few friends and he was married briefly before he died. I'll try track-ing down those friends and his ex-wife, if any of them are still alive. It's possible they have the photos and have no idea that there's a demand for them. It's also possible he left them at Costello's and maybe they were moved to the new building when they knocked down the old, or maybe someone just took them home and they're sitting in a closet."

"That's a lot of maybes, my friend."

"Now you know what my business is all about."

★　★　★　★　★

I called Julia Scully and she gave me a list of a few of Feingersh's friends. There weren't many and she warned me that they might not even be alive or, if they were, their memories might not be that sharp. And she wasn't sure how I might find them, even if they were alive.

"If they're still alive, I'll find them," I said.

"I wish you luck, Henry," she said, "but I'm doubtful you'll find what you're looking for. My guess is they were thrown out in the trash. Remember, back then photographs weren't art and photographers weren't esteemed, as they are today. So many of the photographs I had were rescued from oblivion just because I thought they were beautiful and wanted to keep them for myself, not because I ever thought they'd have any value."

One of the names on her list was Irv Friedman, one of Feingersh's photo editors at a magazine that regularly assigned him work. I checked the Internet and there were some old references to him, but nothing recent. Then I went to the most useful tool I had: the white pages. Sure enough, there was a listing for Irving Friedman. In fact, there were several. When I got to the third one on the list a woman answered. She said she was his wife. And yes, her husband, Irv, was the former editor I was looking for. Not only was he still living but he was still doing some part-time consulting. His wife said he'd be back that afternoon. When I told her I was a journalist doing a story on the state of photography in the fifties she said she was sure he'd see me to talk about the "old days."

Working three cases at once was starting to get to me. I needed a break, something fun to do, something to take my mind off Goldblatt, Donna Recco, Ed Feingersh, and Starr Faithfull. I figured I'd spend a couple hours in a movie theater, one of my favorite places to chill out.

I grabbed a quick lunch at a coffee shop, constantly looking over my shoulder to see if it might be one of Goldblatt's hangouts—it wasn't—then headed over to the multiplex on Second Avenue and 32nd Street, where a Coen Brothers movie, *Inside Llewyn Davis,* about the folk scene in Greenwich Village, was playing. I was about to buy my ticket when my cell phone vibrated. I checked the caller I.D. It was Claudia Bennett.

"It's all set," she said breathlessly, as I backed out of the short line to purchase tickets.

"What's all set?"

"Your meeting with the guy who has the diary. He's even going to meet you in the city, so you won't have to come back out here. He'll be there in a couple hours. He wants to do it in a public place."

"Slow down. First of all, I'm busy this afternoon. Second of all, I like to be in on the planning of the meeting. And third of all, what about the five grand he's supposed to get? You don't have it anymore and I certainly don't have it. And Goldblatt, well, you can forget about him coming up with the cash. He was already burned once by you, and believe me, he's not too happy about coming up a grand short."

"He's willing to wait for the cash until we sell it."

"That sounds fishy to me, Claudia. Why, all of a sudden, would he trust us to pay him off?"

"He's frightened. He just wants out. And he trusts Sid."

"Then he's a damn fool."

"Why do you say that? You don't know Sid. At least you don't know him as well as I do. He's honest. Everyone knows that."

"Listen, Claudia, everyone's honest till they're not. We lie when it suits us to lie. We cheat when it suits us to cheat, and in case you've forgotten, he was a willing participant in ripping me off. There is no such thing as a trustworthy person."

"You're including yourself?"

"I sure as hell am. I'm no different from anyone else. Under the right circumstances, I do what suits me best. That's what makes the world go round, Claudia—greed and self-interest. Sometimes that happens to benefit others. Sometimes not. Even do-gooders do their thing for a selfish reason—because it makes them feel good, virtuous, clean. And religious people, they do good things now because they expect to be rewarded in heaven."

"I think you're wrong, and in this case we don't have to put up any money because he trusts us. We just have to promise to keep him out of it and, when we get paid, pay him."

"I'm not one to look someone else's stupidity in the mouth, so it's fine with me. Get this guy to call me and we'll set something up. What's his name?"

"Tony LaHood."

"Oh, please."

"Really. That's his name."

"Okay, have him call me and I'll take care of the rest. What's the name of the guy I'm going to be dealing with for the diary?"

"You'll have to get that information from Tony. Call me later, to let me know how it went."

I had an uneasy feeling about the whole situation. Something didn't feel right. Okay, it could have been my cynical nature shining through. I have a healthy sense of paranoia that tells me that nothing is as it appears to be, even though sometimes, as rare as that might be, it is. But that way of thinking has kept me relatively healthy this long, so I tend to listen to my gut when it says, "the easier something seems to be, the more difficult it is."

I'd meet with this Tony LaHood, and sure I'd be the go-between for the diary, but would I believe what it is they'd like me to believe, absolutely not. And that night out in Long Beach, with Sidney's fist in my gut, would be all the reminder I needed.

I had to ditch the movie idea so I headed downtown and spent an hour killing time in the St. Mark's Bookshop where I wound up buying a small volume of William Carlos Williams's selected poems, which I'd been meaning to read. It's hard for me to leave a bookstore without something in my hand. Perhaps it takes me back to those days when I used to haunt the local drugstore that also had racks of mass-market paperback books. With a few bucks allowance in my pocket, it was inevitable that I'd drop some of the dough on a book in which I could lose myself for days on end.

At two thirty, I hopped on the train and headed up to meet Irv Friedman, hoping but not necessarily believing that he'd be able to lead me to the Feingersh photos.

Friedman and his wife lived in an immaculately kept pre-war apartment building on Madison Avenue and 88th Street. I was met at the door of their twelfth-floor apartment by Mrs. Friedman, who introduced herself as Madeleine. An attractive, well-put-together, pretty, vivacious woman in her mid- to late seventies, she reminded me very much of Julia Scully. Her auburn hair was cut short, and she couldn't have been friendlier, ushering me into their sunken living room that looked as if it had been furnished in the seventies. Very much like Julia Scully's apartment, the room was filled with art and books, as well as framed black-and-white photographs, some of them very much in the style I'd seen in Julia's apartment. It was the kind of home I would like to have grown up in, the kind of home I had imagined myself having some day in another life.

"May I get you something to drink? Or a snack?"

"No, ma'am, I'm fine," I said.

"Are you sure? It's so cold out there I thought maybe some tea. Or hot chocolate? I keep that around for my grandchildren. They love those little marshmallows I float in the cup."

"That does sound awfully appealing, but I don't want to be any trouble."

"Good. I'll fix you a cup. And it's no trouble at all. Irv will be right out. He's just getting off the phone."

"No rush," I said, sinking into the flower-print sofa.

A moment or two later, Irv Friedman appeared at the top of the two steps leading down into the sunken living room. A small, dapper man, he wore a pair of brown slacks and a white, button-down shirt. His hair was white and combed back, and he too, looked much younger than he had to have been.

"Mr. Swann," he said, extending his hand as he moved toward me. He had a firm handshake. "It's a pleasure to meet you."

"The pleasure's all mine, Mr. Friedman."

"Please. It's Irv. Sit, sit, I'm assuming Madeleine is fixing you something in the kitchen."

"She said something about hot chocolate."

"That's her game, and she's very good at it." He took a seat in the padded leather easy chair, next to the sofa. I could tell it was his usual spot, from the indentation he filled.

"So, you're writing a story."

"Not exactly."

"I thought . . ."

"That's what I told your wife, but it's not really why I'm here."

"So what is it you want?"

"Julia Scully thought you might be able to help me . . ."

"Julia. Julia Scully. I haven't thought about her for years. I haven't heard that name in a while. Lovely woman. Had a bit of a crush on her, actually. Smart. Beautiful. Sweet. The whole package. Where is she? What's she doing now?"

"She's in New York. Lives across town. I think she's doing some writing."

"Well, I'll be damned. Maddy and I are going to have to have her over here some time. But back to what you're here for."

"I've been retained by someone to find something . . ." Before

I could finish Mrs. Friedman arrived with a tray of two cups of hot chocolate, with several marshmallows floating atop, and a plate of sugar cookies.

"Thank you, dear," said Friedman, as he rose to accept the tray and place it on a coffee table in front of us. "Only two cups? Wouldn't you like to join us?"

"No. I've got plenty of things to keep me busy. You and Mr. Swann should talk over your business in private."

"Fine with me, if you stay, Mrs. Friedman. There's nothing private about this discussion."

"No. No. I'll be in the bedroom if you need me, Irv."

As she left, I watched Irv remove the marshmallows and place them on the saucer.

"She sometimes confuses me with our grandchildren," he said, as he took a sip of the hot chocolate. "So, what's the story? Who hired you and what are they looking for?"

"I can't tell you who hired me, but it's to find the lost negatives and photographs of Ed Feingersh. You were a friend of his."

He put down his cup. "Yes, Eddie and I were friends and colleagues, though he wasn't particularly easy to be friends with. He had a bit of a drinking problem, as you probably know. He would sometimes turn belligerent when he was on the sauce. Or worse. Sullen and uncommunicative. On the other hand, he was a genius. A fascinating man who knew just about everything there was to know about photography. I'm sure Julia must have told you he was a bit of a handful. He suffered from horrible bouts of depression. He was also a bit of a loner, other than the time he spent at Costello's, drinking and talking about photography. I don't think I ever knew where the hell he lived, other than it was somewhere out in Brooklyn. But I couldn't even swear to that. He might have had his own place or he might still have been living at home, with his mother. He just didn't talk about those things."

"What about his photographs?"

"I have no idea where they might be. Have you tried the agencies?"

"Dead end."

"Like many alcoholics Ed was very secretive. He didn't let anyone touch his work. If it needed to be cropped, he did it. He even printed his own work. So I suspect those photographs never left his control. It's possible he gave them to someone to hold, someone he trusted, or maybe he rented space or a locker somewhere and kept them there. That would be my best guess. But there's another possibility, too."

"What's that?"

"Eddie didn't consider what he did an art. It was a job. And when the job was over, he didn't really care what happened to the photographs themselves. So, it's also possible he just tossed them in the garbage."

"That doesn't seem like something a man who was so careful about his craft would do."

"Perhaps not, but you'll have to consider that a possibility."

"Did you know his wife?"

"Slightly. She was a model, as I recall. They were an unlikely pair. She was taller than he was and a whole lot prettier. They lived down in the Village. I believe he moved into her apartment. Did Julia tell you she lived just down the block, which was kind of ironic, since she was the ex-girlfriend."

"She mentioned it."

"You might check and see if the woman still lives there. Anywhere else that would be an outrageous possibility, but this is New York City. No one moves from a low rent apartment. We've been here forty years. Bought it for a song in the seventies, now it's worth a small fortune. But we'd never sell because we'd never find anything else even half as nice for the money we'd make. It's like sitting on an oil well but you can't drill because you don't have the tools. Frankly, we could use the money, though I'm sure you wouldn't think that by looking around."

"I don't count other people's money, Irv. I have enough trouble dealing with my own. I suppose I can get the wife's address from Julia. Anything else you can think of?"

He shook his head. "Most of his friends are long gone. You might see if any of the Costellos know anything. There might be a son or daughter left. Maybe he left the photos there. And maybe they still have them stashed somewhere."

"What do you think they'd be worth?"

"I can't say for sure. It would depend on how they were handled. But in this market, I wouldn't be surprised if they'd bring a pretty penny. He's not a household name, though he ought to be, but anything new on the market like that would make quite a splash, especially if there was a 'story' around it. One thing going for it is not only was Ed an incredible photographer, but he died young and he had a mystique about him that would help sell the images. It doesn't surprise me that you were hired to find them. If you can find any of those photographs or negatives, Mr. Swann, it would be like minting money for your employer. But between you and me, I think you're on a fool's errand. The most likely scenario is that those photographs and negatives were destroyed years ago. And besides, if they weren't kept under the right conditions, the chances are they wouldn't be in very good shape, certainly not in good enough shape to be valuable enough to bother with."

"It really doesn't matter to me. There's a bonus if I find them, but I'm getting paid by the day no matter if I find them or not."

"I wish I could help you more, Mr. Swann, but I'm stumped. If you can find his wife and she doesn't know, I'm afraid you're going to just have to collect your check and look for something else to find."

"Well, I appreciate your taking the time, Mr. Friedman," I said, as I rose. I don't know why, but I had a feeling that Friedman was holding back some information and yet I knew I wasn't going to get it out of him. At least not now.

"My pleasure, Mr. Swann. And if you do find them, I'd sure appreciate your letting me know. I'd love to see some of those photos see the light of day. He was an odd little man, but like I said, he was a genius."

17
WHO WROTE THE BOOK
OF LOVE?

There was something about the sound of Tony LaHood's voice that made me dislike him immediately. High-pitched and whiny, it sent chills up and down my spine. It was the kind of voice that told you all about the man before you even laid eyes on him. I knew I could pick him out of a crowd without ever having seen him before. And I was right.

I offered to meet him at the Nathan's on the Amtrak level of Penn Station. I say "offered" but there was really very little choice, since he refused to travel beyond the confines of the station.

"I don't know New York City too good," he claimed, "and I don't want I should get lost."

LaHood's train was due in at six-forty-seven, so I got there a little early, grabbed a hot dog, an order of fries, and a beer, and waited for his train to arrive. As for identification, I told him what I'd be wearing and that I'd be sitting in the back, at a table against the wall, a good vantage point for seeing anyone entering the joint, and believe me, it was a joint. I figured only a moron would have trouble figuring out who I was. And again, I was right.

I recognized him as soon as he walked in. The total opposite of what his name conjured. Thin. Balding. Bent over slightly. Clean-shaven. Squirrelly looking. In his fifties maybe. A face like a hatchet, sharp enough to split wood. He was clutching a leather satchel, the kind of bag school kids used to carry their books in when I was in elementary school. Nervous, his eyes darting around like a bird's, his head jerking after them. He must have looked at me three times without figuring out who I was. This, I thought, isn't going to be easy.

Finally, I put him out of his misery by standing up, moving in front of the table, and waving him over.

"You Swann?" he asked superfluously.

"Yeah. You LaHood?" I said, playing his game.

"Yeah."

"You want something?"

"Huh?"

"To eat."

He considered it as seriously as if I'd asked him whether he wanted to live or die. I could literally see the wheels turning in his head. What kind of idiot doesn't know if he wants something to eat or drink? This, I realized, was the kind.

"Or drink?" I added, just to confuse the matter.

"Nah," he said, and then, "nah," again, and I realized he was answering both questions consecutively. "Let's get down to business. I got a train to catch back. I get the heebie-jeebies being in the city. I got mugged once. That ain't gonna happen again."

I passed on the opportunity to tell him that he was giving me the heebie-jeebies just by standing next to him.

"Fine by me. Let's have a seat."

He looked at the table where I had my coat folded over the back of one of the chairs. I wondered if I'd have to say, "yes, that's the one," but fortunately he saved me the trouble by nodding and heading toward the chair opposite me.

He sat down, carefully placing the bag on the empty chair next to him. But he never took his hand off the handle. I was tempted to entertain both of us with a little small talk, to break the ice, to make him more comfortable, but I didn't want to

prolong this agony any longer than I had to, so I asked the obvious question to get the party started. "You've got the diary?"

"That's what I'm here for, ain't it?"

"And that's what I'm here for, too. Want to give me a look?"

"Huh?"

"Can I see it?"

"Oh, yeah. Sure. You wanna see it."

"Yes," I said slowly, as if I were talking to someone who spoke
little or no English. "I want to see it."

"Sid says you're okay."

"Sid's right. He and I go way back."

"Then you're okay?"

"Yeah. I'm okay. Now, can I see it?"

"Yeah. Okay. You can see it." This was taking twice as long as
it had to, simply because he insisted on repeating a fucked-up
version of everything I said.

He lifted the satchel up off the chair and placed it on the
table. He looked around, behind him, to both sides, and then,
obviously seeing no apparent threat, he unclicked the lock and
opened it. He looked inside, evidently to make sure whatever
he'd packed earlier was still there, then reached in and took out
something wrapped in a Duane Reade plastic bag. He put it on
the table, then put the satchel back down on the chair.

"It's in here," he said, indicating with his hand by pointing
toward the bag.

"So I figured," I said.

He stared at it a moment, as if not sure what to do next. I
didn't want to reach for it and scare him off. I waited. One one-
thousand. Two one-thousand. Three one-thousand. I couldn't
wait any longer. "You gonna open it or should I?"

He pushed it toward me. I figured that meant I could open
it, so I did. When I removed it from the plastic bag I found it
wrapped in a brown paper bag, the kind your mother used to

put lunch in when you were a kid. For a split second, it made me wonder if his mother was the one who wrapped it up for him. Then the idea of this guy actually having parents scared me straight.

"You wrapped this pretty good," I said, unfolding the top and reaching in and removing something from the paper bag.

"It's valuable."

"So I'm told."

There it was: a small, brown leather diary, with a red diagonal stripe running from the top left to the bottom right. The edges of the paper were gold. And there was a small gold lock on it. It felt and looked old.

"What about the key?"

"Didn't find no key. But you don't need one. It's broke. You can just click it open."

He was right. The lock was useless, obviously made so that a child could feel that her secrets were secure. I opened the diary and on the front page someone had written, in what appeared to be a girlish handwriting,

"This is the private property of *Starr Faithfull*"

I carefully turned a few of the pages and saw that in the same handwriting there were dated entries, some less than half a page, others a page or two, all written in a girlish script that tilted so far right at times it looked like the words would tumble off the page. I opened it to the halfway point of the book and the pages were empty. Only a little more than a third of the book had been written in, leading me to believe that it probably was the last diary of Starr Faithfull.

I looked up. LaHood was smiling. "Ya see. It's the real deal."

"Did you read it?"

"Hell, no. I ain't interested in what it says. I just know it's probably worth some dough."

"How much?"

"You know the deal."

"I forgot. Remind me."

For the first time, he looked me in the eye. "Five grand. That's all I'm asking."

"I heard less."

"Where'd you hear that?"

"From Sid. He told me there was a fire sale going on."

"What's that supposed to mean?"

"It means this item is hot."

"You mean like in stolen?"

"Like in dangerous."

"He told you about the break-in?"

"Sid tells me everything. I told you. We're like this," I said, raising two fingers and then slowly moving them together so they touched.

"Oh, yeah." He looked around. I did, too. The only other people in the joint were a derelict in the corner, eating a hot dog, and a couple of college-age kids, their knapsacks on the table, sipping sodas, the detritus of their meal on the table in front of them. I realized it was probably coming to the end of winter break and they were headed back to school, and from the way they were dressed, probably upstate, into more cold weather. "Four grand."

"I heard it was half-price today. Twenty-five hundred."

"You're killing me."

"Thirty-five hundred. But that's it."

"You got it with you?"

"You know I don't. You trust, Sid, right?"

"Yeeee . . . aaahh," he said, tentatively.

"So you know as soon as we make the deal with the other guy, you get your cut." LaHood's eyes began to dart around again, his head following close behind. I wanted to grab his face with my two hands and hold it still, but instead I said, "Look at me, Tony." He did. "You'll get your money as soon as we get ours. Understand?"

"Yeah. I understand."

"And there's no one else here but you and me."

"You mean . . ."

"I mean other than the people eating here."

"Oh."

"Now who is this other guy and how do I contact him?"

"His name's Matty Stern. I don't got no number for him. He contacts me."

"When was the last time he contacted you?"

"Last night."

"Did you tell him about the new arrangement?"

"Yeah."

"But you didn't tell him when and where you were giving me the book, did you?"

"You think I'm crazy?"

"I don't know you well enough to make that assessment, Tony, so I'm just going to ask you straight out, what did you tell Matty Stern?"

"I told him I was handing the book over to someone else who would deal with him."

"Did you tell him my name?"

"Yeah. 'Course I did. How'm I not gonna tell him your name?"

"What else did you tell him about me?"

"I don't know nothing else about you."

"How did you tell him to get in touch with me?"

"Same way I did. Your phone."

"Did he say when he'd be in touch?"

"I didn't ask him that."

"What's he look like?"

"He's a guy."

"I know that, Tony. I want to know what the hell he looks like."

"He's a young guy. Maybe in his late thirties. Kinda tall. Six feet. Got a nice build on him. But not like he's puffed up, if you know what I mean. Like that steroidy kinda thing. 'Cause he's kinda wiry. He was wearin' a suit when I met him. Short, red hair. Kinda fair-skinned. Freckles." He thought for a moment longer. "That's about it."

"Tell me what he told you about why he wants the book and who he's working for."

"He said he's working for the family and they want the book back 'cause it's their property. That's all he said. I didn't ask nothin' more."

"And how did he know you found the book, Tony?"

"I guess 'cause when I found it I thought it might be valuable, you know. Like an antiquey kinda thing. So I told a friend of mine who works the flea market. He took a look at it and he said, 'yeah, it looks pretty old, maybe it's worth something.' He said he'd ask around. I guess that's how this guy Stern found me."

"Did you know who Starr Faithfull was?"

He shook his head, no.

"When did you find out?"

"Find out what?"

"Who she was."

"When my friend got back to me and told me about it. He said he looked her up on the Internet."

"But he didn't tell you he put Stern in touch with you?"

He shook his head in the negative. "Maybe he did, maybe he didn't."

"You never asked him?"

"Why should I?"

"And when he offered you five grand, you got greedy and

181

asked for more."

"I figured it was worth that much it was probably worth more. It was worth a try. It's called bargaining. He coulda just said no."

"And you figure the tossing of your place had to do with the book?"

"I been livin' there more than twenty years, even when times were bad in Long Beach, and nothin' like that ever happened. You tink maybe this was a coincidence?"

I smiled and shook my head, no.

I could see I wasn't going to get anything more out of La-Hood and since he kept looking at his watch, I figured he was in a hurry to get back to Long Beach. I took the book, put it back into the paper bag, then into the plastic bag.

"You ain't gonna cut me outta this thing, are you?"

"Why would I do that?"

"Because you could."

"Yeah. I could. But I wouldn't. Funny thing about me. You don't trust me, I'm more likely to rip you off. Trust me, and I feel obligated to do the right thing. Besides, I'd have Sidney to deal with if I did anything funny, and I wouldn't want that, would I?"

He looked a little puzzled, but somehow he came up with the right answer. "Okay," he said, "I guess I gotta trust you."

He stuck out his hand. There wasn't anything I could do but shake it. It was weak. It was clammy. It told me all I needed to know about Tony LaHood. I could have ripped him off and there wouldn't be any consequences. But that's exactly why I wouldn't.

"I guess that's all there is," he said.

"I guess that's right."

He looked at his watch, grabbed his satchel, and got up. "I can make the train I wanted to. How long you think it'll be before I get my money?"

"I couldn't tell you, Tony. Too many variables."

"Variables?"

"Other things in play. You'll hear from us when you hear from us."

He hesitated a moment, staring at the package in front of me. "Don't worry, it'll be safe with me."

"I hope so. Just be like, careful, man."

"I always am, Tony. I always am."

Only moments after LaHood disappeared from view, Goldblatt, munching on a hot dog, appeared seemingly out of nowhere and sat down across from me. I had warned him to stay out of sight, so as not to spook LaHood, and he'd done a good job of it.

"What a creepy looking guy," he said, his mouthful of food.

"Nice good job of staying out of sight. I wasn't even sure you were here."

"I told you I have a past, Swann. Didn't you believe me? You may not think so, but I'm damn good at disappearing into the woodwork when I have to."

"I probably wasn't listening. What past are you talking about?"

"I can't say directly, but let's just say I did some work for the government."

"Whose government?"

He gave me the stink eye, which is probably what I deserved.

"That it?" he asked.

I nodded, yes.

"Does it look real to you?"

"I'm no expert, but yes, it looks like it could be. But it doesn't matter to us, does it?"

"I guess not," he said. He reached for the bag, but I grabbed it before he could get control.

"I want a little more definitive answer than 'I guess not.' "

"Sure. It doesn't matter to us. We just get it to the guy, get the money, and split it with the girl. So, who is the guy, what's his name?"

"Matty Stern."

"So when and how is Stern supposed to get in touch with us?"

"He didn't say. We'll just have to wait."

"So, you want me to hold onto the book while we wait? I can bury it so deep no one'll find it till we need it."

"No, thanks. I think I'll hold onto it myself."

"You still don't trust me, Swann?"

"I absolutely trust you, Goldblatt," I lied, "but since I'm the point man on this I just think it makes more sense for me to have quick access to the book."

He thought a moment. "Yeah, I guess that's the right move. What're you going to do now?"

"Working three cases at once is taking a lot out of me. I think I'm just gonna go home and crash."

"Yeah. Okay."

"What about you?"

"I've got some meetings a little later."

"Meetings?"

"Yeah. Nothing to do with us. Just some consulting work I'm doing on the side."

I couldn't imagine what kind of consulting work he was into, but the truth is I didn't have the strength to get into it. Besides, the chance of me getting a straight answer was pretty close to nil. I put on my coat, grabbed the package, and jammed it into the large, inside pocket of my coat.

"You'll let me know as soon as you hear?"

"I will. And Goldblatt . . ."

"Yeah."

"Keep yourself free because I'm going to be using you for backup. Something doesn't smell right about this whole deal."

He smiled. I'd made his night. And rather than go and ruin it by saying something else that would certainly be insulting, I just left it at that.

I told Goldblatt to leave the station before I did. As soon as he was out of sight I walked slowly toward the Seventh Avenue exit. When I got to a newsstand about fifty feet away, I stopped and stood in front of the magazine rack, picking up a couple to look at, as I slowly turned to see if there was anyone who might be following me. I wanted to make sure that LaHood had actually left the station and if he had that he wasn't tailed into the city. I didn't see anyone lurking, though that didn't mean that there wasn't anyone there. If they were good, I wouldn't be able to spot them so easily.

After a couple minutes, I headed back toward the Eighth Avenue side of the station and hopped on the F train, which would take me back to West 4th Street and then to the East Village. When I got off at my stop at Second Avenue, I made sure I was the last one up the stairs.

As soon as I got home I hid the book under a floorboard in my closet, then tossed a bunch of my dirty laundry over it. If someone did go to the trouble of tossing my apartment, I doubted they'd find it. Even I shunned the thought of rummaging through that god-awful mess to retrieve it later.

18
JACK IN THE BOX

The next morning when I arrived at Klavan's apartment he met me at the elevator door. He looked irritated.

"There's someone in your office waiting to see you. Been here since nine. Good thing I'm an early riser."

"Who is it?"

"A client of yours."

"Male or female?"

"Male, and very annoying. I told him I didn't know when you'd be in or even if you'd be in, but he insisted on waiting and coming into my office every ten minutes to ask if I'd heard from you, as if I'm your fuckin' secretary. Tell him this isn't a waiting room. Remember, Swann, I've got some very valuable books here and I don't want strange people coming in and out. Especially the kind of people you associate with."

"I understand," I said, "and believe me, I don't like anyone coming here either. At least you don't have to worry about Goldblatt. He hates your guts," I said, heading toward my office space.

"Well," said Klavan, "the feeling's mutual."

It was Jack, and he'd made himself very comfortable sitting in my chair, his feet up on my desk, reading yesterday's newspaper, my yesterday's newspaper. As soon as he saw me, he dropped the paper and a millisecond later when he recognized the look I shot him his feet hit the floor.

"Sorry," he mumbled, as he rose and inched away from my

chair. "I didn't know how long it would be till you got in."

"I don't keep regular hours, Jack. It's one of the reasons I got into this line of work. And just for the record, I don't like drop-ins. And neither does my landlord and friend, Mr. Klavan."

"I get it," he said, moving out of the way as I hung up my coat and re-took my chair. I sat down and put my feet up on the desk, *my* desk, in an obvious attempt to reestablish my territory.

"I put a section of the paper there, so I wouldn't mess anything up," he said, pointing to the spot on my desk where his feet had been.

"So what's up, Jack?"

"I wanted to know if you'd made any progress."

"Depends on how you define progress."

"Do you know where Donna is, what happened to her?"

"Not yet. And we don't know anything 'happened' to her, do we?"

"No. I just meant . . . Do you have any leads?"

"I do."

"Would you share them with me?"

"I don't like working that way, Jack."

"What way?"

"Making clients part of the process."

"Why not?"

"Because clients tend to get in the way. If I tell them too much they try to get involved and it interferes with my train of thought. You don't want to interfere with my train of thought, do you, Jack?"

"No. I just thought . . . maybe I could help."

"Only if you're going to tell me something you didn't tell me before."

"I told you everything."

"Then you've given me all the help you can."

He hesitated a moment. I knew he was holding something back. I kept my mouth shut and waited.

"There's something, I guess, that I didn't tell you. But it really doesn't mean anything."

"Give."

"Well, before she left, she asked to borrow a little money, so I loaned it to her."

"How much is a little?"

"It was really insignificant."

"Twenty bucks is insignificant, Jack."

"It was two thousand."

"And you didn't tell me about this before because . . . ?" I was kicking myself, because this is something I should have gotten out of Jack way earlier. His head dropped. "I was a little embarrassed. I thought you'd think she hustled me for the money and disappeared and that you wouldn't look for her."

I laughed. "Jack, no one hustles someone for two grand, then takes a hike. She borrowed that money to pay for her move, which means she planned it."

"How can you be so sure?"

"Because this is my business, Jack."

"There's something else . . ." He pulled something from his back pocket and handed it to me. It was a flyer for the Brooklyn Academy of Music.

"So?"

"Look at the address."

I did.

"It's addressed to Donna."

"Yeah. So?"

"But that's not her address. It's mine."

"So?"

"She never lived with me, Mr. Swann. There's no possible reason why I would be getting mail addressed to her. And look, it's not even in care of. It's just Donna Recco with my address."

"What do you make of this, Jack?"

"I don't know. But unless someone is playing a cruel joke on me, and I don't know why anyone would, I think maybe Donna put her name on my address and added it to BAM's mailing list."

"Why would she do that?"

"I don't know . . . Maybe it's some kind of signal."

"What kind of signal?"

"That she's coming back to me. That she just wants me to be patient. That she hasn't forgotten me."

"Then you don't need me anymore, Jack, and you can save yourself a lot of dough, though I don't give refunds."

"No. I need you to keep looking. But it . . . it doesn't make sense. What do you think?"

"I think there's either a reasonable explanation for it or she or someone she knows is behind it. I'm not going to speculate which one it is, Jack. But you're going to have to entertain the possibility that this woman is a little *off*." I twirled my finger beside my temple.

"I've known her for two years, Mr. Swann, and she's not *off*."

"Then this just adds to the mystery, Jack, and I'll have to deal with it."

"I'm going a little crazy here, Mr. Swann. I just need to know if there's any chance of finding Donna and bringing her back."

"There's always a chance, Jack." He looked so sad I decided to toss him a bone. "Maybe you can help after all. Does Donna know anyone in either New Jersey or Austin, Texas?"

"Why do you ask about those two places?"

"Because that's where she shipped her stuff."

"How did you find that out?"

"It's my job to find out stuff like that, Jack. Does she?"

"When she first got to New York she had a place in Hoboken.

189

But that was eight years ago. And she had a grandmother in Austin, I think. But she died a couple years ago. Wait, I think she has an uncle who's still there."

"On whose side?"

"Her father's."

"I'm guessing you don't know his name." He shook his head, no. "Well, now that I've found her mother I'm guessing I can find him . . . How many Reccos can there be in Austin?"

"You found her mother?"

"Yup."

"Did she say anything?"

"About?"

"About where Donna is?"

"Said she didn't know."

"That's hard to believe."

"Why's that?"

"Because they were pretty close."

"That's not what her mother says."

"It's not true. Donna spoke to her at least once or twice a week."

"Then she lied to me," I said matter-of-factly.

"You act like you're not surprised."

"Jack, I'm in a business built on lies. If people told the truth, if they lived by the rules, if they paid their bills, if they stayed true to their spouses, if they didn't lie, cheat, and steal, if they didn't have secrets, then I'd be out of business. I'd probably do what you do, make things up and then try to pass them off as the truth."

He sunk his head in his hands. I hoped he wasn't crying. I'm not someone who deals well with emotion, mine or anyone else's. Finally, breaking what was a particularly awkward silence, he said, "I don't know what to do."

"There's nothing you can do, except let me do my job. But

I've got to be honest with you. If this is going to be done right, I might have to go down to Austin. If I do that it's going to cost you more money. I'm not a charitable institution. I don't know if you're prepared to go that far. And before you answer, I want to give you a bit of advice."

"What's that?" he asked, looking up.

"Drop it."

"Drop it?" he said, looking up.

"Yes. Drop it."

"I can't do that. I love her."

"Take it from a neutral party, it's pretty obvious she doesn't feel the same or else she'd be here right now."

His head dropped, his face lost color, as if this was the first time the possibility occurred to him. "What if it wasn't up to her? What if she had to move and it had nothing to do with me?"

"You're hinting at some serious stuff, Jack. Don't you think she'd somehow get word back to you that she's okay?"

He thought for a moment. "What if she can't?"

"I'm not here to debate you. You want me to take this further and you want to pay me, that's fine with me. I'm not Dr. Phil. My job is to do my best to find her for you. You pay, I play."

"How much more are we talking about?"

"At least a grand."

"I can do that."

"She's worth that much to you?"

"More."

"You come up with the money, I'll keep looking. But I want you to think about it overnight. If you still feel that way tomorrow and you have the money, just bring it to me and I'll keep going. And Jack?"

"Yes."

"You're not keeping anything else from me, are you?"

"Like what?"

"Like another reason you're so anxious to find Donna, because it obviously isn't the two grand."

He looked offended, which is the same way I'd look if I were either offended or wanted someone to think I was.

"What other reason could there be?"

"I don't know, Jack, that's why I'm asking you. It could be that Donna has something you want. Or knows something you don't want her to tell."

"That's ridiculous. It's just what I told you in the first place. No more, no less. But you know something," he said, straightening his back, his tone turning a little belligerent, "it doesn't really matter what my reasons are, does it? You're either still on the case or you're not."

"You're absolutely right. So go home, think it over, and then let me know tomorrow if you want me to continue. And if you do, I'll need to see a certified check or cash before I go any further. Understood?"

He got up. His mood seemed to lighten a bit. "Okay. It's a deal. I'll see you tomorrow."

As he walked out the door, I muttered, "Maybe, maybe not." Then I thought, if there was any time it was appropriate now was the time to say, "Hit the road, Jack." Fortunately for me and him, I only thought of that after Jack had already left Klavan's.

As soon as Jack was gone, Klavan popped his head into my office.

"What's with the sad sack?" he asked, as he came in and pulled up a chair.

"His girlfriend skipped out on him."

"Lucky guy."

"He doesn't think so."

"So, let me guess, he hired you to find her."

"Don't look so smug. It was Goldblatt's idea. He got him as a client. And don't say it."

"Say what?" he asked, with feigned innocence.

"That I asked for it by partnering up with Goldblatt. And if you weren't going to say it you were sure thinking it."

"Now you're a mind reader."

"You're an open book, Klavan."

He looked around my office, which was really just an extension of his, and the walls covered with books. He nodded to the shelves, smiled, and said, "Good one, Swann."

"Look, he also came up with the Feingersh case, and that's paying the enormous rent you're charging me."

"So how's it going with that one?"

"Not so great."

"You mean there's someone you can't find?"

"There are a lot of people I can't find, especially if they're not lost. But I've just got a funny feeling about Jack and the disappearance of his girlfriend."

"Do tell."

"I don't know exactly what it is. Maybe it's Jack. Maybe it's that the whole thing is so bizarre. Chick vanishes practically in the middle of the night. Not only does she vanish but so do all her belongings. Everything in her apartment. Poof! Gone. So, it's not like she's been kidnapped. I mean, if she has been it would be the craziest kidnapping on record. So she disappeared voluntarily. And everyone around her is keeping their mouths shut. Either they really don't know where she is or they're protecting her . . . or someone else."

Klavan put his feet up on my desk, but I didn't mind. How could I? After all, it was his desk, not mine.

"Okay, so chances are she left voluntarily. Now, why would she leave voluntarily?"

"To get away from someone."

"That's one possibility. Got another one?"

"To get away from herself."

"What do you mean?"

"Maybe it has nothing to do with Jack. Maybe it's all internal. Maybe she needs to reinvent herself somewhere else because she's not happy with the person she is here."

"That's pretty radical."

"It wouldn't be the first time," I said, thinking back several years to the Janus case, which shook me up so much I left the business. "People are dissatisfied with who they are all the time. They want to be someone else, but rarely do they take any action to make that happen. But it would explain why her belongings were sent to two different storage areas, maybe to hold onto them until she found a place to light and start over again. Keeping one foot in, the other foot out."

"So, what it boils down to is that either she's running away from someone else, who might or might not be Jack, or she's running away from herself."

"Right."

"And that helps you how?"

"Because it means there's no third party involved. It's all Donna. And if she's running from herself, it means she's not trying to erase her tracks because either she doesn't think anybody cares enough to try to find her. Or if they do care too much and it's so urgent that she gets away, she's bound to leave a trail."

"Why's that?"

"Because amateurs leave trails. And she's an amateur. Plus, she's too busy running forward to look back."

"You're a genius, Swann. You've solved the damn case."

"I haven't solved anything. I've just made things a little clearer in my head. Once I get a handle on the why, it makes it a little easier to figure out the where. One thing I've got to do is check out Jack a little better." I looked at Klavan.

"Hey, I just don't have the time right now. What about Gold-blatt?"

"As reluctant as I am to say this, I actually need his help on something else I'm working on."

"You're working on a third case?"

"Yeah. But it should be over soon."

"What is it?"

"I could tell you . . . but then I'd have to kill you."

I'd put my phone on the desk and suddenly it began to dance around crazily. I caught it, answered it, and a gruff, raspy voice asked, "This Swann?"

"It is."

"This is Matty Stern. You've been expecting my call."

"I have."

"You have the book?"

"I do."

"You ready to deal?"

"I am."

"What are you asking?"

"It's bargain day, Matty. We're only asking thirty grand. That's twenty grand less than LaHood was asking."

"That was a joke."

"I'm not laughing, Matty."

"It's our book, you know."

"Maybe. But we found it and we have it, so it's ours, and if you want it, it's going to cost you thirty grand. No negotiation. Take it or leave it. I've got other things to do, so if you fuck around another day the price goes up to thirty-five."

"Okay. We meet tomorrow afternoon, out in Long Beach, in back of the library. Come alone."

"Long Beach doesn't agree with me. And I don't meet at the back of anything. I've got the book, I dictate the terms. We'll meet here in the city, inside the lobby of the Plaza Hotel. High tea-time. That would be three p.m."

"I don't like crowds."

"Too bad."

"I'll be there. You'd better have the damn book."

He hung up before I could beat him to it.

"The Plaza?" said Klavan.

"Yeah."

"Why?"

"*North by Northwest* is one of my favorite flicks," I said, "and besides, I've never been in the bar before."

19
BLACK WIDOW

I wasn't due to meet Stern until three, there wasn't much I could do on the Recco case, so while Klavan was using his well-honed research skills to check out Jack, I decided I would look for Feingersh's ex-wife, whose first name, I learned from Julia Scully, was Alice. The only other things I knew were that she was a former model and that she was married to the man whose photographs I was looking for. If I were lucky, she would have retained Feingersh's name. If not, I'd go back to Friedman and see if he knew anything.

New York City is all about real estate. That's what people talk about. That's what they think about. That's what they dream about. Where they live. Where they lived before. Where they want to live in the future. But no one, and I mean no one, living in a rent controlled or rent stabilized apartment, unless they've won the lottery, ever moves, and so I was hoping that might be the case with Mrs. Feingersh.

Julia had mentioned that while she and Feingersh were dating he lived somewhere in Brooklyn. But when he got married he and his wife moved into an apartment in Greenwich Village, which happened to be down the block from where Julia was living at the time. It was almost sixty years ago, but she still remembered her address and the building where Ed and his bride were living.

Despite the fact that I'm pretty much a lifelong New Yorker, the Village has always given me trouble. While the rest of

Manhattan is laid out in an easy to navigate grid, the Village has its own set of random rules. Some streets amble east for a while, then turn west. They start out going south, then turn west. There is little rhyme or reason and unless you live there or have visited enough to get the hang of it, it always leaves you disoriented, unsure of where you are and where you're going. Maybe that's why I like it: because it is unpredictable and keeps me on my toes.

Julia Scully lived in a building between Bedford and Barrow, and Feingersh and his wife lived a short block away on Commerce, which intersected with Bedford and ran perpendicular to Barrow. I remembered the crescent especially for a restaurant that I used to frequent when dating my wife; the restaurant, called the Grange Hall, was now replaced by a trendy place called Commerce. To walk this area was to fall back into another perhaps not simpler but certainly more interesting time, when artists, writers, poets, and crackpots inhabited the Village. Now, it held what was left of them, as well as the nouveau-riche robber barons who could now afford to live there, and tourists, most of whom had little idea of the interesting history of the area.

When I reached the four-story brownstone that Julia had indicated was where Ed and Alice lived, I was relieved to find it was intact. By the look of it, I suspected it hadn't changed much since the 1950s, since the neighborhood was designated by the city as historical and therefore couldn't be tinkered with much. I didn't expect to find Alice, but when I stepped into the vestibule and checked the mailboxes I was surprised to find a name that might be who I was looking for: Alice Taylor, 2R.

I buzzed, not expecting anyone to be home, so I was surprised when a raspy voice screeching through the intercom, asked, "Who is it?"

"My name is Henry Swann and I'm looking for a woman

who would have been married to the photographer Ed Feingersh."

There was a moment of silence and then I heard a quick series of consecutive clicks, which I realized was the sound of the front door being unlocked. I quickly pressed the weight of my body against it, as I turned the doorknob at the same time.

When I reached the second floor I saw that the door at the end of the hall was already open and a tall, elderly woman dressed in a long, flowered robe was standing in the doorway, her hand on the doorknob, as if ready to slam it shut if she didn't like what she saw.

"I was married to Ed, what do you want? And whatever it is, make it quick, I'm in the middle of watching my favorite soap," she said in a whiskey-soaked voice reminiscent of Tallulah Bankhead, a woman she happened to resemble somewhat.

As I moved closer I said, "I've been hired to track down some of your husband's work."

"I couldn't give a damn about making your life easier. Come on in, before I change my damn mind," she said, not as a request but more as a command. She stepped aside and let me through the door, then shut it and locked it behind me. She was wearing some kind of sweet-smelling perfume that made me wince.

"Straight through, into the living room," she instructed.

I could hear voices coming from the TV and there was a funny smell in the apartment and it wasn't just her perfume. Cats and over-sweet smell of cat litter. Sure enough, when I got to the living room, I was greeted by a couple of cats, meowing and rubbing up against my legs.

"If they bother you, I'll put 'em in the bedroom," she said. "But just remember, they live here, you don't."

"I'll keep that in mind." I was reminded of my wife's cat. When we first started to date, the cat was near death, and she would have to hydrate him with an IV needle, once a day. When she had to leave town for a weekend, I was left with the task. When she came back and found that the cat was still alive, she said later that that's when she fell in love with me.

"Take your coat off, honey. Throw it anywhere. I'm not one for ceremony and besides you won't be here long. You want some tea or coffee or maybe something a little stronger?"

"No thanks."

"Good. I only asked because it seems like the right thing to do. I don't have anything other than booze and seltzer. Too early for that, though. Except maybe special occasions. This isn't a special occasion, is it, honey?"

"It is, if you want it to be."

"Let's see how this goes, before I break out the happy juice. So, you're here about Ed's work."

"That's right," I said, settling into a well-worn wing chair covered with cat hair, as she stepped over and lowered the sound on the TV. I could see her better now and although she was obviously in her late seventies, you could tell that she'd been a beautiful woman. Her face was remarkably unlined, the bone structure still there, and although the apartment was pretty much a mess, she obviously still took care of herself.

"If you don't mind my saying, you look great."

"For a woman my age?"

"For a woman any age."

"Flattery will get you everywhere, honey. But it's all about heredity, honey. I gave up giving a shit years ago."

I looked at the TV. "You could get better reception, you know."

"How's that?"

"Call the cable company. Looks to me like you might need some new wiring."

"How do you know about that kind of shit?"

"I used to work for them in another life."

"Another life, huh? I know about those. So how's this life going for you, honey?"

"Better than that one."

"Yeah, well, lives come and go."

"About Ed's work . . ."

"I hate to burst your bubble, honey, but when I was married to Ed there was no work. At least not the kind of work you're talking about. He was blocked. Couldn't take a damn picture. He was working as an editor and he was either shit-faced or in the shitter. He'd have these dark periods when he left the house and I didn't know when he'd be back."

"Why do you think he was blocked?"

"Damned if I know. Believe me, I tried to inspire him, but the only thing I inspired him to do was kill himself. But don't get me wrong. I don't blame myself. He came to me defective. I just didn't read the packaging careful enough. He was depressed and he drank to deal with the depression and the more he drank the more depressed he became. There was no way I was going to break that cycle, so I decided to join it."

"It's the work before he was blocked I'm interested in."

"Why's that?"

"I don't ask why, I just ask whoever's hiring me, 'how much are you going to pay me?' "

"Things are starting to get interesting. When there's money on the table Alice starts paying attention." She looked at her watch. "It's one o'clock. The bar just opened. Can I get you something?"

"No, thanks."

"That's fine. I don't mind drinking alone."

She got up and disappeared into the kitchen. A moment later, she was back, holding a tumbler of a clear liquid, which I guessed was vodka.

"So, you've been hired to find Eddie's pictures. That's what he called them, you know. 'Pictures.' He tried to make it sound like he wasn't pretentious, but boy did he take that job seriously. Even when he wasn't able to take pictures anymore. He always had an incredible eye. To bad he stopped using it for his own work."

She laughed and held up her glass. "I blame this on Eddie. He didn't like to drink alone. Me, I don't particularly care. But you're not here to listen to me babble. You're looking for his oeuvre. That's what they call it, right?"

"I believe they do."

"Sorry, honey, I haven't the foggiest idea what he did with it. I don't even know if he had it by the time we got together."

"Any idea where it might be?"

"I'm not even sure it is."

"What do you mean?"

"Ed traveled very light in life. When we got married he hardly had any belongings, no furniture, very little in the way of clothing, a few books, that was all. And friends, well most of them were drinking buddies or other photographers, but he wouldn't have left his work with them. The only place he might have kept his work was at his agency, PIX."

"What if he didn't keep the photos there? Isn't there anyplace else you can think of he'd leave them, or anyone he'd leave them with?"

She took another sip of her drink. "I guess it's possible he might have stored some stuff at Costello's, that damn bar he and his cronies used to hang out at all the time. Hell, he might as well have been married to it, not me. But I don't think it's around anymore. But I still am." She laughed and toasted herself.

"It's not. Anyplace else? Anyone else?"

"What makes you so damn sure there are any photos? Eddie was always onto the next project. He didn't care much about what he'd done. It was all about what he was going to do."

"They found those Monroe photos in that warehouse."

One of the cats jumped into my lap.

"Hey, Cutty, get down."

"It's fine."

"You sure."

"Yes. About those Monroe photos . . ." I said as I reflexively started petting the cat.

"I don't know how they got there. My guess? Either he gave them to someone else and they stored them there, or maybe his agency gave away stuff and some of it landed in that warehouse. But you know . . ." She put her drink down on a side table. "If anything of Ed's is found, guess who's got first dibs on it?"

"I don't care who gets what. Don't get me wrong, I enjoy a good fight so long as I'm not in it. In the meantime, I'll string my client along as far as I can stretch it." I winked at her. "Know what I mean?"

She smiled, raised her glass, tipped it toward me, then drained what was left. "A man after my own heart. Why if I were forty years younger . . . You sure you don't want something, honey? Suddenly, I'm feeling kinda social. It's nice to have a man around the house again. I been married three times, but none of 'em stuck."

"Too much woman for them," I said, getting up to leave.

"Ha. Sorry I couldn't be more help, but honey, it's been what, fifty years." She shook her head. "I just can't believe how fast time goes."

"Thanks, anyway."

"My pleasure, honey. And remember if you do find anything let me know so I can put a claim in on it. An old lady with dough, why that's a magnet to those young guys looking for a crack at la vida loca."

20
SWANN MAKES IT
TO THE PLAZA

Next stop was the Plaza Hotel. I'd already alerted Goldblatt, who was thrilled to be in the game again. That would be two days in a row I'd involved him and frankly, though I'd never let on to him, I was glad to have him along.

The plan was simple. I wasn't prepared to exchange the book for the money yet. I wanted to scope this Stern guy out first, see what he was made of, see how serious he was, and try to get some nagging questions answered. The actual exchange, if there were one, would come later. He'd probably be pissed. But I didn't care.

I wanted Goldblatt to hover close by, in case I needed backup. We had a hand signal that would have him quickly appear on the scene if I needed him. Until then, he was to remain invisible, or at least as invisible as was possible for a man who remarkably seemed to take up far more space than his considerable size.

Entering the large, ornate, high-ceiling lobby of the hotel, half a block off Central Park West, there was a bar on the immediate left and then, set against the windows a series of tables and chairs. I told Goldblatt to meet me at the bar half an hour early, so I could brief him.

When I arrived, Goldblatt was already there.

"I'm really pumped for this, Swann," he announced, sipping what he claimed was a Virgin Mary—he bragged that he wanted to have all his wits available. "It's good to see you've finally accepted that we're a team."

"I don't think you should jump to any conclusions, Goldblatt. Let's just take it one day at a time. So you know what to do, right?"

"What am I, retarded or something?"

"Just checking. I expect this to go smoothly, but you never know."

"I'm ready, willing, and able."

I sneered, but didn't say anything. He got the point, I was sure. I checked my watch. "Okay, he'll be here in twenty minutes. I'm going to find a seat back over there. You position yourself so you can see what's going on, away from the bar, please."

"Gotcha, Chief."

"Cut the crap, will ya. This isn't a joke. Wait here ten minutes, then find yourself a seat."

"Gotcha, Chief."

I shook my head and headed toward the back of the lobby, while Goldblatt remained at the bar, finishing what was left of his "virgin" Bloody Mary.

I chose a seat in the corner of the room that still gave me a view of the front entrance and that was conspicuous enough that Goldblatt could find a good perch for himself and still remain anonymous.

I'd told Stern that I'd be reading a copy of the *New York Times,* so I'd purchased one before I got to the hotel. I removed my coat and placed it in the seat next to mine, pulled out the newspaper, spreading several sections of it on the table to discourage anyone else from sitting down, and started to read about the latest scandal plaguing the country, while keeping an eye on the entrance maybe fifty feet in front of me.

A few minutes after I sat down, Goldblatt moved away from the bar and found a seat about thirty feet diagonally from where

I was seated. He winked at me. I refused to acknowledge him.

At precisely three o'clock, a tall, slim, handsome in all the GQ ways, man wearing a camel-haired overcoat, multi-striped knitted scarf, and a fedora, which I thought was a little over the top, walked through the front doors. He stopped a moment, looked around, spotted me holding up the *Times*, and started walking in my direction. Instead of standing up to greet him, I held the newspaper higher, until only my eyes could be seen. When he came within a few feet of me he stopped and, gesturing toward the seat next to mine, asked, "This seat taken?"

"Depends," I said, still holding the newspaper at eye level.

"On what?" he asked.

"On whether you're Matty Stern."

"That depends on whether you're Henry Swann."

"Sit down," I said.

He removed his expensive coat to reveal an even more expensive gray, well-tailored suit. When he unwrapped his scarf, I noted his red and white rep tie. Stern was dressed to intimidate. Unfortunately for him, though I am intimidated by many things, clothing is not one of them.

He picked up my coat gingerly, as if it was in need of being deloused, handed it to me, then sat down, placing his nicely folded overcoat in his lap, his scarf over that.

I made a quick sweep of the lobby. Goldblatt saw what I was doing and did the same. I noticed two men, both standing, one on my left, about twenty-five feet away, the other to my right, about the same distance from me. One was wearing an ill-fitting blue suit that seemed a couple sizes too small, the other was wearing jeans and a black leather jacket. The one in the blue suit was a huge man, with a thick neck. The man in the leather jacket was much slimmer and, though he was a good distance away, he seemed somewhat familiar to me, but I couldn't quite place him. Blue suit was perusing what looked like a touristy pamphlet he'd gotten at the front desk. Leather jacket was holding a copy of the *New York Post*. Neither was reading what they were holding. I knew this because I'd done the very same thing countless times before. Only I was much better at it than they were. I also knew this because every so often I could see them glance in my direction. I assumed they were with Stern and probably a much more effective backup than Goldblatt. I looked over at Goldblatt again and shifted my head ever so slightly in their directions. He nodded discreetly. He'd made them, too.

"Well, Mr. Swann, I believe we have some business to conduct."

"I believe we do."

"You've got the book?"

"I do."

"I don't see any reason to draw this out. I'm sure you have things to do. I know I do. May I see it?"

I crossed my legs and leaned back, trying to look relaxed. "I don't have it with me."

"Excuse me," he said, his eyes popping open, while he moved aggressively forward in his chair. I glanced at the two men, both of whom seemed to stiffen slightly when Stern moved forward. This was going to be fun. "What the hell did you think the point of this meeting was?"

"I thought it was to get to know each other."

"You're playing games with the wrong man, Mr. Swann."

"This is work, not play, Mr. Stern. I know the difference. I'm doing a job and I'm doing it the best way I can. I'm paid to be careful. I'm paid to make sure my client is protected."

"You're not trying to hold me up for more money, are you? Because if you are . . ."

I shook my head. "No. A deal's a deal. It was thirty grand and it still is."

"Then what's the hold-up?"

"I have a few questions I need answered."

"I'm not here to answer your questions. I'm here to get the book."

"You'll get the book, but you'll answer the questions before you do."

"You talk tough, Mr. Swann. The question I ask myself is, can he back it up?"

I smiled. Stood. Started to put my coat on. I looked over at Goldblatt. He wasn't smiling.

"You're prepared to walk away from thirty thousand dollars?"

I put one arm in the sleeve of my coat, then the other.

"All right. What kind of questions?"

I slowly removed one arm, then the other, from my coat, and sat back down, folding it back into my lap.

"About who you are and why you're so anxious to get the diary."

"I'd say that was none of your business. You're just a middle man, and it's best you don't forget it."

"I'd say if you want the diary back you consider it my business. Oh, and for the record, insults don't do much for me or to me. You can't possibly insult me better than I can insult myself. I know what I am and who I am. I live with myself every day, which is punishment enough. Let me give you some advice. Don't fuck with a freelancer, which is what I am. I didn't have this job yesterday and I won't have this job tomorrow, and you can only imagine how little I'm getting for this gig. If you piss me off, and you're getting closer to that point, I walk. And you might not like dealing with the next guy, whoever that is."

He sat back and squeezed his hands together. I knew he was losing patience. I could tell he had a temper and he was trying hard to hold himself back. His eyes made a quick trip to the two men standing on either side of us. I looked at Goldblatt, who had picked up a magazine from a table and was pretending to read it. He saw me looking at him and raised an eyebrow. I nodded my head very slightly, alerting him, I hoped, that everything was fine.

Stern unclenched his hands. "What do you need to know?"

"Who are you and who do you work for?"

"I'm an attorney. I work for the family."

"Whose family?"

"Starr Faithfull's. She has a great-nephew and I represent him."

"What's his name?"

"I'm afraid that's privileged information."

"Why does he want the diary?"

"Because it's rightfully his." He spat the words out like bullets, probably wishing they were.

"That's a lawyer answer, Stern. I want the truth. Why does he suddenly care about his diary enough to pay thirty thousand dollars? And why does he want it bad enough to break into someone's house to find it?"

"I don't know anything about a break-in. And neither does he. As far as his reasons are concerned, he doesn't confide in me. Like you, I'm the hired help. But I'm very good at what I do, Swann, and I'm here to get that diary, as promised. So let's cut the bullshit. What's the best way to get that accomplished?"

"I just want to make sure there's nothing illegal going on here. I'm not sure who the legal owner of this diary is."

"My client is the legal owner."

"This isn't a simple transaction. You wouldn't be bringing those goons over there with you if it was."

"What goons?"

"Those two guys over there," I said, gesturing with my hand, so they could see me.

"I have no idea what you're talking about."

"No idea, huh? Okay. I won't press the matter. If they aren't your guys then there's someone else interested in the diary and you'd better watch your back. But back to our business. If you want the diary I need to know I'm giving it to the rightful owner."

"You're not giving it. You're selling it."

"To the rightful owner? How do I know that?"

"You don't. But what you should know is that I could have you arrested."

"For what?"

"For possession of stolen property."

"Stolen from who? That diary was given to me. And you can't prove otherwise."

"I want that book, Swann. And I've got the thirty thousand dollars here with me to prove it. Now, you're either going to give it to me or . . ."

"Or what? You gonna sue me? You gonna have me arrested? Look, we both know I hold all the cards here. But I'm tired of playing this game. I've got other things to do. I can see I'm not going to get the answers I want but the truth is I have no use for the diary, so I'm going to give it to you. For the money, of course. Here's how it's going to work. You're going to give me the money and an associate of mine will deliver the book to you."

"You've got to be kidding."

"Don't you trust me?"

"Why the hell would I trust you?"

"You want the diary, those are the rules."

"How do I know you even have it?"

It felt like I was in the middle of a bad movie about a kidnapping. Fortunately, I was prepared. Before I'd hidden the book, I'd taken a few photos with my phone, so I took it out and showed them to Stern.

With his thumb and forefinger he eagerly enlarged each of

the three photos, one of the front of the book, one of the first page with Starr's name on it, the last a random page from the book.

He handed it back to me.

"Good enough proof, counselor?"

He nodded. "So how is this going to work?"

"You give me the money and then tell me where you want the book delivered and I'll get it there. Tomorrow. By noon."

"I'm not handing over thirty thousand dollars in cash on the promise of getting the book tomorrow."

"If I walk out of here without a deal, then either I'm going to keep the book or find another buyer. I don't think I'd have a problem with that, do you? Let me give you a scenario, counselor. I find an agent and tell Faithfull's story and then I tell him I have a lost diary. The agent finds a writer who writes the story, sells it to a publisher, and then we've got a book. That book is made into a movie . . . Do you get my drift?"

I could see he was angry and frustrated. He was obviously used to getting his own way and he could see I couldn't be bullied. There was going to be a stalemate unless he made a move. Finally, after almost a minute of silence, he looked up at me and said, "I don't like this, Swann. I don't like it at all."

"That breaks my heart, Matty, but that's the way it's going to be."

"You're playing with the wrong people, Swann."

"It won't be the first time and I doubt it'll be the last."

He paused for a moment then looked me right in the eye. "Have you ever thought about your death, Swann?"

"I think about it all the time."

"I guess a man who does your kind of work would have to. Have you thought about after?"

"After what?"

"After your death."

"I'm guessing it's pretty much nothing. Kind of like being in Topeka."

"I mean the details. Would you prefer to be buried? Cremated?"

"I'd like to be surprised. Besides, it's not like I'm going to know the difference. I'm assuming there's a point in all this talk about death, my death in particular. I've been to the edge and back. It doesn't frighten me as much as you'd like it to. I know how to walk the line. This wouldn't be a not so subtle attempt to intimidate me, would it?"

"Why would I do that?"

"You tell me. But if you are trying to intimidate me, it won't work. Not because I'm brave, because I'm not. And not because I'm not scared, because I'm scared all the time. I walk out of this hotel and I'm scared I'm going to be hit by a car. Or trampled by one of those carriage horses. Or hit by lightning. I lived with it all the time, so trying to scare me is pointless."

"You're a tough man to deal with, Swann."

"To the contrary. Just do things the way I want them and there'll be no problem at all. You'll get your diary and I don't care what the fuck you do with it, and I'll get the money."

"I'm not walking out of here giving you thirty thousand dollars without getting the diary."

I smiled. "How about this? We meet one more time and make the exchange?"

"If you waste my time again, you'll be sorry. Trust me, I can make your life a living hell."

"Too late for that. Here's the deal. We meet tomorrow. Same place, same time. You have the money with you, I have the diary. We make the exchange. I never see you again, you never see me again."

"That'll be a pleasure."

He got up, put on his scarf, his expensive overcoat, gave me a dirty look that I supposed was meant to intimidate me, and walked off. I watched the two goons flanking me. They didn't take their eyes off me, didn't move from their spot. As soon as Stern disappeared through the door, Goldblatt ambled over.

"How'd it go?"

"As well as could be expected."

"He didn't give you the dough."

"He's not stupid."

"Did you find out anything?"

I shook my head. "These guys really want this diary, so it must be important. I just can't help wondering why."

"Maybe we can squeeze some more out of this? Or maybe we should just hold onto it."

I fixed my eyes on his. "I'm only going to say this once, Goldblatt. We're not in this to make more money. We're in this to get the thirty grand, take our share, give the rest to Claudia, and put this behind us. Understood?"

"Yeah, yeah, yeah. I get it. But you've got to admit you're curious."

"Yes, but I know how to deal with that. I want you to stay focused. Now the question is, how do we get rid of those two guys over there? You know they're going to follow me as soon as I leave, so let's see if we can split them up. Find a men's room. Go in, hang out for a couple minutes, then come back here. If I'm still here, we'll go to step two. If not, just go out and do your thing. Go to one of your diners, go to a movie, do whatever the fuck you want. Call me in an hour or so and let me know if the guy is still with you."

"Gotcha."

"And Goldblatt, be careful, will ya. And please, try not to fuck up."

"No problem, Chief. This is my meat and potatoes. I know how to work a tail, I know how to lose a tail."

He gave me the thumbs up, then took off for the bathroom. I watched as the guy in the leather jacket peeled off and trailed after Goldblatt. There was something familiar about him. Something. I just couldn't quite figure out what it was.

Once they were gone, that left the gorilla in the blue suit for me.

I put my coat on and walked slowly toward the front of the hotel, making sure I didn't make eye contact with Mr. Blue Suit. I tossed the newspaper in a trash bin, then moved through the revolving doors to the outside, where I was met by the ever-present sounds of the city.

It was almost five o'clock and offices were beginning to empty, a good time to get lost in a crowd. I walked over to 59th and Lex. Mr. Blue Suit wisely kept about a third of a block between us. Occasionally, just to play with him, I sped up, then slowed down, making believe something in a store window interested me. When I reached 59th and Lex, I started down the subway stairs on the south side of the street. Mr. Blue Suit quickly crossed to the other side and started down the stairs on the north side of the street. He thought he was being cute, but once he started down those stairs I had him. I quickly retraced my steps back up, ducked into the Banana Republic on the corner, and headed straight to the back of the store.

After ten minutes or so, I left the store, looking both ways to make sure he wasn't on the street. When I was certain I was on my own, I hopped a bus down Lex. I got off at 23rd and walked briskly the rest of the way to Klavan's, where I planned to find out if Ross had uncovered anything about Jack.

As I reached Klavan's building and was about to enter, I happened to look across the street. There, leaning against the building, was Mr. Blue Suit.

I was impressed. Either I wasn't as good as I thought I was, or he was a lot smarter than I gave him credit for.

21
CHINESE CHECKERS

"You look a little disconcerted, Swann," Klavan cannily observed as I tossed my coat on one chair and plunked myself down in another. His office is so clean, with everything in its place, that I always feel like I should be wearing white gloves.

"I hate it when I'm inadequate, that I'm not as good as I hope I am."

"That happen often?"

"Too often, way too often."

"What is it this time?"

"I was being tailed. I thought I'd lost him, but he shows up waiting for me outside your building."

"He's no magician. He probably knows where your, or should I say my, office is. It's on your cards, isn't it?"

"I didn't hand him my business card, Ross."

"Easy, big boy."

"Sorry. I'm just a little unnerved. Obviously, I thought I was better than I am."

"You're probably not as hard to find as you think you are. He probably knows where you live, too."

"I doubt that," I said, my mind whirling, trying to figure out how I was going to lose this guy before I got home. "Sometimes I even have trouble finding my way home."

"You're listed, aren't you?"

"Are you kidding? So everyone and his mother can find me? There've been times when I'm only one step ahead of all those guys I used to find for skipping on their bills. And in my business you don't have a lot of satisfied customers. You think I'm going to list my address so just anyone can find me?"

"How do you get away with that?"

"PO box, my friend. And haven't you noticed that I get things delivered here, on occasion?"

"Okay, so he probably doesn't know where you live. But you're going to have to give him the slip when you leave here, unless you plan on never going home again."

"There's a back service entrance, right?"

"Yes. It opens to around the side of the building."

"I can make that work. Did you find out anything about Jack?"

Klavan pulled out a pad. "Jack Kerowak. Born, August 15, 1968, in Long Branch, New Jersey. Father was a schoolteacher, here in New York City. Mother was a nurse's aid. Father was notable in that he was part of the Greenwich Village Beat crowd in the fifties. I found his name, Nick Kerowak, alongside painters like Rothko, Pollock, and de Kooning. He never made it to the big time, though. I'll ask my wife, Mary, if she's ever heard of him. Obviously, she's way too young to be part of that scene, but being a painter she might have heard his name bandied about at some party or art opening. Jack has taught in the past, but I can't find anything that says he's teaching now. But I can only access New York City Public School records, so he might be teaching in a private school. He did have a novel published half a dozen years ago, but it doesn't look like he's ever going to make it to one of my collections. Nothing else comes up right now, and I don't think there's anything here that's going to help you."

"At least what he's told me so far seems to hold up as the truth. That's good because if you turn up one lie it inevitably leads to another. Lies are like fruit flies. They multiply faster than you can count."

I looked at my watch. It was almost seven.

"You going out tonight?" I asked.

"Yeah. Dinner date. With Mary."

"What time are you supposed to meet her?"

"Seven-thirty."

"How would you feel about a little mis-direction?"

"My nipples are hard."

"Here," I said, tossing him my coat. "Try this on. Put the collar up and wear this." I tossed him my watch cap. "Before you step outside, have the doorman hail you a cab. As you see it pulling up to the curb, step outside and make sure you're seen. Then hop in the cab. Quick. Like you're trying to get away from someone."

"And while I'm doing this you'll be?"

"Waiting by the side of the building to make sure he takes the bait. When he does, I'll be on my way."

"If he doesn't?"

"I'll figure out a way to distract him enough so his eyes are off the side of the building."

"You're a master, Swann."

"I do my best."

Klavan sold it well. Wearing my coat and watch cap, he jumped in a cab and my tail, thinking it was me, raced after it, then quickly found a cab of his own to follow.

I headed home with the intention of digging out the diary and seeing if there was anything in it that would explain why it was so valuable. On the way, I stopped and picked up some Chinese food at a local joint. When I got to my building, opened the door, and looked up the landing, there was Claudia Bennett, sitting halfway up the stairs to the second floor, reading a magazine.

"Surprise!" she announced, dropping the magazine and

thrusting her arms toward me.

"How the hell did you get in here?" I asked, climbing the stairs toward her.

"I'm cute. And I look harmless. Cute and harmless-looking people can get in anywhere."

"How did you know where I lived?"

"That's for me to know and you to find out."

"I thought I was anonymous enough no one could ever find me," I mumbled.

"Well, I guess you were wrong."

"You followed me the other day after I left you, didn't you?"

She smiled and cocked her head. "Pretty good, right? Maybe you should hire me to be one of your operatives."

"I don't have operatives."

"Then maybe you can hire me as your personal assistant. I think you could use one. I hope you don't mind my saying this, Swann, but your life is a mess." She looked at what I was holding. "Hope you brought enough for me. I'm starved."

I looked down at the bag of Chinese food in my hand. "Lucky for you my eyes are always bigger than my stomach."

She grabbed my arm. "Let's not stand around wasting time while dinner's getting cold."

Once in my apartment Claudia pronounced the place "a dump"—no surprise to me, I live there—and headed straight to the kitchen. "I guess there's no need to look in a cabinet for dishes," she said, eyeing the dishes piled high in the sink.

"I was going to get around to it," I said, trying not to sound the least bit apologetic, because I wasn't.

"In this century, I hope."

"I haven't been cited by the Board of Health yet."

"I'll take care of this," she said, rolling up her sleeves.

"I think ahead. I've got plastic utensils in here."

"Not on my watch," she said, as she set about washing several mismatched plates, some silverware, and a couple glasses, put them on the kitchen table, and proceeded to dump the Chinese food out of their containers into bowls.

"I usually don't bother," I said. "It saves on washing dishes."

"I can see your dining philosophy but tonight we're going to act like civilized adults and dine, rather than eat out of cartons. You're good with that, right?"

"I guess," I said but the truth was I was kind of getting off on this unexpected show of domesticity and it might be nice to see the bottom of the sink for a change.

"Got any wine?"

"Do I look like a wine drinker?"

She eyed me closely. "Guess not."

"Beer and maybe an old bottle of vodka in the freezer is about the extent of my alcohol repertoire."

"Why am I not surprised?"

We sat, ate, and made small talk about this and that. I knew eventually she'd get to the point of her visit, but I was in no hurry. I wanted to make believe she was actually there to spend time with me. A ridiculous notion, perhaps, but one that was easy to perpetuate as I sat there eating Chinese food off a proper plate, served from a proper bowl—even the rice—and sipping a bottle of Corona, not even caring that I was in my own shabby apartment.

When we finished, she cleared the table—I offered, but she refused—and asked, "Are you a dessert person?"

"I am," I said.

"Me, too. Got anything?"

"Do Hostess cupcakes count?"

"They do if you don't have anything else."

"Then they count." I got up and retrieved them from a cabinet. Tipped the box and the last two emerged.

"I usually eat them two at a time, but I have company so I

think I'm obliged to share."

"Yes. You are."

"Plated?" I asked, innocently.

"Of course," she replied, with a hint of a British accent.

Once we finished and the party was over it was time to get down to business. As much as I wished to prolong the illusion of two people having a pleasant dinner together because they wanted to, eventually I knew the bubble would burst and I wanted to be the one with the pin.

"So, now that we're finished why not tell me what this surprise visit is all about?"

"Because I missed you and wanted to see you?"

"That's a question?"

"No. I missed you and wanted to see you."

I laughed. Not because it was funny, but because it was ridiculous. "Nice try."

"Why do you have that attitude? Don't you think it's possible someone could miss you?"

"Only because just about anything is possible. I'm more interested in what's likely, Claudia. And it's not likely you're here just because you missed me."

"How about if we change that to 'like'? As in, I'm here because I like you."

"Sorry. Even more ridiculous. I may be a lot of things, but likeable and loveable aren't among them."

"What I'm going to say is going to sound like the real reason I'm here and it's not, so maybe I shouldn't say it."

"Say it, Claudia, because we both know it's going to come out in the end, whenever the end is."

"I'm not sure I should," she said, playfully.

"Say it, Claudia, or I'll make you wash the dishes again."

"I doubt you can make me do anything I don't want to do. I'm not the type that can be pushed around, Swannie. You don't mind my calling you that, do you?"

"My grandmother used to say, Henry, don't ever let anyone call you Swannie, it'll make everyone think of Al Jolson."

"Who?"

"Never mind. Call me Swannie, if you like. Now what were you going to say?"

"I was just going to ask if I could take a look at the diary, but now it's going to seem like that's why I came."

"Frankly, I don't care why you came. You're here and it's been fun and if you want to see what's in the book, you have every right to see what's in the book, since this is your play, not mine."

"Goodie," she squealed, getting up, then leaning over to give me a peck on the cheek, a peck, quite frankly, that left me wanting more. But I wasn't going to ask for it. At least not then. "Where is it?"

I went into my bedroom and returned with the diary. By that time, she'd cleared the dishes and was sitting on my couch. She patted the empty space next to her and I sat down. I removed the book from the Duane Reade bag, then the brown paper bag.

"That's old, all right," said Claudia as she leaned over my shoulder to get a closer look. I smelled her hair. It smelled freshly shampooed. Some kind of fruity smell, I couldn't quite identify.

I opened the book so she could see Starr's name.

"And it really is hers, isn't it?"

"Unless it's not."

"What's that supposed to mean?"

"Ever hear the word *forgery*?"

"Why would anyone go to the trouble of forging the diary of a girl who's been dead over half a century, a girl no one's ever heard of?"

I looked her straight in the eye and made a face.

"Okay, but we're not talking about the original Declaration of Independence here. How much could this thing be worth?"

"Value is only determined by what someone is willing to pay for it. Right now, the value is thirty grand. That only changes if someone is willing to pay more for it. My question is, why's it worth even that much?"

"Let's read it and see. How many pages did she fill?"

I thumbed through it about a quarter of the way before the writing stopped.

"It's not that much," she said, "and we've got time, right?"

"I live here."

"And I'm your guest," she said, snuggling closer to me, putting her arm between mine and my side, as if we had a relationship we did not have.

We read the diaries, turning the pages slowly, until both of us had digested what was on each of them. In a girlish script, Starr wrote about her emotional and everyday life in overheated, emotional prose, and her "deep thoughts," if you could call them that, about herself, her "boyfriends," most of whom it was obvious were using her, her casual drug use, as well as her hopes and dreams, which were, in the end, pretty banal. They were the hopes and dreams of any teenager, although she was well past that stage. Until we got to near the end of the diary entries, when she started to get more serious. She spoke of one lover using only initials, A.P., as someone, much older than she was, that she really cared about, lusted after, in fact. But at some point it became clear he was moving himself out of the picture. He was obviously wealthy and prominent and as she kept writing, Starr became more and more enraged at his indifference toward her. At one point, she wrote about trying to get back at him. "The only thing A.P. cares about is his money and his reputation. Well, if he's not careful he'll lose both. He's going to rue the day he trifled with me," she wrote. "I know where he keeps some very valuable and important things and if they go missing, well maybe he'll start to see things my way. In the end, he'll know I was right—that we are meant to be together."

Claudia looked up. "Jeez, this chick had some problems."

"You think?"

"This is starting to get good. There are only a few more pages left. Let's see what she did."

We turned back to the diary and together we read it till the end. The last paragraph was the kicker.

"I've taken what A.P. thinks is his most valuable possession. He doesn't know that it's really me. I've hidden it along with some of the nice things he's given me, in a place he'll never find it, never that is, until he realizes that he can't toy with my affections. That I have feelings and that he can't just use me and throw me away, like he does everyone else.

"The funny thing is, it's hidden right under his nose, but he'll never see it, because he's too busy looking for other things, things that don't matter . . ."

"Jeez, what do you think it is that she hid and where did she hide it?"

"I have no idea, but it doesn't matter, Claudia. Whoever wants this diary knows something was missing and thinks this," I patted the book, which now sat in my lap, "will tell them where it is."

"It's so vague, how could anyone think this book could lead them to whatever this thing is?"

"They'd have to know a lot about the person she's talking about, where he lived, where he worked. Of course, they have no idea what's in this book. They can only be speculating that it gives clues as to where this thing might be. For all Stern knows, he and whoever's hired him will be paying thirty grand for nothing. But the thing is, this hint about hiding it right under

223

his nose wouldn't help us, but it sure might give a lead to someone who knows the whole story."

"What should we do?"

"Just what we planned to do. Sell the diary to Stern."

"But it might be worth so much more."

"To someone else, maybe. To us, not so much."

"Come on, Swann."

"Hogs get fat, pigs get slaughtered."

"Okay. I get your point."

"At least we now know why someone might want this diary."

"So, when does the deal go down?"

"Tomorrow afternoon."

"Can I come?"

"Not a chance."

"Why not?"

"Because this is not a spectator sport. It's enough I've got Goldblatt involved."

"You'd take him and not me."

"That's right. He's my . . ." I choked on the word, but I still said it, "partner."

"I'm your employer."

"Don't push it, Claudia."

She leaned in against me and yawned.

"Sleepy?" I asked, knowing damn well it was more than that.

"Well, I don't know about sleepy, but I think I'd like to go to bed."

"You think it's so easy?"

"What?"

"To seduce me?"

She looked me in the eye and smiled. Her eyes, too. They smiled. Okay, it was that easy, and she knew it.

Afterwards, when it was over, when we were lying next to each other, naked, our bodies touching slightly, listening to the sounds of a garbage truck moving slowly up my street, the metallic sound of cans hitting the side of the truck as it swallowed up yesterday's trash, Claudia nuzzled her head close to mine. Her hair still had that sweet fruity smell. Her skin was soft and warm. I pressed my cheek against hers, rough against smooth but it seemed to fit.

"Do you sleep with all your clients, Swannie?" she asked, caressing my chest.

"Whenever I get the chance."

"Even the male clients?"

"I draw the line somewhere."

"And that's where?"

"That's one of the wheres."

"I should get a list of the others."

"It would be a short list."

"You're probably not as tough and cynical as you'd like people to believe."

"I may not be as tough, but believe me, I am as cynical, maybe more, than people might believe. I thought you were sleepy."

"Not so much anymore," she said, rolling on top of me.

It seems the night was not yet over.

22
THE MORNING AFTER THE NIGHT BEFORE

The phone woke me up and an unfamiliar male voice said, "I've got that information you're looking for." At first, blinking away sleep, I didn't know what he meant and so I was silent, as Claudia slept heavily beside me.

"The guy was in here last night. The reporter dude, remember? The one you wanted me to call you about. Got a pencil?"

I recognized who he was now. It was the bartender at the former Costello's bar. "Sure," I said, reaching over to the night-stand for something to write with and on. I came up with a pen and the back of a Verizon telephone bill envelope.

"His name's Elliot Ravetz. He gave me his address. I told him about you. He said you should just stop by. He's home most of the time when he's not at the bar."

The address was on the Upper West Side, near Riverside Park. I thanked him, hung up, put my hand on Claudia's soft, warm, naked shoulder, and squeezed gently. She rolled over, her eyes still closed. She reached out for me, but I was already half out of bed.

"What time is it?" she asked, her eyes still closed.

"Eight-thirty."

"What's the rush?"

"Gotta work."

"You work?"

"On occasion. When I'm unlucky enough to have something to do."

She sat up in bed, letting the blankets drop to her waist. Her breasts were amazing. Small but firm, with light brown, longish nipples. Her dancer's body shunned fat, and so a couple of her ribs showed. She raised her arms and stretched, giving me an excellent view of what I was going to miss. I didn't want to be tempted back into bed, so I tossed her her top, which was on a chair next to the bed. "Get dressed."

"You could just go and leave me here, so I can keep sleeping. Or you could come back to bed," she purred.

"Don't take this personally, but I'm not leaving you here alone with the diary, and as tempting as it is to give in to the latter, I really do have things I've got to get done."

"Would you at least settle on breakfast, just so I don't feel used and abused?"

"Why do I feel I was the one being used?"

"That's not the way I remember it," she said, stretching her arms toward the ceiling.

"Okay. I'll spring for breakfast. But let's do it now, because I don't have that much of the day to screw around with," I said, throwing her her leggings while I then proceeded to pull on my jeans.

"Mind if I shower?" she asked, as she stepped gingerly out of bed. "Boy, it's cold in here. Don't you believe in turning on the heat?"

"Heat? We don't need no stinkin' heat. But because you're a guest I will close the window and sure, take a shower," I said, part of me wanting to reverse the dressing process and join her. "I can resist anything but temptation," Oscar Wilde used to say and all too often that is the case for me. But today, I had too many other things on my mind to give in to temptation, no matter how tempting it might be.

I didn't want to leave the diary in my apartment—if Claudia found me, so could someone else, or so could someone else she told—so I decided to take it with me. While she was in the shower, I retrieved it from its hole in my closet and stashed it in my peacoat pocket. We had a quick, somewhat awkward (I think she was pissed I didn't trust her, but that was only because I *didn't* trust her) breakfast at the local diner, after which I stuffed her in a cab, handed her a twenty, and gave the driver instructions to take her to Penn Station.

I made a move to kiss her goodbye but pulled back. The wise words of Robert Frost, "It was only a small commitment anyway, like a kiss," crossed my mind but I decided even that was more of a commitment than I wanted to make. Claudia was beautiful and smart, but I didn't trust her. I don't know why. I just didn't. Maybe it's because I don't trust anyone anymore, not even myself. In my mind, everything is temporary. Everything has an expiration date. You get too attached and you're bound to pay for it in the end, whenever that is. I'd paid enough in my life. I didn't think I was owed anything, but I certainly didn't think I owed anything to anybody else.

Ravetz lived in one of those nondescript, pre-war high-rises that dotted West End Avenue and Riverside Drive. His building was on 89th Street, halfway down the block. It was obvious from the updating of the lobby and the fact that there was no uniformed doorman that it was one of those buildings that had started out as a rental but had turned co-op as soon as the landlord could accumulate enough apartments to meet the requirements. Those who bought real estate back in the seventies and eighties, at the insider prices, made a windfall profit if they sold. Those who didn't, those who preferred to remain at stabilized prices, had a roof over their heads at a reasonable price, but no equity. I often wondered what I would have done given the opportunity. But in the end, whatever I'd chosen, it probably would have been the wrong thing, so why torture myself with what-ifs?

Ravetz had to be close to eighty if not over that, but the man who answered the door looked at least ten or fifteen years younger. Close to six-feet tall, he was lean except for a slightly protruding belly, his face barely lined. He still had his hair, though it was gray, thinning, and obviously hadn't seen a brush or comb in days. Ditto a razor. He was wearing a button-down blue Oxford shirt and baggy jeans, held up by red and white suspenders.

"Come on in," he said, in a raspy but surprisingly strong, vibrant voice.

He took my coat and hung it in an almost empty front closet. He ushered me into the smallish living room made smaller by the numerous piles of books, which obviously couldn't fit on the wall-to-wall shelves that lined the room. It reminded me a little of Klavan's, only without the class and organization. There were a few framed magazine covers on the wall, as well as a print or two, and a black-and-white photograph that looked familiar, though I couldn't quite place it. Other than the books, the room seemed well-organized and almost gave off the feel of a motel room.

"In case you're wondering, other than the books, why the place is in such good condition, it's because I'm a control freak. I'm told it comes with the alcoholic territory. We like everything in its place, except our lives. Being neat gives me the illusion I'm in control, which of course, I'm not. How about you? You in control, Mr. Swann?"

"Hardly ever," I replied, looking around for a suitable place to sit. My eyes settled on a worn-out easy chair in a corner of the room, but before I could set my ass down I got a disapproving look from Ravetz, followed by a, "Sorry, that's my chair, son. Fits my ass perfectly. Took years to get that accomplished. Sofa's almost as comfortable. Why don'tcha try that."

I did, while he plopped down in his chair.

"Someday I'm gonna get out of this shit-hole, but when I do, this baby," he tapped the worn-down arms of the chair, "goes with me. I'd offer you something, but unless you want water, you'd be sorely disappointed. I'm not even sure I've got any ice, not that you'd need it on a day like today."

"I'm good. You don't drink anymore?"

"Gave it up twenty-five years ago. Cold turkey. None of that AA crap for me. I don't share my toothbrush, my feelings, or my life with anyone."

"And yet you frequent the Overlook."

"It gets me out of the house and keeps me connected to my past. Not that it was all that great, but the older I get the more enticing it becomes. Besides, I like making idle chatter with anonymous folks I'll never see again, and then getting the hell out of there. I like my privacy. I haven't had someone come looking for me in twenty years, and that was my ex-wife looking for her alimony check. So to what do I owe this visit? And who the hell are you?"

"I'm a private investigator," I said, giving myself far more gravitas than I deserved. Somehow, telling this guy I was a skip-tracer by trade didn't seem right. Hell, it never seems right. "I've been hired to find some photos, if they exist, and the guy who took them used to hang out at Costello's. I was told you were a patron, too, and I thought you might know him."

"Believe me, son, if this guy hung out at Costello's, I knew him. Wanna give me his name?"

"Ed Feingersh."

He smiled. "Eddie. Yeah. I knew him all right. At one time in his life he pretty much lived there. Hell, so did I. Who hired ya?"

"I'm not supposed to say."

"Oh, yeah. Confidentiality. I know all about that. I was a

reporter for almost forty years. For the *New York Post* before that sonuvabitch Murdoch came in and turned it into a right-wing shit-rag. I worked for Dorothy Schiff, with Pete Hamill, Max Lerner, Leonard Lyons, Murray Kempton, who was the best damn columnist I ever read. Breslin, too, though he came and went with the breeze. I'll bet you never even heard of half of them."

"You'd lose."

"You don't look old enough to know about them."

"My father read the *Post* and the *News*. He couldn't figure out what wing he was in. I thought about becoming a journalist for about ten minutes."

"You made the right decision, my friend. Journalism is down the tubes. Won't be any newspapers in ten years. Everything's the damn Internet. But hell, you aren't here to hear me bitch about the future. It is what it is and that's all that it is. You're here about the past. That's a place I like to live. Tell me more."

"After Ed died all his photographs seem to have disappeared, except for the Monroe ones they found a while back. The person who hired me thinks they exist somewhere and he wants to get his hands on them. I thought you might know something about where they might be."

"You speak to his wife?"

"Yes."

"No help?"

"No."

"Who else?"

"His former girlfriend, Julia Scully."

"Julia Scully. Great broad. She's still around, huh?"

"She is."

"Before you leave, maybe you could tell me how to get in touch with her."

"Sure thing. She doesn't live far from here. You'd think you two would have bumped into each other."

"Told ya. I don't get out much. The legs don't work so good anymore. They say I need a knee replacement but at my age I'll go with what got me here."

"Got any idea what might have happened to those photos?"

"Why are you asking me?"

"I thought he might have talked about them, or mentioned where he kept them."

"We talked about a lot of things, son, but at the time both of us were drinking pretty good, so a lot of it didn't make sense and what might have is long forgotten. You know, Eddie and I weren't so different."

"How's that?"

"We both drank to hide depression. The only difference is, I realized it and got help. I've been sober twenty-five years, but I told you that, didn't I? Anyway, now it's just pills to keep me alive and relatively sane. Poor Eddie was never able to make the connection. Maybe he just liked drinking too much. Truth is, it was fun. Hanging out with all those guys till late at night. Shootin' the breeze. Work. Women. Sports. That's what we talked about. What else was there? He was a fascinating guy. He'd come up with these crazy ideas for shots and somehow he'd pull them off. He had no fear. It wasn't a surprise that he died young. I thought it would be one of his crazy stunts that would kill him. What was a surprise was how old he got to be."

"How well did you know him?"

"We spent a lot of time together, but I didn't know him all that well. No one did is my guess. He never talked about himself, just what he did and what he wanted to do. Never anything personal. I didn't even know where he lived—hell, if I'd given it any thought I would have said he lived at Costello's. Many's the night he closed the joint."

"But the photos . . ."

"Oh, yeah, the photos. As I recall, he mostly worked out of a darkroom at his agency, PIX, and I would guess that he left the photos there."

I shook my head. "Could he have left any of his photos at Costello's?"

"It's possible, I suppose. But if he did, they were probably lost in one of the moves."

"Or with his family?"

"Also possible. But you've spoken to his wife, so obviously she doesn't have them, or else you wouldn't be here. I don't even know if he had any other family. My reporter's instinct tells me that if they haven't surfaced by now, they're never going to. Don't mind my asking if you have any other leads, do you?"

"A couple, maybe," I said, not because I did but because maybe saying it out loud would mean they'd come to me.

"Mind my asking what they are? Just my newsman's curiosity, that's all."

I looked at him. He had this strange smile on his face. It bothered me a little. I didn't know how to read him. Something told me there was more going on, but maybe I was too ready to see conspiracies where there were none. I'd fallen into that trap before, and I wasn't about to let it happen again.

"I'd rather not say."

He put his hands up. "No problem. I get it."

"Well, thanks for your time," I said, as I got up, put on my coat, and started toward the door.

"Anytime, son. I don't get many visitors so this kinda breaks up my day."

It was only when I was out on the street that I realized I'd forgotten to give him Julia's information. But then, maybe it wasn't all that important to him, since he hadn't bothered to ask me for it again.

23
ALL THINGS BEING EQUAL, WHICH THEY NEVER ARE

I didn't want Goldblatt involved in the Faithfull situation anymore, but once in, there seemed to be little way of keeping him out.

Once again, we met at the Plaza bar before the meet, this time an hour earlier because I didn't want to underestimate Stern and his flunkies. I was pretty sure they were smart enough not to come into a situation blind and I wanted to make sure we were prepared, especially Goldblatt. I didn't want him freelancing and messing things up.

Goldblatt appeared wearing a tie and jacket, as well as a clean white shirt. He almost looked presentable, except for part of his shirt hanging out over his belt. He made me smile. No matter who he tried to be he couldn't hide who he was.

"Looking very dapper today, Goldblatt."

"Thanks," he said, preening a little as he fingered the knot of his rep tie.

"What's the occasion? Got a job interview?"

"I like to look my best when there's money involved. So, what's the plan?" he said, as he plunked his ass down on the seat and immediately grabbed a handful of assorted nuts.

"The plan is simple. He gives me the dough, I give him the book."

"I still don't know why this asshole is willing to pay that much money for this book."

"You were."

"That's different."

"How's that?"

"I saw the potential."

"Maybe he does, too."

"I doubt that." He looked at me closely. "You know, don't you?"

"What are you talking about?"

"You know why he wants the book. You read it, didn't you, and you figured it out?"

"What would you like to drink?"

"Stop avoiding the question. What's in it?"

"Twelve-year-old girl stuff."

"My ass."

I didn't want to tell him. I swear I didn't. But he was like a bulldog. I knew he'd never let it go and it was getting closer to the time Stern would show up and I wasn't quick enough to lie to him, so I told him the truth.

"I knew it!" he said, slapping his thigh hard enough so that the sound echoed through the enormous room. Or at least it seemed that way to me. "Let's get the fuck out of here."

"What are you talking about?"

"You heard me. Either we're renegotiating or we're holding onto that book."

"No to both harebrained ideas. We're taking the money and running with it."

"So what? You can hand it over to your sweetheart and she can buy herself a few new tutus? Not on my watch."

"Goldblatt, I know you're not going to believe it when I tell you this, but it's the truth. I've got a bad feeling about this diary. I don't know why, but I do. I think the best thing we can do is get rid of it, take our cut, give what we promised to Claudia, and walk away."

"What kind of bad feeling?"

"I don't know. It's just a feeling. We don't have anything to gain by holding onto it. We're not going to squeeze anything else out of Stern and going back on our deal is just going to piss him off. And the information in that book, if it means anything at all, means nothing to us. It would do us absolutely no good. Trust me on this."

Goldblatt looked dejected. He was silent for a moment, then brightened and said, "I guess I'll have that drink now."

I marveled at his recuperative powers. How bad could it be if he was asking for something to ingest?

"Look," I said, trying to smooth the waters a little, "we've still got the Feingersh thing. We're making good money on that, right?"

"Yeah," he said, his eyes searching for the bartender who was at the other end of the bar.

"How much have we racked up now?"

"Eight grand," he said, grabbing another handful of nuts.

"Not bad, right?"

"No. Not bad," he said, popping a few nuts into his mouth. He had remarkably good aim, probably from having so much practice putting things in his mouth. "How we doing on that thing? You know we get a nice bonus if we find the stuff."

"I wouldn't get my heart set on that. I'm making progress, but there's a good chance there are no photos or negatives left."

"But you're not finished yet, right?"

"I think we can still wring a couple more days out of it," I said, trying to mollify him. For some reason, I felt sorry for him. He'd had his heart set on a big score and this wasn't going to be it. But it might even be more than that. Like everyone else, Goldblatt had spent his life pursuing the American Dream. The Big Score. But it wasn't only the money. It was the satisfaction that he was right. He saw big money, possibly even fame, in this Starr Faithfull diary, and now he was letting it go, giving it to someone else to run with. It was that, as much as the money, I think, that was bugging him.

It was at that moment that I stopped feeling sorry for him . . . and for me . . . and started feeling *almost* grateful that we were partners. Not so much for his sake, but for mine. He would keep me moving forward, toward Fitzgerald's green light at the other end of the harbor. It was something I needed and something I couldn't always provide for myself. Goldblatt, damn him, all 290 pounds of him, would be my muse!

I took my hand and put it on his shoulder, squeezing it slightly.

"What's your problem?" he asked.

"Nothing," I said. "I just wanted to let you know the drinks are on me. Dinner, too."

"You going soft on me, Swann?" he asked.

"Not on your life," I said.

I slid the book, still wrapped in the Duane Reade bag, secured by a rubber band to hold it together, out from under my jacket and handed it to him. "Hold onto this until I give you the signal. Then bring it over to us."

"What's the signal?"

"I'll take my hand like this," I said, holding it out in front of me, "and do this." I demonstrated, flexing it in a come-hither movement.

"You mean, like, come on over."

"You read my fucking mind. Sometimes, Goldblatt, you're scary. It's like we share the same brain."

"Fuck you, Swann."

At two forty-five, after downing one beer to Goldblatt's three, I found a seat against the wall and waited for Stern. At precisely three o'clock, he waltzed through the doors, looked around, spotted me, and headed over. I looked around, but I didn't see the other two guys. Did he feel secure enough to come alone? Or were they were waiting for him right outside the lobby?

"Got the book?" he asked brusquely.

"I do. Got the money?"

He patted his side pocket.

"Sit down," I said.

"Why? We have something to discuss?"

"Yes."

"I thought we did all our talking yesterday, Swann. Let's make this as simple as possible. l hand over the cash, you hand over the book. Then we never have to see each other again."

"I think we'll do it my way," I said, sinking into my seat.

He hesitated a moment and then, seeing no other way, he joined me.

"Let's get this over with."

"I don't see your goons. They wouldn't be waiting outside for me, would they?"

"I told you yesterday, I don't travel around with goons. I wouldn't even know where to find a goon."

"You live in the biggest city of goons in the world, Stern, you should be able to come up with a couple."

He pulled out a large manila envelope and held it in front of him, waving it slightly. "This is what you want, now where's the book?"

I looked over to the bar, ready to give the signal. Goldblatt wasn't there. That sonuvabitch, I thought. I never should have trusted him with the book. I'll kill that fat bastard when I get my hands on him. I looked around the room but he wasn't there. I looked back at Stern. It seemed like he was getting a little nervous, but no more nervous than I was.

"The book, Swann?"

"My associate has it and he seems to have slipped out for the moment."

"Are you fucking kidding me?"

He stood up and tucked the envelope back into his jacket. I expected his goons to come out of the woodwork, lead me out of the building, like they did to Cary Grant in *North by Northwest*, take me into the park, and beat the shit out me until I bled. I looked around for some help. A security guard. A hotel official. No one. But no one was coming toward me, either.

"You'll pay for this, Swann!" Stern hissed, as he turned his back and began to walk away.

There was no way I could convince him that I was the victim here, not him, and so I simply stood up and watched him walk away. But just as he'd taken no more than half a dozen steps, out of the corner of my eye, I spotted Goldblatt lumbering back into the room. He was actually fiddling with his pants zipper.

"Wait," I yelled out to Stern, who stopped dead in his tracks and spun around. "He's here."

"Who?"

"My partner. With the book."

"You've got to be kidding me. What kind of game are you playing here?"

Goldblatt, a surprised look on his face, joined us. "What's going on?" he asked, so innocently I didn't know whether to punch him in the mouth or pat him reassuringly on the shoulder.

"Where the hell were you?"

"I had to take a leak."

"In the middle of this you had to take a leak."

"I'm sorry. Three beers do that to me. I saw you guys talking. I figured I had a few minutes. Besides, didn't you see me give you the high sign?"

"No, I didn't see you give me any fucking high sign."

"Well, I did," he said, so innocently, I could have punched him in the face.

"If you two girls could stop fighting, I'd just as soon make this deal and get the hell out of here," said Stern.

I turned to Stern, shot him a "fuck you" look, then back to Goldblatt. "Give me the book."

"It's in my coat, over there," he said, pointing to a seat at the bar.

"You left it in the open?"

"I told the bartender to keep an eye on it."

"Get it," I hissed, out of the side of my mouth.

"That's some backup you've got there," Stern said, as Goldblatt waddled back to the bar.

"Fucking interns," I replied.

Goldblatt returned, carrying his coat in one hand and the Duane Reade bag in the other.

"Did he give you the money?"

"Not yet," I said, turning to Stern. "But he's about to."

"I want to see the book first."

"Fair enough." I nodded to Goldblatt and he removed the diary from the plastic bag, then held it up for Stern to see.

"I need to hold it."

"And I need to hold the money," I said.

Reluctantly, he pulled a brown manila envelope from his inside jacket pocket. "The money's in here."

"I'm sure it is, but I need to actually see it."

He opened it, thrust it toward me, and I got a brief look at the contents. He wasn't fooling around. There was cash there and plenty of it.

I took the Duane Reade bag from Goldblatt and removed the book. I opened it to the page with Starr Faithfull's name on it, then to another page of her writing.

"Good enough?" I asked.

"Yeah. I guess so." He handed me the dough and I handed him the book and the plastic bag. "I won't need that," he said, pushing the bag back into my hand. He paged through the

book, until he got to the final entries. I knew what he was looking for.

"How much do you think there is?" I asked, as I handed the
envelope to Goldblatt, who immediately started counting the
money.

He looked up. "What are you talking about?"

"How much do you think she stole from your client's ances-
tor?"

"I still don't know what you're talking about."

I shrugged. "Starr Faithfull. That's why your client wants the
book. Something was taken from the family and they want it
back. And they think the answer's in the book."

"That's none of your business now, Swann. We're finished
here."

"You're right, it is none of my business."

He turned and walked away. Alone. I was puzzled. Why hadn't
he brought those two goons with him? And if they weren't with
him, who were they with and why were they following me and
Goldblatt?

When we got outside, Goldblatt was jubilant.

"Our first real deal," he bubbled, as we stood under the
overhang, facing the glass house of the Apple store across the
street.

"Just remember, it's not all ours."

"I know. I know. But three grand of it is. That's fifteen
hundred for you and fifteen hundred for me."

"What about the money you owe your 'investors'?"

"All taken care of. Let's celebrate."

"Like how?"

"I don't know. How about dinner at a nice joint."

"It's four o'clock in the afternoon. Later? I've got some things
to take care of."

"Come on, Swann, don't rain on my parade."

"I've got to get the money to Claudia."

"She can wait till tomorrow."

"I've got other cases."

"The Jack thing? You're not still wasting your time with that, are you?"

"I am. And there's the Feingersh case."

"How you doing with that one?"

"Lots of dead ends. I'm not so sure our employer is going to be very happy. By the way, who is he?"

"I can't say."

"Can't or won't?"

"What does it matter?"

"We're partners, aren't we? Are partners supposed to keep secrets from each other?"

"Like you don't have secrets from me."

"Well, maybe we ought to start trusting each other, now that we're in the black."

"You know that ain't gonna happen."

"What do you mean?"

"I mean you're never going to fully trust me. And that's okay. As long as I know that, I don't mind."

"You don't mind that I don't trust you?"

"That's right. It keeps me on my toes. Besides, it gives me something to work for. Someday I know I'll earn your trust." He reached out and pinched my cheek, before I could pull away. Turns out, he was pretty quick for a big man. Maybe some of those stories had a grain of truth to them.

"Hey!"

"Aw, you know you love me, Swann. Stop fighting it."

He went to give me a hug, but this time I managed to elude him. He had the weight, but I had the speed.

"You're a very strange man, Goldblatt. Very strange."

"I pride myself on that. Maybe I ought to put that on my business cards."

"Yeah. That'll bring in tons of business." I looked at my watch. "I gotta go."

"Go where?"

"I've got a hunch about something. I'm going to go back to my office and check it out."

"You know, that reminds me, I think we ought to get an office together, not that mouse hole you have in Klavan's place."

"I'm fine where I am and you're fine where you are."

"Okay. For the time being, maybe. But face it, Swann, there's going to come a time, whether you like it or not, when we're going to move in together . . ." He put his arm around my shoulder and for some reason, I don't know why, it almost felt comfortable.

24
ANTEING UP

As I stepped off the elevator and into Klavan's apartment, Angie was just putting on her coat.

"Ange, just the person I wanted to see."

"It's five o'clock, Mr. Swann."

"I know. Quitting time. But what if I gave you fifty bucks to stay another hour to do something for me?"

"Fifty bucks cash or fifty bucks on a check that might bounce?"

"Ange, honey, when has a check I've ever given you bounced?"

"Never. But that's because Mr. Klavan pays me, not you. But I have, on occasion, had the opportunity to glance at your checking statement and let me tell you, Mr. Swann, it's pretty anemic."

"Anemic, yes. But in the course of your snooping I'm sure you've also seen that all my bills are paid. Late, maybe, but paid. And lately, I've done better than that. They've been paid on time. But regardless," I pulled out my wallet and picked out two twenties and a ten, "this time it's in cash."

She took it and stared at the bills for a moment.

"They're real, Angie."

"I know. I just want it to sink in."

"Funny girl."

"Okay, I'm done," she said, sticking the cash in her jeans

244

pocket and peeling off her coat. "What is it you want me to do?"

"I want you to find out as much as you can about Ed Feingersh, Julia Scully, Irv Friedman, and Elliot Ravetz. See if there's anything that ties them together. And I'm also interested in the Feingersh Marilyn Monroe photos. I want to know who found them and where they were found."

"And you expect me to do all that in an hour?"

"You're killing me, Ange. Okay, overtime is double. How's that? And now you know I'm good for it."

Klavan wasn't there, so I decided to catch a quick nap on his couch. Before I could close my eyes, my phone buzzed. It was Claudia.

"Did you get it?"

"I did."

"All of it?"

"Yes."

"And he took the book?"

"Of course."

"That's great, Swann. Thank you so much. I'd give you a big hug, but I'm out in Long Beach. When will I see you?"

I knew she wanted me to say that she should hop on the train and come in, or that I'd be out there on the next train, but that wasn't going to happen.

"How about tomorrow?"

"Not tonight?"

"I'm beat, Claudia. And I've got some other business I've got to take care of. Why don't we have dinner tomorrow night. I'll have the cash, don't worry."

"I'm not worried."

I laid down on the plush couch in Klavan's living room, shut my eyes, but I couldn't sleep. One case appeared to be over, but there was still Feingersh and finding Donna Recco. It was between Hoboken and Austin, and although Hoboken was closer, my gut told me Austin was her more likely destination. And since Jack had okayed a trip down there, I knew I had to go. I was tired and worn-out, but sometimes a sense of responsibility rears its ugly head, which meant I was going to get my ass down to Austin to look for Donna. It was Wednesday and I had nothing planned for the weekend, so that's when I would head down there. That decided, I was finally able to close my eyes and catch a short nap, only to be awakened in what seemed only minutes later, by Angie, who stood over me, her coat on, waving a piece of paper in my face.

"What time is it?"

"Time for me to leave."

I looked at my watch. "Six o'clock. Man, I was out like a light."

"Here's everything I could find, and it wasn't much."

I closed my eyes again. "The long and short of it, please."

I heard the door open. I knew who it was by the familiar thud on the carpet. Klavan.

"What's going on here?" he asked.

"Join the party," I said. "Angie was just delivering some information I asked her to get."

"Anyone for a drink?" asked Klavan.

"I'm good," I said.

"Me, too," said Angie.

"Drinking alone never stopped me. Keep talking. I'm all ears," Klavan said, as he moved toward the bar at the other end of the room.

Angie pulled over a chair and sat down. "Those Feingersh photos were found in a New York warehouse in 1987. It doesn't say who found them, but they were purchased by an archivist named Michael Ochs as part of a larger lot of unexamined materials. You want to hear something kind of interesting?"

"Sure. Why not?"

"Michael Ochs was . . ."

"The brother of a protest-folksinger named Phil Ochs, who committed suicide," said Klavan, as he returned holding a glass of what I guessed was whiskey on the rocks.

"How'd you know that?" asked Angie.

"I'm a lot smarter than I look," said Klavan, as he pulled up a chair. Feeling a little too much like a patient, I sat up on the couch. "I've run into him some over the years. We've even bid on some of the same items. The fact that he bought a whole bunch of the material leads me to believe that stuff was probably stored in that warehouse, unclaimed, and then sold off."

"Anyway," continued Angie, reading from the paper in her hand, "Ochs sold his entire collection, which, by the way, was worth millions, in 2007 to Getty Images."

"Which brings me right back to where I was before. But if the people at Getty knew how valuable those images were, they certainly would have looked through their own archives to see if there were other Feingersh images, right?"

"You bet your ass they would," said Klavan, who was drinking from the glass while stroking his bald head. "And you, my friend, are indeed, right back where you started from."

"There's more, if you want to hear it," said Angie.

"Shoot," I said.

"Well, you asked me to look up those names, too, to see if there were any connections. And it seems there might be. I think Scully, Friedman, and Ravetz all worked at the same photography magazine back in the early sixties. I found their names on the masthead."

"Really," I said. "That's very interesting, because when I spoke to them, none of them mentioned that they'd worked together. Ravetz intimated he didn't even know Julia was still alive. But that doesn't seem very likely, since they live less than a mile from each other." My mind was racing, trying to make connections, the same way I did when I was installing cable a couple years earlier. I thought back to my interview with Scully. Something she said started to resonate. "Poker with the boys." Could these possibly be two of the boys she was talking about?

"You're onto something, aren't you?" said Klavan. He pointed to my head. "I can see you thinking."

"It's that apparent, huh? I think I know where those negatives are."

"That would be big, man. You gonna share that information with us?"

"Not until I'm sure. Angie," I said, taking out my wallet, "you've earned yourself a little bonus. Here's an extra twenty."

Angie took the money, happily, and suddenly I was wide awake. It was just after six o'clock. Not too late, I thought, to pay a visit to Julia Scully.

Before I did, I called Goldblatt. "Tell me who hired you in the Feingersh case."

"Wish I could."

"What's that supposed to mean?"

"Okay, the truth is, I never met the guy. Everything was done over the phone."

"You trusted someone you never even met? That's hard to believe."

"I met a check for one week's worth of work. That was enough for me."

"Who signed the check?"

"It was a cashier's check."

"And that didn't seem strange to you?"

"Nope. Collectors are sometimes like that. They like to remain anonymous."

"Next time, if there is a next time, we meet our clients, face to face."

"What'sa matter, your social life isn't full enough you've got to actually meet people who pay you up front?"

I didn't answer. I didn't have to.

"What a nice surprise," said Julia Scully, who was waiting for me at her front door. Once again, she was dressed casually but eloquently, in a white button-down Oxford shirt, camel's hair sweater, and black trousers.

"Thanks for seeing me again on such short notice."

"Come in, please. I was just sitting down to dinner, but I can set another place."

"No thanks. I don't want to interrupt you, but I promise, it won't take long."

"Oh, please, don't worry. That's what microwaves were made for. We can sit in the living room."

She led the way, past all her photographs. I stopped to look at one in particular. It was a shot that showed a submarine submerging. I hadn't noticed it the first time I'd visited. But now I did and I was sure it was a Feingersh.

We sat across from each other. I took a chair, she the sofa.

"Have you made any progress?" she asked.

"I think I have."

"Oh, that's wonderful. Do you mean you've actually found the photographs?"

"I think I have. In a way. I met with your friends, Irv Friedman and Elliot Ravetz." I watched her face. Her expression didn't change. That was a dead giveaway. She didn't ask about either of them. I knew why and I knew I was onto something. She was waiting for me to continue. So, I did. "I have a feeling the three of you know each other pretty well."

"I knew Irv, of course, but it's been years since I've seen him. How is he? And is he still married to, I think her name is Madeleine?"

"I think you know how he is. You worked with him on the magazine?"

"Yes, that's true. But as I said, that was years ago."

"And Elliot Ravetz worked for the same magazine, didn't he?"

"I believe he might have. But people came and went. He might have been a freelancer."

"But you knew him."

"Vaguely, I suppose. Where is all this leading, Mr. Swann? I feel like I'm being accused of something."

"Not yet. But I think you're lying about not seeing them recently. In fact, I believe you see them pretty regularly, Julia. I think, if I checked around, I'd find that the three of you are in that poker game you mentioned. You know, the one downtown that you play in every month."

She said nothing.

"Here's what I think, Julia. I think the three of you cooked up this elaborate scheme to jack up the prices of the photographs. I think one of the three of you, probably you, have those photographs, or at least some of them, and I think you're holding them off the market until the value is right. And then, just like the Monroe photos, they'll suddenly appear. And you know, I think if I looked even further, I'd find that one of you, if not all three of you, is behind hiring me."

"Why on earth would we do that?"

"Because you knew I wouldn't find them, because you guys have them. After my search came up empty, you could leak that to the newspapers, which would bring Ed back into the news, which would then send the value of those photos through the roof. Am I getting close?"

She smiled. "I really don't know what you're talking about, Mr. Swann, but I will say that you do have a wonderful imagination."

"That might be true. But I'm not imagining this. You know, Julia, I don't really care that you used me. I got paid, Goldblatt got paid, and from what I've seen of the three of you, all of you charming, by the way, I think you guys deserve to win the lottery. Why shouldn't you have some extra money in your golden years, to do with what you'd like? And who's hurt by it, except maybe me. But I'm getting paid, too, so no harm no foul. So you know what I'm going to do?"

"What?"

"Nothing. I'm just going to walk away, like nothing ever happened. But I'm going to do it only if you agree to two things."

"Not that I'm admitting to anything, but I'm just curious, what would those two things be?"

"First of all, I want you to cut his wife in on anything you get for the photos. Why shouldn't she share in it? And believe me, she could use it. She's a lot worse off than you three."

"And the second thing?"

"No publicity. I don't want anyone knowing you hired me. I don't want anyone to know there was any kind of search going on. You want to bring those photos back onto the market, fine with me. I hope you make a fortune. But you're not going to make it by making me look bad. Either you announce that I found them or you don't. But if you don't, then you're on your own."

"Do you play poker, Mr. Swann?"

"On occasion."

"Well, you should do it more often. You're probably very good at it."

"I don't gamble because I hate losing, Julia, and any time you get into a game like that, especially with players like you, there's always the chance of coming up short. That's a chance I don't want to take." I got up. "Now, I'll leave you to your dinner. And please say hello to Irv and Elliot for me. And the next time you have one of your poker games, I wouldn't mind being invited. Just to watch, though. Oh, and you don't need to walk me to the door. I know my way out, and your dinner is getting cold."

25
SAVE THE LAST DANCE
FOR ME

As soon as I stepped outside Julia's building, I was immediately assaulted by the wind, whipping in from the Hudson. Another cold icy night. I buttoned up my coat, pulled my watch cap out of my pocket, and put it on. I was, in a sense, in the middle of nowhere. It was a several block walk to the Broadway subway line and I thought it a better idea to wait for the 57 bus, which would take me all the way across town, where I could hook up with the Number 5 train.

The stop was only a block away, and as I stood huddled against the wall of the bus shelter, I thought about how much of what just happened I'd tell Goldblatt. I was feeling pretty good about myself. As far as I was concerned, the case was over. I knew where those photographs were and yet I wasn't going to do anything about it. I hate feigning failure, but in this situation I'd do it. If I told him the truth, Goldblatt would be livid, thinking he'd lost out on the bonus. But I knew there would have been no bonus. Ravetz, Scully, and Friedman had concocted this plan and knew I wouldn't be able to find the photos. I could lie to Goldblatt and tell him I wasn't able to track them down, that they were probably destroyed. But I also knew that when they did surface, and I knew they would, he'd know I was lying. So, the truth, or some version of it, was the best thing I could do.

I looked up to see the 57 bus, turning down 72nd and West End, just as it began to snow again. I could see the flakes dancing in the headlights of the bus, as it pulled closer. It skidded to a stop. I got on, slipped my Metro card into the slot, then moved toward the back of the nearly empty bus. Just as it was about to pull away, I heard a banging on the door. The driver opened it and a large man, bundled up in a heavy down coat, a muffler, and a watch cap similar to mine, stepped in. He paid the fare in change, then looked down the aisle of the bus. His eyes seemed to light on me for a moment, and then he found a seat several rows behind me, the move of a pro.

I recognized him. He was the bigger goon from the Plaza Hotel, the one I lost outside Klavan's apartment house. What the hell was he doing still following me? Obviously, he wasn't working for Stern. Stern had his book, I had the money. But if not Stern, who was he working for?

I thought about approaching him, but instead I decided to let it play out. I'd lead him on a merry ride, but I'd make sure to lose him before I got home.

When the bus reached 57th and Lexington Avenue, I pushed the yellow tape; the bell rang, then I moved to the front of the bus, as if I were getting off. Out of the corner of my eye, I watched as he got up, too, and moved to the back-door exit. The bus stopped, I started to get off, slowly. The goon stepped off before I did. I turned to the driver and said, "Sorry, my mistake. I thought this was Second Avenue," then stepped back on. He quickly closed the door and pulled away, leaving the goon on the sidewalk. As the bus moved forward, I watched as the big man tried to keep up. But we had a head of steam and made the light across Third Avenue, leaving the goon panting and stranded, as the light changed. By the time we reached Second Avenue, he was nowhere in sight. I got off and grabbed a cab downtown to St. Mark's Bookshop, walking the rest of the way back to my apartment, stopping only to pick up some Indian food on 6th Street.

Once home, I called Goldblatt to fill him in.

"So the gravy train has come to an end," he sighed.

"That's right."

"You sure you can't find those photos?"

"If they still exist, they're someplace no one left alive knows about."

"Yeah, well, okay, we didn't do too bad. I think it totals up to about eight grand. Plus expenses."

There was a knock on my door.

"Gotta go. There's someone at the door."

"Who?"

"I don't know. And since I didn't buzz anyone up, I'd better check on it."

"Hey, call me later."

"You worried about me, Goldblatt?"

"You're my partner."

I hung up the phone, afraid that Goldblatt would get all gooey, not that I'd believe a word of it. I moved toward the door, on the way picking up a baseball bat I had in the corner for emergencies, like big goons finding out where I lived. I would have looked through the peephole if I had one that actually worked.

"Who's there?"

"Claudia."

I opened the door. She was wearing knee-high boots over black tights, with an oversized, off-white cable knit sweater.

"How'd you get in?"

"Have you looked at that pathetic thing you call a lock?" She pulled a credit card from her pocket and waved it in my face.

"Jesus, Claudia, there's a buzzer downstairs. Try using it."

"I didn't think I had to," she said, moving past me as she took off her coat and hung it on the coatrack beside the front door.

"Why's that?"

"Because of this," she said, as she kissed me on the mouth.

"Not good enough. Next time, if there is a next time, use the buzzer instead of a credit card. Okay?"

"Whatever you say, boss."

"I told you I'd see you tomorrow."

"I never listen to whatever anyone tells me. I always do what I want. That's something you should know about me."

"Not an especially attractive feature."

She shrugged. "I've got others that make up for that."

"I know. But you're here for business, aren't you?"

"Sad to say, I am. My dad really needs to hand over that money or else . . . well, you know or else what."

"I've got a pretty good imagination. Have a seat and I'll get the dough."

I went into the bedroom and when I came back, Claudia was seated on the couch, whispering into her phone. When she saw me, she said, "Bye," and quickly hung up.

"I'd ask who that was, but it's none of my business."

"Just my dad. I wanted to tell him everything was okay."

"Where's Sidney?"

"Why do you ask?"

"Just curious."

"I wouldn't know."

"Funny, because I took a look out my window and there's a guy across the street who looks remarkably like him."

She looked like the kid caught with his hand in the cookie jar.

"I can't help myself, Claudia. I'm a suspicious guy. Now you could just tell the truth, or even make up something. Like, I'm going to be carrying home a lot of money and I didn't want to do it alone."

"That's what it is."

"Then why not just tell me Sidney's downstairs waiting to ride shotgun?"

"It never occurred to me to tell you. I mean it just didn't seem important."

"Maybe it's not. But you still should have mentioned it."

"You don't have to make a big deal out of it," she said, moving closer and putting her arm around me.

I was pissed. I knew what she wanted. But I wasn't going to make it easy for her to get it.

She moved to kiss me. Normally, I wouldn't have minded that. But this time, I knew that it didn't mean what I wanted it to mean so I moved to the side, just as she was about to make contact.

Instead of acting all hurt, she just smiled. She knew she wasn't fooling me and she was smart enough to know when to throw in her hand and deal out a new one.

"I guess you know why I'm really here."

"I do. What are you really going to do with the money, Claudia? I mean, we're not talking millions here, but it's a tidy, little sum."

"You know what it's for."

"I know what you told me it's for, but I know that's not true, so I was just wondering. New car? A trip to the Caribbean? Or are you the investment type? No, wait, I don't think you are. I take you for a woman who doesn't like to delay gratification."

"You think you're a pretty good judge of character, don't you?"

"Sometimes it takes me a little longer, but yeah, in the end I can usually figure out people pretty good. But then, being cynical and always believing in the worst instincts in people usually pays off in coming to the right conclusion. Have a seat. I'll be right back with your money."

I went into the kitchen and opened the freezer, which was

bare except for a couple of old phone books. Someone once told me that an empty refrigerator eats a lot of electricity. I believed them and so I stuff the phone books in there instead of food. I took out the large envelope of cash, minus the percentage for Goldblatt and me.

When I walked back into the living room, Claudia was sitting on the couch. So was Sidney, who'd removed his coat and hung it on my coatrack.

"A little cold out there, Sid?"

"Yeah. Cold."

I slowly inched toward where I'd leaned the baseball bat against the wall near the door. It's not that I would use it—the idea of crunching bones and blood flying through the air didn't appeal to me—but I wanted to have something in my hand in case Sid decided to get a little rough, though I couldn't understand why, since I had the dough in my hand and was about to turn it over.

"You don't trust me, Claudia? You thought I wouldn't give you the money? That I had a weapon in the kitchen. Honey, even my knives are way too dull to draw blood."

She smiled. "I didn't think so, but I figured Sid came all the way in with me, he might as well feel useful. Besides, he was getting cold out there."

"It's getting a little chilly in here. Feel useful, Sid?"

"Sure."

"I'm happy." I moved away from the bat, toward the couch. "Here, Claudia, and I'd be disappointed if you didn't count it. Twenty-seven grand, just like we agreed on. Unless, of course, Sid's here to take back the three grand that was my commission."

"No. You earned that," she said, taking the envelope from me. "And I'm not going to waste my time and yours counting it. I'm sure you wouldn't short me."

"It's not beneath me, honey, but I promise you, it's all there, so I guess our business is concluded. And I'm sure you're going to give LaHood his share."

"Of course."

She got up. So did Sidney.

"I'd say it's been a pleasure," said Claudia, as she pulled on her coat, "but I don't think that's what you want to hear."

"No, it's not. But since we're parting on such a nice note, you might as well come clean."

"What are you talking about?"

"The book. It's a forgery, isn't it?"

The beginnings of a smile crept across her lips, which she then quickly pursed. "Whatever would make you think that?"

"The whole thing was an elaborate scam, wasn't it? And a good one, I might say. I wish I had all the details."

"There are no details, darling."

She moved toward the door, with Sidney in the lead. When she got there, she turned, moved toward me, kissed me firmly and sweetly on the mouth, then whispered in my ear, "You're a very smart man, Henry Swann. Thank you."

"And you're good, Claudia, you really are."

After they left, I plopped down on the couch, leaned back, propped my legs up on my coffee table, which was really just a crate I'd rescued from the street and refinished poorly, and put my hands behind my head. I was a smart man, but sometimes I wasn't smart enough soon enough. But, in the end, I wasn't the one being taken and the truth was, I liked Claudia, and maybe even Sidney, a lot more than I liked Matty Stern.

★ ★ ★ ★ ★

AUSTIN, TEXAS

★ ★ ★ ★ ★

"That depends a good deal on where you want to get to."
—Lewis Carroll, *Alice's Adventures in Wonderland*

26
DEEP IN THE HEART
OF TEXAS

I was down to one job, and that one job had taken me to Austin, Texas. On the plane, I read up on a city I'd heard plenty about but had never visited. The capital of Texas, Austin lies practically right, square in the middle of the state. It is the eleventh most populous city in the U.S. and fourth most populous city in the state of Texas. In 1839, Austin officially took over from Houston as the state capital.

Residents are called Austinites and they are made up of government employees, university faculty and staff, college students, musicians, high-tech workers, blue collar workers, and businesspeople. This particular mix makes it the most liberal city in the state. The arts scene is huge, with the Austin City Limits Music Festival and the South by Southwest music and film festival.

This, along with a map of the city I picked up at Barnes and Noble before I took off, was more than enough to get me through a quick trip, which I hoped would end with me finding Donna Recco, or at least getting me closer to finding her.

First, I had to find her uncle. It wasn't difficult finding Reccos in the phone book, because there was only one: Salvatore Recco. He lived not far from one of the three man-made lakes inside the city limits, Lady Bird Lake, which, obviously, was named for First Lady Lady Bird Johnson.

Stepping into the airport, I was suddenly immersed in a sea of cowboy boots and blue jeans. As far as the jeans, I fit right in. The cowboy boots, not so much. But I wasn't going to be there long, so it was a little like stepping into the scene of a movie. I missed New York already, but it was only one night. That's what I kept telling myself as I made my way through the airport, looking for a place to rent a car.

After getting pretty good directions from the cute redhead at the rental agency, I headed straight for Salvatore Recco's. When I got to the address, I found a well-manicured lawn and a ranch-style house on a street of other perfect houses, which only intensified my imperfectness.

I parked my car a couple houses away, then brazenly walked up to the door and knocked. Since it was early afternoon and a cloudless day, the temperature in the mid-seventies, I didn't really expect to find anyone home. I was wrong. Only moments after I knocked, the door opened and I was faced with a woman wearing pink pants, a flower-print blouse, and the biggest, blondest hair I'd ever seen.

"May I help you?" she asked, in that Texas twang that makes everyone sound sweet and inviting.

"I sure hope so. I'm looking for Salvatore Recco."

She smiled. "No one calls him that, honey. It's Sal, although that's not always what I call him."

"I won't ask what that is," I said.

"Well, y'all come on in. Sal's in the back, trying to do some gardening. He's not very good at it, but that doesn't stop him. I'm Marilyn," she said, offering me a well-manicured hand, her nails long and red. On the second finger of her left hand, there was a huge diamond ring, as well as a smaller diamond-encrusted wedding ring. "Who shall I say is calling?" she asked, as she led me through the house, toward the backyard.

"I'll just introduce myself, if you don't mind."

"Suit yourself, honey."

Funny thing about southerners, they're way too friendly and

accommodating. But under that veneer of friendliness there always seems to be suspicion lurking, which gives a sense that outsiders aren't really welcome. Maybe that's why I prefer New Yorkers, where the hostility and cynicism is right out in the open.

As she led me through the enormous house, decorated as if it were the set of a 1950s western, she asked, "Where ar'ya from, darlin'?"

"New York City."

"No kiddin'. I love New York. I make Sal take me up there at least once a year to do some shoppin'. I love that Bloomingdale's and Saks Fifth Avenue. We got those stores down here, along with Neiman Marcus, but it ain't nothin' like it is up there."

When I got out back, to a yard that seemed to be the size of a city block, Sal wasn't working in the garden; instead, he was seated on a lawn chair, a beer in his hand, watching a large, flat-screen TV that had been hooked up on the patio. It was tuned, of course, to the football game, the University of Texas versus Penn State.

"Sal, honey, this is . . . I don't know his name."

"It's Henry Swann."

"This here's Mr. Henry Swann and he's lookin' to talk to you."

"Pull up a seat," said Sal, pointing to another lawn chair a few feet away. "Marilyn, bring this fella a cold one, will ya."

"Where you from?" asked Sal, without taking his eyes off the screen.

"New York City," I said, as I pulled up a lawn chair and sat down beside him.

"I shoulda guessed. I'm pretty good with accents. You a Giant fan?"

"Not really."

"You don't like football?"

"I can take it or leave it."

"How 'bout a little bet on the game? Penn State's ahead by three. I'll give you a touchdown. Just to make it a little interesting."

"I don't think I'll be here that long, Mr. Recco."

"Why's that? And what the hell are you here for?"

"I'm looking for your niece, Donna."

"What for? She ain't in no trouble, is she?"

"No trouble at all. I'm just looking to talk to her. Do you know where she is?"

"At this particular moment?"

"In general."

"She's probably hanging out somewhere downtown with her cousin."

"That would be?"

"Edie. My daughter. Why'd you say you were looking for her?"

"I just need to give her a message."

"You want I should give it to her?"

"No. I really need to talk to her. Do you know where I can find her?"

"I don't think I should just hand out that kind of information to a stranger. You don't expect me to do that, do you?"

"No. I don't. But if you could get her a message, maybe she'd talk to me."

He took another swig of beer and looked back at the screen. "We're drivin'. Tell you what, what if I give you two touchdowns. That means you're seven points in the black."

"I don't think so. About that message . . ."

"What you want me to say?"

"That Henry Swann would just like to meet up with her for a few minutes. That it's important. That it would mean a lot to Jack."

"Who the hell's Jack?"

"She'll know."

"Damn, damn, damn!"

I looked at the screen. The UT quarterback had fumbled the ball. Penn State picked it up.

"See, you shoulda took me up on those two touchdowns."

"It's early in the game."

"Yeah. But I don't like what I'm seein'." He turned to me. "Let's say I was going to deliver that message to Donna. And let's say she agreed to talk to you. How would she do that?"

"She can pick the place. I'm leaving town in the morning, but I'm wide open after I leave here until my plane leaves at 11 a.m."

"Gimme your number."

I handed him my card, which had my cell number on it.

He took it and shoved it in the pocket of his shorts. "I'll see if I can get ahold of her. In the meantime, Marilyn's cookin' up some burgers, you're welcome to stick around and have somethin' to eat."

"I appreciate the hospitality, but I think I'll head back into town. Now you'll give Donna that message, right?"

"I sure will, son."

I left Salvatore and Marilyn Recco, but I didn't leave emptyhanded. I had the name of his daughter and I figured there was a good chance Donna was staying with her. So, I hopped in my car, pulled out my smartphone, went straight to whitepages .com, and typed in Edie Recco. An address came up, and then I map quested the address in a neighborhood called Spyglass-Barton's Bluff. With that information, I headed straight back into town.

The area where Edie lived turned out to be a narrow strip of land that ran between Mopac Expressway and Barton Creek, in southwest Austin. It seemed like the area had been built up in solely the past twenty years, and it was filled with offices, single-family homes, and large complexes of condominiums. It was in one of these condominiums that Edie Recco resided.

I parked the car, then headed to Edie's building. I waited at the door till someone came out, then I scooted in. I found a board with resident apartment numbers, then headed up to 14C, Edie's apartment.

I buzzed and it was Donna, not Edie, who answered. I recognized her from the photos Jack had provided me with. She was wearing jeans and a tank top and her dark hair was pulled back in a ponytail. She didn't seem to be wearing any makeup and, if anything, she was even prettier than her photos.

"Yes?"

"Donna, I'd like to speak to you for a few minutes."

She started to shut the door on me, but ever since my skip-trace days my natural reflex is to stick my foot forward, which is just what I did, stopping the door from closing.

"I'm no danger to you, Donna. I promise."

Coming from somewhere back in the apartment I heard, "Who is it, Donna?"

"It's for me, Edie. You don't have to come out."

"How did you find me?" she whispered, in a voice that had a slight Texas twang to it, which surprised me, since she wasn't from Texas and had only been down there a couple weeks. But then I remembered she was an actress, many of whom are sponges taking on not only accents but various character traits.

"It's what I do."

"Jack sent you, didn't he?"

"He didn't actually send me, Donna, since he doesn't know where you are. Can I come in and we can talk about this?"

"I guess . . ."

"Ten minutes, and then I'll leave. I promise."

She hesitated a moment, then the door opened slowly.

"Ten minutes. That's it."

"I promise."

I walked into a spacious living room, with a terrific view of the city. She motioned to a couch. I sat. She sat as far away from me as possible, in a chair angled to face the couch and the wall of windows. Her body language was obvious. Stiff. Her hands folded in her lap. Her back up straight. She didn't want me there and she was being protective. That was to be expected. I really wasn't there to attack her and I would let her know that.

"Jack loves you. He doesn't understand why you disappeared without leaving a word for him."

"I'm sorry. I didn't mean to hurt him. But this is just what I didn't want."

"What's that?"

"Him trying to find me. It's pointless."

"Why's that, Donna?"

"Because I'm not coming back. At least not to him."

"Did he do something to you?"

"What's your name?"

"Henry Swann."

"Who are you? What do you do? What are you to Jack?"

"I find people. Like I said, Jack hired me to find you."

"You can't make me go back."

"That's not why I'm here, Donna. Look," I said, leaning forward so that only the tip of my ass was still on the seat. "I don't know the guy, but he seems to be okay. But in my experience *seems like* is a very dangerous term. Very few people are what they seem. If Jack is a danger to you, I want to know."

"He's no danger."

I could see what Jack saw in her. Not only was she very pretty, but she also had a vulnerability about her that was appealing. But along with this vulnerability there was a steeliness, a toughness. This wasn't some flaky chick who didn't know what she was doing. But I also got the sense that she didn't always know why she was doing it.

"He didn't hire me to kidnap you and bring you back. And if you don't want him to know where you are, I won't tell him. I don't even have to tell him I found you, if you don't want me to."

"Then why don't you just leave?"

"Because Jack's in pain. He's in pain because he doesn't understand why you left him the way you did."

"I'm sorry about that."

"You can do something about it, Donna."

"Like what?"

"Jack needs to know that you're sorry. And he needs to know why you did it, Donna. Why you left him. I'm not saying that's going to make him whole, because it's not."

Suddenly, I began to hate myself for what I was becoming: a third-rate Dr. Phil. But still, I kept going.

"He thinks I'm coming back, doesn't he?"

"He hopes you will."

She shook her head. "I don't think so."

"Tell me why, Donna, so I can tell him, so I can understand it. Didn't love him?"

She looked at me, without blinking. I wondered what was going on in her mind. And when she told me, I still didn't know.

"I don't know what love is."

"I'm not sure anyone does. It's kind of like that court definition of pornography. You know it when you feel it."

"I care for him very much. But I'm not sure I'm capable of loving anyone."

"Does Jack know that?"

She shook her head.

"What do you want me to tell him, Donna?"

She was silent a moment. I could see tears starting to well in her eyes. I wanted to go over and put my arm around her. To comfort her. I don't know why. It wasn't as if I knew her. It wasn't as if I should have cared. But for some reason, I did. I could see she was in pain, but I wasn't sure she was in touch with that pain, that she knew where it was coming from. I didn't know if she was near tears because of Jack or because of her. In the end, it didn't matter because it was her business. And Jack's. My business was to find her, which I did. Now it was to see if I could get any answers for Jack. Or maybe even see if there was any possibility of returning.

"I don't know if I want you to tell him anything." She took a breath, then exhaled slowly. "It would probably be best if he didn't even know that you found me, that you know where I am."

"I can do that, Donna," I said, though I'd already kept my mouth shut about one of my cases, maybe even two, so the idea of playing deaf, dumb, and blind to another didn't really sit well with me. Like most people, I was only as good as my last success. To Goldblatt, of course, it didn't matter, because it was all about the money. And all three cases were winners in that respect. But to me, it was more than that. The only thing that keeps me going is thinking that in some way, however meaningless and pathetic it might be to others, I am successful. The question was, could the notion that in each case I found what I was looking for, that I'd solved a mystery, be enough to sustain me. I didn't know. Facing the truth is sometimes hard. I knew that the reason I took jobs finding people was the hope that eventually I could find myself. Donna's confusion echoed my own. And so that's why I didn't know if I could or couldn't ignore Donna's request.

"Can you do that?"

"I have to think about it, Donna."

"What does that mean?"

"I was hired by Jack to find you. Implicit in that was to either talk you into coming back or find out why you won't. It's also implicit that I tell him whether or not I found you. Doing what you ask would be lying to him, breaking our contract. And the truth is, I try to stay out of all the other shit that surrounds the situations I'm thrust into."

"I'll just move someplace else. I've done it before, you know."

"I do know. And that's your business. You do what you have to do."

"But if he hired you again you'd find me again, wouldn't you?"

I nodded.

She lowered her head. "I don't want to move again." She looked up. "What about doing the right thing?"

"Who's to say what the right thing is, Donna? You? Me? Jack? There are all kinds of right things."

"Jack . . . and you, have no right to interfere in my life. I'm not married to Jack. I can do what I want. And what I want is to be out of New York and away from him."

"What are you afraid of, Donna?"

"That's none of your business."

"I'm going to give you a little advice, Donna, and then I'm going to get on my way and I'm going to honor your request."

"You are?"

"Yes. But here's the advice, Donna, and like any free advice it's worth exactly what you pay for it. There are demons in your head and, from personal experience, because I've had my share, I can tell you they don't just fade away. You either deal with them or they stay with you forever. Some of us do exactly what you're doing, run or hide or try to make believe nothing's wrong. But it doesn't work. I'm not saying you belong with Jack. No one knows that for sure. But you're going to keep running unless you face those demons and deal with them."

She looked up at me. The tears back in her eyes. She didn't know whether to attack, retreat, or acquiesce. That was okay. I wasn't looking for any kind of answer.

"I do suggest one thing, Donna." She looked at me with her big, brown eyes.

"What's that?"

"That at some point you contact Jack, I don't care how, and give him some kind of answer. Otherwise, this is going to stick with him way too long. If you care about him at all, you'll give him some kind of explanation. Something he can live with. Something that allows him to move on. It doesn't even have to be the truth, but it has to be truthful. You know what I mean?"

She nodded.

"You're not evil, Donna."

She looked up at me as if she knew what I meant but didn't necessarily believe what I was saying was true.

"How do you know?"

"I'm a pretty good judge of character, that's how," I said, lying my ass off. It wasn't the first time and it wouldn't be the last.

"I'm happy here. I don't want to leave. But I will if you tell him. And then you'll have to live with it."

"I've lived with a lot worse, Donna. You can't threaten me with anything I haven't been threatened with before. What you do with your life is your business. And who knows if Jack is the right person for you. It doesn't matter. I'll keep your secret, and I'll live with it."

"Thank you," she said, getting up out of her chair and approaching me. She hugged me. Her hair smelled good. Maybe she was better off here in Texas. Maybe she had made the right decision. Only time would tell. And as for Jack, well, I'd think of something to tell him. It wouldn't be the truth, but it would be something.

★ ★ ★ ★ ★

NEW YORK CITY

★ ★ ★ ★ ★

"The facts will appear with the shining of the dawn."
—Aeschylus, *Agamemnon*

27
HOPE SPRINGS ETERNAL . . . OR DOES IT?

All that was left to me now was to face Jack and give him the news. What was I going to tell him? That I'd found Donna and that she refused to come back, that she refused to see him, that she didn't even want him to know where she was? That was the truth, but that wasn't what I would tell Jack. It wasn't because I liked him, though I might if I got to know him. It wasn't because I wanted to spare his feelings, because I didn't know him. More likely, it was because I'd made a promise to Donna, who was not my client, whom I had no allegiance to, who wasn't paying me a cent. Why did I choose Donna over Jack?

These are the questions I pondered on the plane ride back. And I would be lying if I said that by the time we landed at Kennedy I had any of the answers. What I did have were plenty of rationalizations about why I was going to do what I was going to do. I would be keeping a promise. I would be saving Jack's feelings. I would be preventing a possible ugly scene, if Jack did what I thought he'd do, go down and confront Donna. That was a scenario in which no one came out the winner.

Although I dreaded it, I decided to be a man and report back to Jack face to face. And what better place than the very diner we'd met weeks earlier. Trying to avoid getting into it over the phone, I sent Jack an email giving him time and place. The email he sent back asked for details. I ignored him.

For a moment, I contemplated having Goldblatt accompany me, but I knew that would do no good for anyone. I decided I wouldn't even tell him what I was planning until after the deed was done. I was sure that in this case he would side with me, after all he wasn't thrilled at my deal with Jack and he certainly didn't see this case as a cash cow.

After a restless night's sleep, I was ensconced in the window of the Silver Star Diner Monday morning, nursing a cup of coffee, at nine-fifteen. As it happened, it was Martin Luther King, Jr. Day, so there was no school, which meant Jack would have no trouble making the appointment.

At precisely nine-thirty, Jack burst through the door, spied me sitting at my table, and rushed right over. In one smooth motion he removed his coat and tossed it over a chair, taking the one opposite me.

"You found her?"

"Slow down, Jack. How about . . ." but before I could finish my sentence, the elderly waiter was by our table asking the very question I was about to pose. Jack shook his head, no.

"She's in Austin?"

Let the lies begin.

"No, Jack, she's not."

"But you know where she is?" he said, moving forward in his chair so that his face was only inches from mine.

"No, not exactly."

"What's that supposed to mean?"

I had too much pride to admit to complete failure, and so I had concocted what I thought of as an acceptable lie, if there is ever such a thing. I doubted it would mollify Jack, but it would take me off the case and at this point, that's all I wanted.

"I don't know where she is, Jack, but I did find out some information that I think you ought to have."

"What kind of information?"

"I was able to get a message from Donna."

"What kind of message?"

"Jack, you either let me talk to you my way or I'm going to leave. I don't need to be interrupted every thirty seconds, so shut the fuck up and let me talk."

"I'm sorry," he said, moving back in his chair.

"That's better," I said. I was stalling. Hoping the words I'd rehearsed came out the right way, the way that would forestall Jack from pursuing Donna any further.

"Okay, Jack, you have to prepare yourself to hear this."

"I'm prepared."

"Okay. First of all, Donna is safe. Second of all, she's truly sorry she put you through this . . ."

"Then you have seen her."

"No. I don't know where she is. But I've spoken to her on the phone."

"You have a number for her."

"No."

"But she called you, or you called her, so you must have a number."

"She called from a public phone, Jack. Hard to believe, but there still are such things."

"Is she coming back?"

I hesitated a moment. I didn't think she would. Ever. But should I tell Jack that? Or should I leave a ray of hope for him to grab onto? What is hope, anyway? It's a tool. Something that gets us from one day to the next. But what about false hope? Is that destructive, does it stop us from moving on? For me, the hope that someday I can get my life together. That someday I can find myself and be there for my son if he needs me. That is essential. Without it, I would only fall into that lake of despair. And drown. This is what went through my mind when Jack asked me that question. And it informed the answer I gave him.

"She didn't say, Jack. She's confused. She needs time to work

279

things out."

"Maybe I can help her."

"No. You can't. You need to be patient, Jack, and you need to get on with your life. Maybe Donna will come back, maybe not. But if and when she does, you . . . and she . . . will be different people. If you still want each other, it'll happen."

"Do you think she'll come back?" he asked, with that bit of hope in his voice that wanted me to say yes, needed me to say, yes.

"You're asking for my opinion, Jack?"

"Yes. I am."

"I don't think so. But that doesn't mean she won't."

He was silent for a moment. For two. "I think she will. I think she'll come back."

I smiled. I was off the hook. At least I hoped so.

28
WHAT GOES AROUND
COMES AROUND

We were pretty much back where we started from. The same greasy spoon Italian restaurant where our partnership was hatched. Why? Because Goldblatt had suggested it and I was too worn out to fight him on it.

"So," he said, digging into his baked ziti, which looked more like a dish of cheap macaroni and cheese to me. "Not bad for our first couple weeks as partners. Fifteen grand split two ways, seventy-five hundred big ones apiece."

"That would be a fifty-fifty split."

"Yeah. Isn't that what we agreed on?"

"No."

"Are you sure?"

"Yes. I'm sure."

"I coulda sworn . . ."

"Cut the crap, Goldblatt."

"Listen, Swann, if this is going to work, if we're going to be partners, then we have to be equal partners. Otherwise, there's the risk of bad feelings on one side. My side, to be precise."

"What about my bad feelings about splitting things with you fifty-fifty, especially since I'm out there doing all the work, taking all the risks?"

"What risks? I don't see a mark on you."

"Psychological wounds, Goldblatt. The kinds of wounds you can't see."

"What? You're gonna tell me you suffer from post-traumatic

281

syndrome? You gonna pull that card on me?"

"I didn't give it a name. You can't possibly understand it unless you're doing it. I'm trying to solve puzzles and just because you put a puzzle together, doesn't mean you always get the answers. And I need answers. I need to know there are answers."

"So, ask me a question and I'll give you the answer."

I smiled. Because he was funny. Because he was right. Just because I found the answer wouldn't mean my life would be solved, that I'd be put back together. But like the gift I gave Jack, the gift of hope, I needed something to keep me going. And maybe Goldblatt was my gift. Maybe it would be Goldblatt that would keep me going.

Would it be worth fifty percent?

We'll see.

ABOUT THE AUTHOR

Charles Salzberg is a freelance writer who lives in New York City. His first novel, *Swann's Last Song,* was nominated for a Shamus Award for Best First P.I. Novel. He is also the author of *Swann Dives In* and *Devil in the Hole.* He teaches writing in New York City and is a Founding Member of the New York Writers Workshop.